VAMPIRE ACADEMY

For my urban fantasy grrrls, Jackie and Caitlin.

VAMPIRE ACADEMY

RICHELLE MEAD

Vampire Academy

RAZORBILL

Published by the Penguin Group
Penguin Young Readers Group
345 Hudson Street, New York, New York 10014, USA.
Penguin Group (USA) Inc., 375 Hudson Street, New York, New York 10014, USA.
Penguin Group (Canada), 90 Eglinton Avenue East, Suite 700, Toronto,
Ontario, Canada M4P 2Y3 (a division of Pearson Penguin Canada Inc.)
Penguin Books Ltd, 80 Strand, London WC2R 0RL, England
Penguin Ireland, 25 St Stephen's Green, Dublin 2, Ireland
(a division of Penguin Books Ltd)
Penguin Group (Australia), 250 Camberwell Road, Camberwell,
Victoria 3124, Australia (a division of Pearson Australia Group Pty Ltd)
Penguin Books India Pvt Ltd, 11 Community Centre, Panchsheel Park,
New Delhi – 110 017, India
Penguin Group (NZ), 67 Apollo Drive, Mairangi Bay, Auckland 1311,
New Zealand (a division of Pearson New Zealand Ltd)
Penguin Books (South Africa) (Pty) Ltd, 24 Sturdee Avenue,
Rosebank, Johannesburg 2196, South Africa

Penguin Books Ltd, Registered Offices: 80 Strand, London WC2R 0RL, England

30

Library of Congress Cataloging-in-Publication Data is available

Printed in the United States of America

ONE

I FELT HER FEAR BEFORE I heard her screams.

Her nightmare pulsed into me, shaking me out of my own dream, which had had something to do with a beach and some hot guy rubbing suntan oil on me. Images—hers, not mine—tumbled through my mind: fire and blood, the smell of smoke, the twisted metal of a car. The pictures wrapped around me, suffocating me, until some rational part of my brain reminded me that this wasn't *my* dream.

I woke up, strands of long, dark hair sticking to my forehead.

Lissa lay in her bed, thrashing and screaming. I bolted out of mine, quickly crossing the few feet that separated us.

"Liss," I said, shaking her. "Liss, wake up."

Her screams dropped off, replaced by soft whimpers. "Andre," she moaned. "Oh God."

I helped her sit up. "Liss, you aren't there anymore. Wake up."

After a few moments, her eyes fluttered open, and in the dim lighting, I could see a flicker of consciousness start to take over. Her frantic breathing slowed, and she leaned into me, resting her head against my shoulder. I put an arm around her and ran a hand over her hair.

"It's okay," I told her gently. "Everything's okay."

"I had that dream."

"Yeah. I know."

We sat like that for several minutes, not saying anything else. When I felt her emotions calm down, I leaned over to the nightstand between our beds and turned on the lamp. It glowed dimly, but neither of us really needed much to see by. Attracted by the light, our housemate's cat, Oscar, leapt up onto the sill of the open window.

He gave me a wide berth—animals don't like dhampirs, for whatever reason—but jumped onto the bed and rubbed his head against Lissa, purring softly. Animals didn't have a problem with Moroi, and they all loved Lissa in particular. Smiling, she scratched his chin, and I felt her calm further.

"When did we last do a feeding?" I asked, studying her face. Her fair skin was paler than usual. Dark circles hung under her eyes, and there was an air of frailty about her. School had been hectic this week, and I couldn't remember the last time I'd given her blood. "It's been like . . . more than two days, hasn't it? Three? Why didn't you say anything?"

She shrugged and wouldn't meet my eyes. "You were busy. I didn't want to—"

"Screw that," I said, shifting into a better position. No wonder she seemed so weak. Oscar, not wanting me any closer, leapt down and returned to the window, where he could watch at a safe distance. "Come on. Let's do this."

"Rose—"

"Come *on*. It'll make you feel better."

I tilted my head and tossed my hair back, baring my neck. I saw her hesitate, but the sight of my neck and what it offered proved too powerful. A hungry expression crossed her face, and her lips parted slightly, exposing the fangs she normally kept hidden while living among humans. Those fangs contrasted oddly with the rest of her features. With her pretty face and pale blond hair, she looked more like an angel than a vampire.

As her teeth neared my bare skin, I felt my heart race with a mix of fear and anticipation. I always hated feeling the latter, but it was nothing I could help, a weakness I couldn't shake.

Her fangs bit into me, hard, and I cried out at the brief flare of pain. Then it faded, replaced by a wonderful, golden joy that spread through my body. It was better than any of the times I'd been drunk or high. Better than sex—or so I imagined, since I'd never done it. It was a blanket of pure, refined pleasure, wrapping me up and promising everything would be right in the world. On and on it went. The chemicals in her saliva triggered an endorphin rush, and I lost track of the world, lost track of who I was.

Then, regretfully, it was over. It had taken less than a minute.

She pulled back, wiping her hand across her lips as she studied me. "You okay?"

"I . . . yeah." I lay back on the bed, dizzy from the blood loss. "I just need to sleep it off. I'm fine."

Her pale, jade-green eyes watched me with concern. She stood up. "I'm going to get you something to eat."

My protests came awkwardly to my lips, and she left before I could get out a sentence. The buzz from her bite had lessened as soon as she broke the connection, but some of it still lingered in my veins, and I felt a goofy smile cross my lips. Turning my head, I glanced up at Oscar, still sitting in the window.

"You don't know what you're missing," I told him.

His attention was on something outside. Hunkering down into a crouch, he puffed out his jet-black fur. His tail started twitching.

My smile faded, and I forced myself to sit up. The world spun, and I waited for it to right itself before trying to stand. When I managed it, the dizziness set in again and this time refused to leave. Still, I felt okay enough to stumble to the window and peer out with Oscar. He eyed me warily, scooted over a little, and then returned to whatever had held his attention.

A warm breeze—unseasonably warm for a Portland fall—played with my hair as I leaned out. The street was dark and relatively quiet. It was three in the morning, just about the only time a college campus settled down, at least somewhat. The house in which we'd rented a room for the past eight months sat on a residential street with old, mismatched houses. Across the road, a streetlight flickered, nearly ready to burn out. It still cast enough light for me to make out the shapes of cars and buildings. In our own yard, I could see the silhouettes of trees and bushes.

And a man watching me.

I jerked back in surprise. A figure stood by a tree in the yard, about thirty feet away, where he could easily see through the window. He was close enough that I probably could have thrown something and hit him. He was certainly close enough that he could have seen what Lissa and I had just done.

The shadows covered him so well that even with my heightened sight, I couldn't make out any of his features, save for his height. He was tall. Really tall. He stood there for just a moment, barely discernible, and then stepped back, disappearing into the shadows cast by the trees on the far side of the yard. I was pretty sure I saw someone else move nearby and join him before the blackness swallowed them both.

Whoever these figures were, Oscar didn't like them. Not counting me, he usually got along with most people, growing upset only when someone posed an immediate danger. The guy outside hadn't done anything threatening to Oscar, but the cat had sensed something, something that put him on edge.

Something similar to what he always sensed in me.

Icy fear raced through me, almost—but not quite—eradicating the lovely bliss of Lissa's bite. Backing up from the window, I jerked on a pair of jeans that I found on the floor, nearly falling over in the process. Once they were on, I grabbed my coat and Lissa's, along with our wallets. Shoving my feet into the first shoes I saw, I headed out the door.

Downstairs, I found her in the cramped kitchen, rummaging through the refrigerator. One of our housemates, Jeremy, sat at the table, hand on his forehead as he stared sadly at a calculus book. Lissa regarded me with surprise.

"You shouldn't be up."

"We have to go. Now."

Her eyes widened, and then a moment later, understanding clicked in. "Are you . . . really? Are you sure?"

I nodded. I couldn't explain how I knew for sure. I just did.

Jeremy watched us curiously. "What's wrong?"

An idea came to mind. "Liss, get his car keys."

He looked back and forth between us. "What are you—"

Lissa unhesitatingly walked over to him. Her fear poured into me through our psychic bond, but there was something else too: her complete faith that I would take care of everything, that we would be safe. Like always, I hoped I was worthy of that kind of trust.

She smiled broadly and gazed directly into his eyes. For a moment, Jeremy just stared, still confused, and then I saw the thrall seize him. His eyes glazed over, and he regarded her adoringly.

"We need to borrow your car," she said in a gentle voice. "Where are your keys?"

He smiled, and I shivered. I had a high resistance to compulsion, but I could still feel its effects when it was directed at another person. That, and I'd been taught my entire life that using it was wrong. Reaching into his pocket, Jeremy handed over a set of keys hanging on a large red key chain.

"Thank you," said Lissa. "And where is it parked?"

"Down the street," he said dreamily. "At the corner. By Brown." Four blocks away.

"Thank you," she repeated, backing up. "As soon as we leave, I want you to go back to studying. Forget you ever saw us tonight."

He nodded obligingly. I got the impression he would have walked off a cliff for her right then if she'd asked. All humans were susceptible to compulsion, but Jeremy appeared weaker than most. That came in handy right now.

"Come on," I told her. "We've got to move."

We stepped outside, heading toward the corner he'd named. I was still dizzy from the bite and kept stumbling, unable to move as quickly as I wanted. Lissa had to catch hold of me a few times to stop me from falling. All the time, that anxiety rushed into me from her mind. I tried my best to ignore it; I had my own fears to deal with.

"Rose . . . what are we going to do if they catch us?" she whispered.

"They won't," I said fiercely. "I won't let them."

"But if they've found us—"

"They found us before. They didn't catch us then. We'll just drive over to the train station and go to L.A. They'll lose the trail."

I made it sound simple. I always did, even though there

was nothing simple about being on the run from the people we'd grown up with. We'd been doing it for two years, hiding wherever we could and just trying to finish high school. Our senior year had just started, and living on a college campus had seemed safe. We were so close to freedom.

She said nothing more, and I felt her faith in me surge up once more. This was the way it had always been between us. I was the one who took action, who made sure things happened— sometimes recklessly so. She was the more reasonable one, the one who thought things out and researched them extensively before acting. Both styles had their uses, but at the moment, recklessness was called for. We didn't have time to hesitate.

Lissa and I had been best friends ever since kindergarten, when our teacher had paired us together for writing lessons. Forcing five-year-olds to spell *Vasilisa Dragomir* and *Rosemarie Hathaway* was beyond cruel, and we'd—or rather, *I'd*—responded appropriately. I'd chucked my book at our teacher and called her a fascist bastard. I hadn't known what those words meant, but I'd known how to hit a moving target.

Lissa and I had been inseparable ever since.

"Do you hear that?" she asked suddenly.

It took me a few seconds to pick up what her sharper senses already had. Footsteps, moving fast. I grimaced. We had two more blocks to go.

"We've got to run for it," I said, catching hold of her arm.

"But you can't—"

"*Run.*"

It took every ounce of my willpower not to pass out on the sidewalk. My body didn't want to run after losing blood or while still metabolizing the effects of her saliva. But I ordered my muscles to stop their bitching and clung to Lissa as our feet pounded against the concrete. Normally I could have out-run her without any extra effort—particularly since she was barefoot—but tonight, she was all that held me upright.

The pursuing footsteps grew louder, closer. Black stars danced before my eyes. Ahead of us, I could make out Jeremy's green Honda. Oh God, if we could just make it—

Ten feet from the car, a man stepped directly into our path. We came to a screeching halt, and I jerked Lissa back by her arm. It was *him*, the guy I'd seen across the street watching me. He was older than us, maybe mid-twenties, and as tall as I'd figured, probably six-six or six-seven. And under different circumstances—say, when he wasn't holding up our desperate escape—I would have thought he was hot. Shoulder-length brown hair, tied back in a short ponytail. Dark brown eyes. A long brown coat—a duster, I thought it was called.

But his hotness was irrelevant now. He was only an obstacle keeping Lissa and me away from the car and our freedom. The footsteps behind us slowed, and I knew our pursuers had caught up. Off to the sides, I detected more movement, more people closing in. God. They'd sent almost a dozen guardians to retrieve us. I couldn't believe it. The queen herself didn't travel with that many.

Panicked and not entirely in control of my higher reasoning, I acted out of instinct. I pressed up to Lissa, keeping her behind me and away from the man who appeared to be the leader.

"Leave her alone," I growled. "Don't touch her."

His face was unreadable, but he held out his hands in what was apparently supposed to be some sort of calming gesture, like I was a rabid animal he was planning to sedate.

"I'm not going to—"

He took a step forward. Too close.

I attacked him, leaping out in an offensive maneuver I hadn't used in two years, not since Lissa and I had run away. The move was stupid, another reaction born of instinct and fear. And it was hopeless. He was a skilled guardian, not a novice who hadn't finished his training. He also wasn't weak and on the verge of passing out.

And man, was he fast. I'd forgotten how fast guardians could be, how they could move and strike like cobras. He knocked me off as though brushing away a fly, and his hands slammed into me and sent me backwards. I don't think he meant to strike that hard—probably just intended to keep me away—but my lack of coordination interfered with my ability to respond. Unable to catch my footing, I started to fall, heading straight toward the sidewalk at a twisted angle, hip-first. It was going to hurt. A *lot*.

Only it didn't.

Just as quickly as he'd blocked me, the man reached out and caught my arm, keeping me upright. When I'd steadied myself, I noticed he was staring at me—or, more precisely, at my neck. Still disoriented, I didn't get it right away. Then, slowly, my free hand reached up to the side of my throat and lightly touched the wound Lissa had made earlier. When I pulled my fingers back, I saw slick, dark blood on my skin. Embarrassed, I shook my hair so that it fell forward around my face. My hair was thick and long and completely covered my neck. I'd grown it out for precisely this reason.

The guy's dark eyes lingered on the now-covered bite a moment longer and then met mine. I returned his look defiantly and quickly jerked out of his hold. He let me go, though I knew he could have restrained me all night if he'd wanted. Fighting the nauseating dizziness, I backed toward Lissa again, bracing myself for another attack. Suddenly, her hand caught hold of mine. "Rose," she said quietly. "Don't."

Her words had no effect on me at first, but calming thoughts gradually began to settle in my mind, coming across through the bond. It wasn't exactly compulsion—she wouldn't use that on me—but it was effectual, as was the fact that we were hopelessly outnumbered and outclassed. Even I knew struggling would be pointless. The tension left my body, and I sagged in defeat.

Sensing my resignation, the man stepped forward, turning his attention to Lissa. His face was calm. He swept her a bow and managed to look graceful doing it, which surprised me considering his height. "My name is Dimitri Belikov," he said. I could hear a faint Russian accent. "I've come to take you back to St. Vladimir's Academy, Princess."

TWO

MY HATRED NOTWITHSTANDING, I HAD to admit Dimitri Beli-whatever was pretty smart. After they'd carted us off to the airport to and onto the Academy's private jet, he'd taken one look at the two of us whispering and ordered us separated.

"Don't let them talk to each other," he warned the guardian who escorted me to the back of the plane. "Five minutes together, and they'll come up with an escape plan."

I shot him a haughty look and stormed off down the aisle. Never mind the fact we *had* been planning escape.

As it was, things didn't look good for our heroes—or heroines, rather. Once we were in the air, our odds of escape dropped further. Even supposing a miracle occurred and I did manage to take out all ten guardians, we'd sort of have a problem in getting off the plane. I figured they might have parachutes aboard somewhere, but in the unlikely event I'd be able to operate one, there was still that little issue of survival, seeing as we'd probably land somewhere in the Rocky Mountains.

No, we weren't getting off this plane until it landed in backwoods Montana. I'd have to think of something then, something that involved getting past the Academy's magical wards and ten times as many guardians. Yeah. No problem.

Although Lissa sat at the front with the Russian guy, her fear sang back to me, pounding inside my head like a hammer. My concern for her cut into my fury. They couldn't take her back *there*, not to that place. I wondered if Dimitri might have hesitated if he could feel what I did and if he knew what I knew. Probably not. He didn't care.

As it was, her emotions grew so strong that for a moment, I had the disorienting sensation of sitting in her seat—in her *skin* even. It happened sometimes, and without much warning, she'd pull me right into her head. Dimitri's tall frame sat beside me, and my hand—*her* hand—gripped a bottle of water. He leaned forward to pick up something, revealing six tiny symbols tattooed on the back of his neck: *molnija* marks. They looked like two streaks of jagged lightning crossing in an X symbol. One for each Strigoi he'd killed. Above them was a twisting line, sort of like a snake, that marked him as a guardian. The promise mark.

Blinking, I fought against her and shifted back into my own head with a grimace. I hated when that happened. Feeling Lissa's emotions was one thing, but slipping into her was something we both despised. She saw it as an invasion of privacy, so I usually didn't tell her when it happened. Neither of us could control it. It was another effect of the bond, a bond neither of us fully understood. Legends existed about psychic links between guardians and their Moroi, but the stories had never mentioned anything like this. We fumbled through it as best we could.

Near the end of the flight, Dimitri walked back to where I sat and traded places with the guardian beside me. I pointedly turned away, staring out the window absentmindedly.

Several moments of silence passed. Finally, he said, "Were you really going to attack all of us?"

I didn't answer.

"Doing that . . . protecting her like that—it was very brave." He paused. "*Stupid*, but still brave. Why did you even try it?"

I glanced over at him, brushing my hair out of my face so I could look him levelly in the eye. "Because I'm her guardian." I turned back toward the window.

After another quiet moment, he stood up and returned to the front of the jet.

When we landed, Lissa and I had no choice but to let the commandos drive us out to the Academy. Our car stopped at the gate, and our driver spoke with guards who verified we weren't Strigoi about to go off on a killing spree. After a minute, they let us pass on through the wards and up to the Academy itself. It was around sunset—the start of the vampiric day—and the campus lay wrapped in shadows.

It probably looked the same, sprawling and gothic. The Moroi were big on tradition; nothing ever changed with them. This school wasn't as old as the ones back in Europe, but it had been built in the same style. The buildings boasted elaborate, almost churchlike architecture, with high peaks and stone carvings. Wrought iron gates enclosed small gardens and doorways here and there. After living on a college campus, I had a new appreciation for just how much this place resembled a university more than a typical high school.

We were on the secondary campus, which was divided into lower and upper schools. Each was built around a large open quadrangle decorated with stone paths and enormous, century-old trees. We were going toward the upper school's quad, which had academic buildings on one side, while dhampir dormitories and the gym sat opposite. Moroi dorms sat on one of the other ends, and opposite them were the administrative buildings that also served the lower school. Younger students lived on the primary campus, farther to the west.

Around all the campuses was space, space, and more space. We were in Montana, after all, miles away from any real city. The air felt cool in my lungs and smelled of pine and wet, decaying leaves. Overgrown forests ringed the perimeters of the Academy, and during the day, you could see mountains rising up in the distance.

As we walked into the main part of the upper school, I broke from my guardian and ran up to Dimitri.

"Hey, Comrade."

He kept walking and wouldn't look at me. "You want to talk now?

"Are you taking us to Kirova?"

"*Headmistress* Kirova," he corrected. On the other side of him, Lissa shot me a look that said, *Don't start something*.

"Headmistress. Whatever. She's still a self-righteous old bit—"

My words faded as the guardians led us through a set of doors—straight into the commons. I sighed. Were these people *really* so cruel? There had to be at least a dozen ways to get to Kirova's office, and they were taking us right through the center of the commons.

And it was breakfast time.

Novice guardians—dhampirs like me—and Moroi sat together, eating and socializing, faces alight with whatever current gossip held the Academy's attention. When we entered, the loud buzz of conversation stopped instantly, like someone had flipped a switch. Hundreds of sets of eyes swiveled toward us.

I returned the stares of my former classmates with a lazy grin, trying to get a sense as to whether things had changed. Nope. Didn't seem like it. Camille Conta still looked like the prim, perfectly groomed bitch I remembered, still the self-appointed leader of the Academy's royal Moroi cliques. Off to the side, Lissa's gawky near-cousin Natalie watched with wide eyes, as innocent and naive as before.

And on the other side of the room . . . well, that was interesting. Aaron. Poor, poor Aaron, who'd no doubt had his heart broken when Lissa left. He still looked as cute as ever—maybe more so now—with those same golden looks that complemented hers so well. His eyes followed her every move. Yes. Definitely not over her. It was sad, really, because Lissa had never really been all that into him. I think she'd gone out with him simply because it seemed like the expected thing to do.

But what I found most interesting was that Aaron had

apparently found a way to pass the time without her. Beside him, holding his hand, was a Moroi girl who looked about eleven but had to be older, unless he'd become a pedophile during our absence. With plump little cheeks and blond ringlets, she looked like a porcelain doll. A very pissed off and evil porcelain doll. She gripped his hand tightly and shot Lissa a look of such burning hatred that it stunned me. What the hell was that all about? She was no one I knew. Just a jealous girlfriend, I guessed. I'd be pissed too if my guy was watching someone else like that.

Our walk of shame mercifully ended, though our new setting—Headmistress Kirova's office—didn't really improve things. The old hag looked exactly like I remembered, sharp-nosed and gray-haired. She was tall and slim, like most Moroi, and had always reminded me of a vulture. I knew her well because I'd spent a lot of time in her office.

Most of our escorts left us once Lissa and I were seated, and I felt a little less like a prisoner. Only Alberta, the captain of the school's guardians, and Dimitri stayed. They took up positions along the wall, looking stoic and terrifying, just as their job description required.

Kirova fixed her angry eyes on us and opened her mouth to begin what would no doubt be a major bitch session. A deep, gentle voice stopped her.

"Vasilisa."

Startled, I realized there was someone else in the room. I hadn't noticed. Careless for a guardian, even a novice one.

With a great deal of effort, Victor Dashkov rose from a corner chair. *Prince* Victor Dashkov. Lissa sprang up and ran to him, throwing her arms around his frail body.

"Uncle," she whispered. She sounded on the verge of tears as she tightened her grip.

With a small smile, he gently patted her back. "You have no idea how glad I am to see you safe, Vasilisa." He looked toward me. "And you too, Rose."

I nodded back, trying to hide how shocked I was. He'd been sick when we left, but this—this was *horrible*. He was Natalie's father, only about forty or so, but he looked twice that age. Pale. Withered. Hands shaking. My heart broke watching him. With all the horrible people in the world, it didn't seem fair that this guy should get a disease that was going to kill him young and ultimately keep him from becoming king.

Although not technically her uncle—the Moroi used family terms very loosely, especially the royals—Victor was a close friend of Lissa's family and had gone out of his way to help her after her parents had died. I liked him; he was the first person I was happy to see here.

Kirova let them have a few more moments and then stiffly drew Lissa back to her seat.

Time for the lecture.

It was a good one—one of Kirova's best, which was saying something. She was a master at them. I swear that was the only reason she'd gone into school administration, because

I had yet to see any evidence of her actually *liking* kids. The rant covered the usual topics: responsibility, reckless behavior, self-centeredness. . . . Bleh. I immediately found myself spacing out, alternatively pondering the logistics of escaping through the window in her office.

But when the tirade shifted to me—well, that was when I tuned back in.

"You, Miss Hathaway, broke the most sacred promise among our kind: the promise of a guardian to protect a Moroi. It is a great trust. A trust that you violated by selfishly taking the princess away from here. The Strigoi would love to finish off the Dragomirs; *you* nearly enabled them to do it."

"Rose didn't kidnap me." Lissa spoke before I could, her voice and face calm, despite her uneasy feelings. "I wanted to go. Don't blame her."

Ms. Kirova *tsk*ed at us both and paced the office, hands folded behind her narrow back.

"Miss Dragomir, you could have been the one who orchestrated the entire plan for all I know, but it was still *her* responsibility to make sure you didn't carry it out. If she'd done her duty, she would have notified someone. If she'd done her duty, she would have kept you safe."

I snapped.

"I *did* do my duty!" I shouted, jumping up from my chair. Dimitri and Alberta both flinched but left me alone since I wasn't trying to hit anyone. Yet. "I did keep her safe! I kept her safe when none of *you*"—I made a sweeping gesture around the room—"could do it. I took her away to protect her. I did what I had to do. You certainly weren't going to."

Through the bond, I felt Lissa trying to send me calming messages, again urging me not to let anger get the best of me. Too late.

Kirova stared at me, her face blank. "Miss Hathaway, forgive me if I fail to see the logic of how taking her out of a heavily guarded, magically secured environment is protecting her. Unless there's something you aren't telling us?"

I bit my lip.

"I see. Well, then. By my estimation, the only reason you left—aside from the novelty of it, no doubt—was to avoid the consequences of that horrible, destructive stunt you pulled just before your disappearance."

"No, that's not—"

"And that only makes my decision that much easier. As a Moroi, the princess must continue on here at the Academy for her own safety, but we have no such obligations to you. You will be sent away as soon as possible."

My cockiness dried up. "I . . . what?"

Lissa stood up beside me. "You can't do that! She's my guardian."

"She is no such thing, particularly since she isn't even a guardian at all. She's still a novice."

"But my parents—"

"I know what your parents wanted, God rest their souls,

but things have changed. Miss Hathaway is expendable. She doesn't deserve to be a guardian, and she will leave."

I stared at Kirova, unable to believe what I was hearing. "Where are you going to send me? To my mom in Nepal? Did she even know I was gone? Or maybe you'll send me off to my *father*?"

Her eyes narrowed at the bite in that last word. When I spoke again, my voice was so cold, I barely recognized it.

"Or maybe you're going to try to send me off to be a blood whore. Try that, and we'll be gone by the end of the day."

"Miss Hathaway," she hissed, "you are out of line."

"They have a bond." Dimitri's low, accented voice broke the heavy tension, and we all turned toward him. I think Kirova had forgotten he was there, but I hadn't. His presence was way too powerful to ignore. He still stood against the wall, looking like some sort of cowboy sentry in that ridiculous long coat of his. He looked at me, not Lissa, his dark eyes staring straight through me. "Rose knows what Vasilisa is feeling. Don't you?"

I at least had the satisfaction of seeing Kirova caught off guard as she glanced between us and Dimitri. "No . . . that's impossible. That hasn't happened in centuries."

"It's obvious," he said. "I suspected as soon as I started watching them."

Neither Lissa nor I responded, and I averted my eyes from his.

"That is a gift," murmured Victor from his corner. "A rare and wonderful thing."

"The best guardians always had that bond," added Dimitri. "In the stories."

Kirova's outrage returned. "Stories that are centuries old," she exclaimed. "Surely you aren't suggesting we let her stay at the Academy after everything she's done?"

He shrugged. "She might be wild and disrespectful, but if she has potential—"

"Wild and disrespectful?" I interrupted. "Who the hell are you anyway? Outsourced help?"

"Guardian Belikov is the princess's guardian now," said Kirova. "Her *sanctioned* guardian."

"You got cheap foreign labor to protect Lissa?"

That was pretty mean of me to say—particularly since most Moroi and their guardians were of Russian or Romanian descent—but the comment seemed cleverer at the time than it really was. And it wasn't like I was one to talk. I might have been raised in the U.S., but my parents were foreign-born. My dhampir mother was Scottish—red-haired, with a ridiculous accent—and I'd been told my Moroi dad was Turkish. That genetic combination had given me skin the same color as the inside of an almond, along with what I liked to think were semi-exotic desert-princess features: big dark eyes and hair so deep brown that it usually looked black. I wouldn't have minded inheriting the red hair, but we take what we get.

Kirova threw her hands up in exasperation and turned to him. "You see? Completely undisciplined! All the psychic bonds and *very* raw potential in the world can't make up for that. A guardian without discipline is worse than no guardian."

"So teach her discipline. Classes just started. Put her back in and get her training again."

"Impossible. She'll still be hopelessly behind her peers."

"No, I won't," I argued. No one listened to me.

"Then give her extra training sessions," he said.

They continued on while the rest of us watched the exchange like it was a Ping-Pong game. My pride was still hurt over the ease with which Dimitri had tricked us, but it occurred to me that he might very well keep me here with Lissa. Better to stay at this hellhole than be without her. Through our bond, I could feel her trickle of hope.

"Who's going to put in the extra time?" demanded Kirova. "You?"

Dimitri's argument came to an abrupt stop. "Well, that's not what I—"

Kirova crossed her arms with satisfaction. "Yes. That's what I thought."

Clearly at a loss, he frowned. His eyes flicked toward Lissa and me, and I wondered what he saw. Two pathetic girls, looking at him with big, pleading eyes? Or two runaways who'd broken out of a high-security school and swiped half of Lissa's inheritance?

"Yes," he said finally. "I can mentor Rose. I'll give her extra sessions along with her normal ones."

"And then what?" retorted Kirova angrily. "She goes unpunished?"

"Find some other way to punish her," answered Dimitri. "Guardian numbers have gone down too much to risk losing another. A girl, in particular."

His unspoken words made me shudder, reminding me of my earlier statement about "blood whores." Few dhampir girls became guardians anymore.

Victor suddenly spoke up from his corner. "I'm inclined to agree with Guardian Belikov. Sending Rose away would be a shame, a waste of talent."

Ms. Kirova stared out her window. It was completely black outside. With the Academy's nocturnal schedule, *morning* and *afternoon* were relative terms. That, and they kept the windows tinted to block out excess light.

When she turned back around, Lissa met her eyes. "Please, Ms. Kirova. Let Rose stay."

Oh, Lissa, I thought. *Be careful.* Using compulsion on another Moroi was dangerous—particularly in front of witnesses. But Lissa was only using a tiny bit, and we needed all the help we could get. Fortunately, no one seemed to realize what was happening.

I don't even know if the compulsion made a difference, but finally, Kirova sighed.

"If Miss Hathaway stays, here's how it will be." She turned to me. "Your continued enrollment at St. Vladimir's is strictly probationary. Step out of line *once*, and you're gone. You will attend all classes and required trainings for novices your age. You will also train with Guardian Belikov in every spare moment you have—before *and* after classes. Other than that, you are banned from all social activities, except meals, and will stay in your dorm. Fail to comply with any of this, and you will be sent . . . away."

I gave a harsh laugh. "Banned from all social activities? Are you trying to keep us apart?" I nodded toward Lissa. "Afraid we'll run away again?"

"I'm taking precautions. As I'm sure you recall, you were never properly punished for destroying school property. You have a lot to make up for." Her thin lips tightened into a straight line. "You are being offered a very generous deal. I suggest you don't let your attitude endanger it."

I started to say it wasn't generous at all, but then I caught Dimitri's gaze. It was hard to read. He might have been telling me he believed in me. He might have been telling me I was an idiot to keep fighting with Kirova. I didn't know.

Looking away from him for the second time during the meeting, I stared at the floor, conscious of Lissa beside me and her own encouragement burning in our bond. At long last, I exhaled and glanced back up at the headmistress.

"Fine. I accept."

THREE

SENDING US STRAIGHT TO CLASS after our meeting seemed beyond cruel, but that's exactly what Kirova did. Lissa was led away, and I watched her go, glad the bond would allow me to keep reading her emotional temperature.

They actually sent me to one of the guidance counselors first. He was an ancient Moroi guy, one I remembered from before I'd left. I honestly couldn't believe he was still around. The guy was so freaking old, he should have retired. Or died.

The visit took all of five minutes. He said nothing about my return and asked a few questions about what classes I'd taken in Chicago and Portland. He compared those against my old file and hastily scrawled out a new schedule. I took it sullenly and headed out to my first class.

1st Period	Advanced Guardian Combat Techniques
2nd Period	Bodyguard Theory and Personal Protection 3
3rd Period	Weight Training and Conditioning
4th Period	Senior Language Arts (Novices)
	—Lunch—
5th Period	Animal Behavior and Physiology
6th Period	Precalculus

7th Period   *Moroi Culture 4*

8th Period   *Slavic Art*

Ugh. I'd forgotten how long the Academy's school day was. Novices and Moroi took separate classes during the first half of the day, which meant I wouldn't see Lissa until after lunch—if we had any afternoon classes together. Most of them were standard senior classes, so I felt my odds were pretty good. Slavic art struck me as the kind of elective no one signed up for, so hopefully they'd stuck her in there too.

Dimitri and Alberta escorted me to the guardians' gym for first period, neither one acknowledging my existence. Walking behind them, I saw how Alberta wore her hair in a short, pixie cut that showed her promise mark and *molnija* marks. A lot of female guardians did this. It didn't matter so much for me now, since my neck had no tattoos yet, but I didn't want to ever cut my hair.

She and Dimitri didn't say anything and walked along almost like it was any other day. When we arrived, the reactions of my peers indicated it was anything but. They were in the middle of setting up when we entered the gym, and just like in the commons, all eyes fell on me. I couldn't decide if I felt like a rock star or a circus freak.

All right, then. If I was going to be stuck here for a while, I wasn't going to act afraid of them all anymore. Lissa and I had once held this school's respect, and it was time to remind everyone of that. Scanning the staring, openmouthed novices, I looked for a familiar face. Most of them were guys. One caught my eye, and I could barely hold back my grin.

"Hey Mason, wipe the drool off your face. If you're going to think about me naked, do it on your own time."

A few snorts and snickers broke the awed silence, and Mason Ashford snapped out of his haze, giving me a lopsided smile. With red hair that stuck up everywhere and a smattering of freckles, he was nice-looking, though not exactly hot. He was also one of the funniest guys I knew. We'd been good friends back in the day.

"This *is* my time, Hathaway. I'm leading today's session."

"Oh yeah?" I retorted. "Huh. Well, I guess this is a good time to think about me naked, then."

"It's *always* a good a time to think about you naked," added someone nearby, breaking the tension further. Eddie Castile. Another friend of mine.

Dimitri shook his head and walked off, muttering something in Russian that didn't sound complimentary. But as for me . . . well, just like that, I was one of the novices again. They were an easygoing bunch, less focused on pedigree and politics than the Moroi students.

The class engulfed me, and I found myself laughing and seeing those I'd nearly forgotten about. Everyone wanted to know where we'd been; apparently Lissa and I had become legends. I couldn't tell them why we'd left, of course, so I offered up a lot of taunts and wouldn't-you-like-to-knows that served just as well.

The happy reunion lasted a few more minutes before the adult guardian who oversaw the training came over and scolded Mason for neglecting his duties. Still grinning, he barked out orders to everyone, explaining what exercises to start with. Uneasily, I realized I didn't know most of them.

"Come on, Hathaway," he said, taking my arm. "You can be my partner. Let's see what you've been doing all this time."

An hour later, he had his answer.

"Not practicing, huh?"

"Ow," I groaned, momentarily incapable of normal speech.

He extended a hand and helped me up from the mat he'd knocked me down on—about fifty times.

"I hate you," I told him, rubbing a spot on my thigh that was going to have a wicked bruise tomorrow.

"You'd hate me more if I held back."

"Yeah, that's true," I agreed, staggering along as the class put the equipment back.

"You actually did okay."

"What? I just had my ass handed to me."

"Well, of course you did. It's been two years. But hey, you're still walking. That's something." He grinned mockingly.

"Did I mention I hate you?"

He flashed me another smile, which quickly faded to something more serious. "Don't take this the wrong way. . . . I mean, you really are a scrapper, but there's no way you'll be able to take your trials in the spring—"

"They're making me take extra practice sessions," I explained. Not that it mattered. I planned on getting Lissa and me out of here before these practices really became an issue. "I'll be ready."

"Extra sessions with who?"

"That tall guy. Dimitri."

Mason stopped walking and stared at me. "You're putting in extra time with Belikov?"

"Yeah, so what?"

"So the man is a *god*."

"Exaggerate much?" I asked.

"No, I'm serious. I mean, he's all quiet and antisocial usually, but when he fights . . . wow. If you think you're hurting now, you're going to be dead when he's done with you."

Great. Something else to improve my day.

I elbowed him and went on to second period. That class covered the essentials of being a bodyguard and was required for all seniors. Actually, it was the third in a series that had started junior year. That meant I was behind in this class too, but I hoped protecting Lissa in the real world had given me some insight.

Our instructor was Stan Alto, whom we referred to simply as "Stan" behind his back and "Guardian Alto" in formal settings. He was a little older than Dimitri, but not nearly as tall, and he always looked pissed off. Today, that look intensified when he walked into the classroom and saw me sitting there. His eyes widened in mock surprise as he circled the room and came to stand beside my desk.

"What's this? No one told me we had a guest speaker here today. Rose Hathaway. What a privilege! How very *generous* of you to take time out of your busy schedule and share your knowledge with us."

I felt my cheeks burning, but in a great show of self-control, I stopped myself from telling him to fuck off. I'm pretty sure my face must have delivered that message, however, because his sneer increased. He gestured for me to stand up.

"Well, come on, come on. Don't sit there! Come up to the front so you can help me lecture the class."

I sank into my seat. "You don't really mean—"

The taunting smile dried up. "I mean *exactly* what I say, Hathaway. Go to the front of the class."

A thick silence enveloped the room. Stan was a scary instructor, and most of the class was too awed to laugh at my disgrace quite yet. Refusing to crack, I strode up to the front of the room and turned to face the class. I gave them a bold look and tossed my hair over my shoulders, earning a few sympathetic smiles from my friends. I then noticed I had a larger audience than expected. A few guardians—including Dimitri—lingered in the back of the room. Outside the Academy, guardians focused on one-on-one protection. Here, guardians had a lot more people to protect *and* they had to train the novices. So rather than follow any one person around, they worked shifts guarding the school as a whole and monitoring classes.

"So, Hathaway," said Stan cheerfully, strolling back up to the front with me. "Enlighten us about your protective techniques."

"My . . . techniques?"

"Of course. Because presumably you must have had some sort of plan the rest of us couldn't understand when you took an underage Moroi royal out of the Academy and exposed her to constant Strigoi threats."

It was the Kirova lecture all over again, except with more witnesses.

"We never ran into any Strigoi," I replied stiffly.

"Obviously," he said with a snicker. "I already figured that out, seeing as how you're still alive."

I wanted to shout that maybe I could have defeated a Strigoi, but after getting beat up in the last class, I now suspected I couldn't have survived an attack by Mason, let alone an actual Strigoi.

When I didn't say anything, Stan started pacing in front of the class.

"So what'd you do? How'd you make sure she stayed safe? Did you avoid going out at night?"

"Sometimes." That was true—especially when we'd first run away. We'd relaxed a little after months went by with no attacks.

"*Sometimes*," he repeated in a high-pitched voice, making my answer sound incredibly stupid. "Well then, I suppose you slept during the day and stayed on guard at night."

"Er . . . no."

"No? But that's one of the first things mentioned in the chapter on solo guarding. Oh wait, you wouldn't know that because *you weren't here.*"

I swallowed back more swear words. "I watched the area whenever we went out," I said, needing to defend myself.

"Oh? Well that's something. Did you use Carnegie's Quadrant Surveillance Method or the Rotational Survey?"

I didn't say anything.

"Ah. I'm guessing you used the Hathaway Glance-Around-When-You-Remember-To Method."

"No!" I exclaimed angrily. "That's not true. I watched her. She's still alive, isn't she?"

He walked back up to me and leaned toward my face. "Because you got *lucky.*"

"Strigoi aren't lurking around every corner out there," I shot back. "It's not like what we've been taught. It's safer than you guys make it sound."

"Safer? *Safer?* We are at war with the Strigoi!" he yelled. I could smell coffee on his breath, he was so close. "One of them could walk right up to you and snap your pretty little neck before you even noticed him—and he'd barely break a sweat doing it. You might have more speed and strength than a Moroi or a human, but you are nothing, *nothing,* compared to a Strigoi. They are deadly, and they are powerful. And do you know what makes them more powerful?"

No way was I going to let this jerk make me cry. Looking

away from him, I tried to focus on something else. My eyes rested on Dimitri and the other guardians. They were watching my humiliation, stone-faced.

"Moroi blood," I whispered.

"What was that?" asked Stan loudly. "I didn't catch it."

I spun back around to face him. "Moroi blood! Moroi blood makes them stronger."

He nodded in satisfaction and took a few steps back. "Yes. It does. It makes them stronger and harder to destroy. They'll kill and drink from a human or dhampir, but they want Moroi blood more than anything else. They seek it. They've turned to the dark side to gain immortality, and they want to do whatever they can to keep that immortality. Desperate Strigoi have attacked Moroi in public. Groups of Strigoi have raided academies exactly like this one. There are Strigoi who have lived for thousands of years and fed off generations of Moroi. They're almost impossible to kill. And *that* is why Moroi numbers are dropping. They aren't strong enough—even with guardians—to protect themselves. Some Moroi don't even see the point of running anymore and are simply turning Strigoi by choice. And as the Moroi disappear . . ."

". . . so do the dhampirs," I finished.

"Well," he said, licking sprayed spit off his lips. "It looks like you learned something after all. Now we'll have to see if you can learn enough to pass this class and qualify for your field experience next semester."

Ouch. I spent the rest of that horrible class—in my seat,

thankfully—replaying those last words in my mind. The senior-year field experience was the best part of a novice's education. We'd have no classes for half a semester. Instead, we'd each be assigned a Moroi student to guard and follow around. The adult guardians would monitor us and test us with staged attacks and other threats. How a novice passed that field experience was almost as important as all the rest of her grades combined. It could influence which Moroi she got assigned to after graduation.

And me? There was only one Moroi I wanted.

Two classes later, I finally earned my lunch escape. As I stumbled across campus toward the commons, Dimitri fell into step beside me, not looking particularly godlike—unless you counted his godly good looks.

"I suppose you saw what happened in Stan's class?" I asked, not bothering with titles.

"Yes."

"And you don't think that was unfair?"

"Was he right? Do you think you were fully prepared to protect Vasilisa?"

I looked down at the ground. "I kept her alive," I mumbled.

"How did you do fighting against your classmates today?"

The question was mean. I didn't answer and knew I didn't need to. I'd had another training class after Stan's, and no doubt Dimitri had watched me get beat up there too.

"If you can't fight *them*—"

"Yeah, yeah, I know," I snapped.

He slowed his long stride to match my pain-filled one. "You're strong and fast by nature. You just need to keep yourself trained. Didn't you play any sports while you were gone?"

"Sure," I shrugged. "Now and then."

"You didn't join any teams?"

"Too much work. If I'd wanted to practice that much, I'd have stayed here."

He gave me an exasperated look. "You'll never be able to really protect the princess if you don't hone your skills. You'll always be lacking."

"I'll be able to protect her," I said fiercely.

"You have no guarantees of being assigned to her, you know—for your field experience *or* after you graduate." Dimitri's voice was low and unapologetic. They hadn't given me a warm and fuzzy mentor. "No one wants to waste the bond—but no one's going to give her an inadequate guardian either. If you want to be with her, then you need to work for it. You have your lessons. You have me. Use us or don't. You're an ideal choice to guard Vasilisa when you both graduate—if you can prove you're worthy. I hope you will."

"Lissa, call her Lissa," I corrected. She hated her full name, much preferring the Americanized nickname.

He walked away, and suddenly, I didn't feel like such a badass anymore.

By now, I'd burned up a lot of time leaving class. Most everyone else had long since sprinted inside the commons for lunch, eager to maximize their social time. I'd almost made it back there myself when a voice under the door's overhang called to me.

"Rose?"

Peering in the voice's direction, I caught sight of Victor Dashkov, his kind face smiling at me as he leaned on a cane near the building's wall. His two guardians stood nearby at a polite distance.

"Mr. Dash—er, Your Highness. Hi."

I caught myself just in time, having nearly forgotten Moroi royal terms. I hadn't used them while living among humans. The Moroi chose their rulers from among twelve royal families. The eldest in the family got the title of "prince" or "princess." Lissa had gotten hers because she was the only one left in her line.

"How was your first day?" he asked.

"Not over yet." I tried to think of something conversational. "Are you visiting here for a while?"

"I'll be leaving this afternoon after I say hello to Natalie. When I heard Vasilisa—and you—had returned, I simply had to come see you."

I nodded, not sure what else to say. He was more Lissa's friend than mine.

"I wanted to tell you . . ." He spoke hesitantly. "I understand the gravity of what you did, but I think Headmistress

Kirova failed to acknowledge something. You *did* keep Vasilisa safe all this time. That is impressive."

"Well, it's not like I faced down Strigoi or anything," I said.

"But you faced down some things?"

"Sure. The school sent psi-hounds once."

"Remarkable."

"Not really. Avoiding them was pretty easy."

He laughed. "I've hunted with them before. They aren't *that* easy to evade, not with their powers and intelligence." It was true. Psi-hounds were one of many types of magical creatures that wandered the world, creatures that humans never knew about or else didn't believe they'd really seen. The hounds traveled in packs and shared a sort of psychic communication that made them particularly deadly to their prey—as did the fact that they resembled mutant wolves. "Did you face anything else?"

I shrugged. "Little things here and there."

"Remarkable," he repeated.

"Lucky, I think. It turns out I'm really behind in all this guardian stuff." I sounded just like Stan now.

"You're a smart girl. You'll catch up. And you also have your bond."

I looked away. My ability to "feel" Lissa had been such a secret for so long, it felt weird to have others know about it.

"The histories are full of stories of guardians who could feel when their charges were in danger," Victor continued.

"I've made a hobby of studying up on it and some of the ancient ways. I've heard it's a tremendous asset."

"I guess." I shrugged. *What a boring hobby,* I thought, imagining him poring over prehistoric histories in some dank library covered in spiderwebs.

Victor tilted his head, curiosity all over his face. Kirova and the others had had the same look when we'd mentioned our connection, like we were lab rats. "What is it like—if you don't mind me asking?"

"It's . . . I don't know. I just sort of always have this hum of how she feels. Usually it's just emotions. We can't send messages or anything." I didn't tell him about slipping into her head. That part of it was hard even for me to understand.

"But it doesn't work the other way? She doesn't sense you?"

I shook my head.

His face shone with wonder. "How did it happen?"

"I don't know," I said, still glancing away. "Just started two years ago."

He frowned. "Near the time of the accident?"

Hesitantly, I nodded. The accident was *not* something I wanted to talk about, that was for sure. Lissa's memories were bad enough without my own mixing into them. Twisted metal. A sensation of hot, then cold, then hot again. Lissa screaming over me, screaming for me to wake up, screaming for her parents and her brother to wake up. None of them had, only me.

And the doctors said that was a miracle in itself. They said I shouldn't have survived.

Apparently sensing my discomfort, Victor let the moment go and returned to his earlier excitement.

"I can still barely believe this. It's been so long since this has happened. If it did happen more often . . . just think what it could do for the safety of all Moroi. If only others could experience this too. I'll have to do more research and see if we can replicate it with others."

"Yeah." I was getting impatient, despite how much I liked him. Natalie rambled a lot, and it was pretty clear which parent she'd inherited *that* quality from. Lunch was ticking down, and although Moroi and novices shared afternoon classes, Lissa and I wouldn't have much time to talk.

"Perhaps we could—" He started coughing, a great, seizing fit that made his whole body shake. His disease, Sandovsky's Syndrome, took the lungs down with it while dragging the body toward death. I cast an anxious look at his guardians, and one of them stepped forward. "Your Highness," he said politely, "you need to go inside. It's too cold out here."

Victor nodded. "Yes, yes. And I'm sure Rose here wants to eat." He turned to me. "Thank you for speaking to me. I can't emphasize how much it means to me that Vasilisa is safe—and that you helped with that. I'd promised her father I'd look after her if anything happened to him, and I felt like quite the failure when you left."

A sinking sensation filled my stomach as I imagined him wracked with guilt and worry over our disappearance. Until now, I hadn't really thought about how others might have felt about us leaving.

We made our goodbyes, and I finally arrived inside the school. As I did, I felt Lissa's anxiety spike. Ignoring the pain in my legs, I picked up my pace into the commons.

And nearly ran right into her.

She didn't see me, though. Neither did the people standing with her: Aaron and that little doll girl. I stopped and listened, just catching the end of the conversation. The girl leaned toward Lissa, who seemed more stunned than anything else.

"It looks to *me* like it came from a garage sale. I thought a precious Dragomir would have standards." Scorn dripped off the word *Dragomir*.

Grabbing Doll Girl by the shoulder, I jerked her away. She was so light, she stumbled three feet and nearly fell.

"She does have standards," I said, "which is why you're done talking to her."

FOUR

WE DIDN'T HAVE THE ENTIRE commons' attention this time, thank God, but a few passing people had stopped to stare.

"What the hell do you think you're doing?" asked Doll Girl, blue eyes wide and sparkling with fury. Up close now, I was able to get a better look at her. She had the same slim build as most Moroi but not the usual height, which was partly what made her look so young. The tiny purple dress she wore was gorgeous—reminding me that I was indeed dressed in thrift-shop wear—but closer inspection led me to think it was a designer knockoff .

I crossed my arms across my chest. "Are you lost, little girl? The elementary school's over on west campus."

A pink flush spread over her cheeks. "Don't you ever touch me again. You screw with me, and I'll screw you right back."

Oh man, what an opening that was. Only a head shake from Lissa stopped me from unleashing any number of hilarious comebacks. Instead, I opted for simple brute force, so to speak.

"And if you mess with either of us again, I'll break you in half. If you don't believe me, go ask Dawn Yarrow about what

I did to her arm in ninth grade. You were probably at nap time when it happened."

The incident with Dawn hadn't been one of my finer moments. I honestly hadn't expected to break any bones when I shoved her into a tree. Still, the incident had given me a dangerous reputation, in addition to my smartass one. The story had gained legendary status, and I liked to imagine that it was still being told around campfires late at night. Judging from the look on this girl's face, it was.

One of the patrolling staff members strolled by right then, casting suspicious eyes at our little meeting. Doll Girl backed off, taking Aaron's arm. "Come on," she said.

"Hey, Aaron," I said cheerfully, remembering he was there. "Nice to see you again."

He gave me a quick nod and an uneasy smile, just as the girl dragged him off. Same old Aaron. He might be nice and cute, but aggressive he was not.

I turned to Lissa. "You okay?" She nodded. "Any idea who I just threatened to beat up?"

"Not a clue." I started to lead her toward the lunch line, but she shook her head at me. "Gotta go see the feeders."

A funny feeling settled over me. I'd gotten so used to being her primary blood source that the thought of returning to the Moroi's normal routine seemed strange. In fact, it almost bothered me. It shouldn't have. Daily feedings were part of a Moroi's life, something I hadn't been able to offer her while living on our own. It had been an inconvenient situation, one that left me weak on feeding days and her weak on the days in between. I should have been happy she would get some normality.

I forced a smile. "Sure."

We walked into the feeding room, which sat adjacent to the cafeteria. It was set up with small cubicles, dividing the room's space in an effort to offer privacy. A dark-haired Moroi woman greeted us at the entrance and glanced down at her clipboard, flipping through the pages. Finding what she needed, she made a few notes and then gestured for Lissa to follow. Me she gave a puzzled look, but she didn't stop me from entering.

She led us to one of the cubicles where a plump, middle-aged woman sat leafing through a magazine. She looked up at our approach and smiled. In her eyes, I could see the dreamy, glazed-over look most feeders had. She'd probably neared her quota for the day, judging from how high she appeared to be.

Recognizing Lissa, her smile grew. "Welcome back, Princess."

The greeter left us, and Lissa sat down in the chair beside the woman. I sensed a feeling of discomfort in her, a little different from my own. This was weird for her too; it had been a long time. The feeder, however, had no such reservations. An eager look crossed her face—the look of a junkie about to get her next fix.

Disgust poured into me. It was an old instinct, one that had been drilled in over the years. Feeders were essential to Moroi life. They were humans who willingly volunteered to be a regular blood source, humans from the fringes of society who gave their lives over to the secret world of the Moroi. They were well cared for and given all the comforts they could need. But at the heart of it, they were drug users, addicts to Moroi saliva and the rush it offered with each bite. The Moroi—and guardians—looked down on this dependency, even though the Moroi couldn't have survived otherwise unless they took victims by force. Hypocrisy at its finest.

The feeder tilted her head, giving Lissa full access to her neck. Her skin there was marked with scars from years of daily bites. The infrequent feedings Lissa and I had done had kept my neck clear; my bite marks never lasted more than a day or so.

Lissa leaned forward, fangs biting into the feeder's yielding flesh. The woman closed her eyes, making a soft sound of pleasure. I swallowed, watching Lissa drink. I couldn't see any blood, but I could imagine it. A surge of emotion grew in my chest: longing. Jealousy. I averted my eyes, staring at the floor. Mentally, I scolded myself.

What's wrong with you? Why should you miss it? You only did it once every day. You aren't addicted, not like this. And you don't want to be.

But I couldn't help myself, couldn't help the way I felt as I recalled the bliss and rush of a vampire's bite.

Lissa finished and we returned to the commons, moving toward the lunch line. It was short, since we only had fifteen minutes left, and I strolled up and began to load my plate with french fries and some rounded, bite-size objects that looked vaguely like chicken nuggets. Lissa only grabbed a yogurt. Moroi needed food, as dhampirs and humans did, but rarely had an appetite after drinking blood.

"So how'd classes go?" I asked.

She shrugged. Her face was bright with color and life now. "Okay. Lots of stares. A *lot* of stares. Lots of questions about where we were. Whispering."

"Same here," I said. The attendant checked us out, and we walked toward the tables. I gave Lissa a sidelong glance. "You okay with that? They aren't bothering you, are they?"

"No—it's fine." The emotions coming through the bond contradicted her words. Knowing I could feel that, she tried to change the subject by handing me her class schedule. I looked it over.

1ˢᵗ Period	Russian 2
2ⁿᵈ Period	American Colonial Literature
3ʳᵈ Period	Basics of Elemental Control
4ᵗʰ Period	Ancient Poetry
	—Lunch—
5ᵗʰ Period	Animal Behavior and Physiology
6ᵗʰ Period	Advanced Calculus
7ᵗʰ Period	Moroi Culture 4
8ᵗʰ Period	Slavic Art

"Nerd," I said. "If you were in Stupid Math like me, we'd have the same afternoon schedule." I stopped walking. "Why are you in elemental basics? That's a sophomore class."

She eyed me. "Because seniors take specialized classes."

We fell silent at that. All Moroi wielded elemental magic. It was one of the things that differentiated living vampires from Strigoi, the dead vampires. Moroi viewed magic as a gift. It was part of their souls and connected them to the world.

A long time ago, they had used their magic openly, averting natural disasters and helping with things like food and water production. They didn't need to do that as much anymore, but the magic was still in their blood. It burned in them and made them want to reach out to the earth and wield their power. Academies like this existed to help Moroi control the magic and learn how to do increasingly complex things with it. Students also had to learn the rules that surrounded magic, rules that had been in place for centuries and were strictly enforced.

All Moroi had a small ability in each element. When they got to be around our age, students "specialized" when one element grew stronger than the others: earth, water, fire, or air. Not specializing was like not going through puberty.

And Lissa . . . well, Lissa hadn't specialized yet.

"Is Ms. Carmack still teaching that? What she'd say?"

"She says she's not worried. She thinks it'll come."

"Did you—did you tell her about—"

Lissa shook her head. "No. Of course not."

We let the subject drop. It was one we thought about a lot but rarely spoke of.

We started moving again, scanning the tables as we decided where to sit. A few pairs of eyes looked up at us with blatant curiosity.

"Lissa!" came a nearby voice. Glancing over, we saw Natalie waving at us. Lissa and I exchanged looks. Natalie was sort of Lissa's cousin in the way Victor was sort of her uncle, but we'd never hung out with her all that much.

Lissa shrugged and headed in that direction. "Why not?"

I followed reluctantly. Natalie was nice but also one of the most uninteresting people I knew. Most royals at the school enjoyed a kind of celebrity status, but Natalie had never fit in with that crowd. She was too plain, too uninterested in the politics of the Academy, and too clueless to really navigate them anyway.

Natalie's friends eyed us with a quiet curiosity, but she didn't hold back. She threw her arms around us. Like Lissa, she had jade-green eyes, but her hair was jet black, like Victor's had been before his disease grayed it.

"You're back! I knew you would be! Everyone said you were gone forever, but I never believed that. I knew you couldn't stay away. Why'd you go? There are so many stories about why you left!" Lissa and I exchanged glances as Natalie prattled on. "Camille said one of you got pregnant and went off to have an abortion, but I knew that couldn't be true. Someone else said you went off to hang out with Rose's mom, but I figured Ms. Kirova and Daddy wouldn't have been so upset if you'd turned up there. Did you know we might get to be roommates? I was talking to . . ."

On and on she chatted, flashing her fangs as she spoke. I smiled politely, letting Lissa deal with the onslaught until Natalie asked a dangerous question.

"What'd you do for blood, Lissa?"

The table regarded us questioningly. Lissa froze, but I immediately jumped in, the lie coming effortlessly to my lips.

"Oh, it's easy. There are a lot of humans who want to do it."

"Really?" asked one of Natalie's friends, wide-eyed.

"Yup. You find 'em at parties and stuff. They're all looking for a fix from something, and they don't really get that a vampire's doing it: most are already so wasted they don't remember anyway." My already vague details dried up, so I simply shrugged in as cool and confident a way as I could manage. It wasn't like any of them knew any better. "Like I said, it's easy. Almost easier than with our own feeders."

Natalie accepted this and than launched into some other topic. Lissa shot me a grateful look.

Ignoring the conversation again, I took in the old faces, trying to figure out who was hanging out with whom and how power had shifted within the school. Mason, sitting with a group of novices, caught my eye, and I smiled. Near him, a group of Moroi royals sat, laughing over something. Aaron and the blond girl sat there too.

"Hey, Natalie," I said, turning around and cutting her off. She didn't seem to notice or mind. "Who's Aaron's new girlfriend?"

"Huh? Oh. Mia Rinaldi." Seeing my blank look, she asked, "Don't you remember her?"

"Should I? Was she here when we left?"

"She's always been here," said Natalie. "She's only a year younger than us."

I shot a questioning look at Lissa, who only shrugged.

"Why is she so pissed off at us?" I asked. "Neither of us know her."

"I don't know," answered Natalie. "Maybe she's jealous about Aaron. She wasn't much of anybody when you guys left. She got *really* popular *really* fast. She isn't royal or anything, but once she started dating Aaron, she—"

"Okay, thanks," I interrupted. "It doesn't really—"

My eyes lifted up from Natalie's face to Jesse Zeklos's, just as he passed by our table. Ah, Jesse. I'd forgotten about him. I liked flirting with Mason and some of the other novices, but Jesse was in an entirely different category. You flirted with the other guys simply for the sake of flirting. You flirted with Jesse in the hopes of getting semi-naked with him. He was a royal Moroi, and he was so hot, he should have worn a WARNING: FLAMMABLE sign. He met my eyes and grinned.

"Hey Rose, welcome back. You still breaking hearts?"

"Are you volunteering?"

His grin widened. "Let's hang out sometime and find out. If you ever get parole."

He kept walking, and I watched him admiringly. Natalie and her friends stared at me in awe. I might not be a god in the Dimitri sense, but with this group, Lissa and I *were* gods— or at least former gods—of another nature.

"Oh my gawd," exclaimed one girl. I didn't remember her name. "That was *Jesse*."

"Yes," I said, smiling. "It certainly was."

"I wish I looked like you," she added with a sigh.

Their eyes fell on me. Technically, I was half-Moroi, but my looks were human. I'd blended in well with humans during our time away, so much so that I'd barely thought about my appearance at all. Here, among the slim and small-chested Moroi girls, certain features—meaning my larger breasts and more defined hips—stood out. I knew I was pretty, but to Moroi boys, my body was more than just pretty: it was sexy in a risqué way. Dhampirs were an exotic conquest, a novelty all Moroi guys wanted to "try."

It was ironic that dhampirs had such an allure here, because slender Moroi girls looked very much like the super-skinny runway models so popular in the human world. Most humans could never reach that "ideal" skinniness, just as Moroi girls could never look like me. Everyone wanted what she couldn't have.

Lissa and I got to sit together in our shared afternoon classes but didn't do much talking. The stares she'd mentioned certainly did follow us, but I found that the more I talked to people, the more they warmed up. Slowly, gradually, they seemed to remember who we were, and the novelty—though not the intrigue—of our crazy stunt wore off.

Or maybe I should say, they remembered who *I* was. Because I was the only one talking. Lissa stared straight ahead, listening but neither acknowledging nor participating in my attempts at conversation. I could feel anxiety and sadness pouring out of her.

"All right," I told her when classes finally ended. We stood outside the school, and I was fully aware that in doing so, I was already breaking the terms of my agreement with Kirova. "We're not staying here," I told her, looking around the campus uneasily. "I'm going to find a way to get us out."

"You think we could really do it a second time?" Lissa asked quietly.

"Absolutely." I spoke with certainty, again relieved she couldn't read my feelings. Escaping the first time had been tricky enough. Doing it again would be a real bitch, not that I couldn't still find a way.

"You really would, wouldn't you?" She smiled, more to herself than to me, like she'd thought of something funny. "Of course you would. It's just, well . . ." She sighed. "I don't know if we should go. Maybe—maybe we should stay."

I blinked in astonishment. "What?" Not one of my more eloquent answers, but the best I could manage. I'd never expected this from her.

"I saw you, Rose. I saw you talking to the other novices during class, talking about practice. You miss that."

"It's not worth it," I argued. "Not if . . . not if *you* . . ." I couldn't finish, but she was right. She'd read me. I *had* missed the other novices. Even some of the Moroi. But there was more to it than just that. The weight of my inexperience, how much I'd fallen behind, had been growing all day.

"It might be better," she countered. "I haven't had as many . . . you know, things happening in a while. I haven't felt like anyone was following or watching us."

I didn't say anything to that. Before we'd left the Academy, she'd always felt like someone was following her, like she was being hunted. I'd never seen evidence to support that, but I had once heard one of our teachers go on and on about the same sort of thing. Ms. Karp. She'd been a pretty Moroi, with deep auburn air and high cheekbones. And I was pretty sure she'd been crazy.

"You never know who's watching," she used to say, walking briskly around the classroom as she shut all the blinds. "Or who's following you. Best to be safe. Best to *always* be safe." We'd snickered amongst ourselves because that's what students do around eccentric and paranoid teachers. The thought of Lissa acting like her bothered me.

"What's wrong?" Lissa asked, noticing that I was lost in thought.

"Huh? Nothing. Just thinking." I sighed, trying to balance my own wants with what was best for her. "Liss, we can stay, I guess . . . but there are a few conditions."

This made her laugh. "A Rose ultimatum, huh?"

"I'm serious." Words I didn't say very much. "I want you to stay away from the royals. Not like Natalie or anything, but you know, the others. The power players. Camille. Carly. That group."

Her amusement turned to astonishment. "Are you serious?"

"Sure. You never liked them anyway."

"*You* did."

"No. Not really. I liked what they could offer. All the parties and stuff."

"And you can go without that now?" She looked skeptical.

"Sure. We did in Portland."

"Yeah, but that was different." Her eyes stared off, not really focused on any one thing. "Here . . . *here* I've got to be a part of that. I can't avoid it."

"The hell you do. Natalie stays out of that stuff."

"Natalie isn't going to inherit her family's title," she retorted. "I've already got it. I've got to be involved, start making connections. Andre—"

"Liss," I groaned. "You *aren't* Andre." I couldn't believe she was still comparing herself to her brother.

"He was always involved in all that stuff."

"Yeah, well," I snapped back, "he's *dead* now."

Her face hardened. "You know, sometimes you aren't very nice."

"You don't keep me around to be nice. You want nice, there are a dozen sheep in there who would rip each other's throats to get in good with the Dragomir princess. You keep me around to tell you the truth, and here it is: Andre's dead. You're the heir now, and you're going to deal with it however you can. But for now, that means staying away from the other royals. We'll just lie low. Coast through the middle. Get involved in that stuff again, Liss, and you'll drive yourself . . ."

"*Crazy*?" she supplied when I didn't finish.

Now I looked away. "I didn't mean . . ."

"It's okay," she said, after a moment. She sighed and touched my arm. "Fine. We'll stay, and we'll keep out of all that stuff. We'll 'coast through the middle' like you want. Hang out with Natalie, I guess."

To be perfectly honest, I didn't want any of that. I wanted to go to all the royal parties and wild drunken festivities like we'd done before. We'd kept out of that life for years until Lissa's parents and brother died. Andre should have been the one to inherit her family's title, and he'd certainly acted like it. Handsome and outgoing, he'd charmed everyone he knew and had been a leader in all the royal cliques and clubs that existed on campus. After his death, Lissa had felt it was her family duty to take his place.

I'd gotten to join that world with her. It was easy for me, because I didn't really have to deal with the politics of it. I was a pretty dhampir, one who didn't mind getting into trouble and pulling crazy stunts. I became a novelty; they liked having me around for the fun of it.

Lissa had to deal with other matters. The Dragomirs were one of the twelve ruling families. She'd have a very powerful place in Moroi society, and the other young royals wanted to get in good with her. Fake friends tried to schmooze her and get her to team up against other people. The royals could bribe and backstab in the same breath—and that was just with *each other*. To dhampirs and non-royals, they were completely unpredictable.

That cruel culture had eventually taken its toll on Lissa. She had an open, kind nature, one that I loved, and I hated to see her upset and stressed by royal games. She'd grown fragile since the accident, and all the parties in the world weren't worth seeing her hurt.

"All right then," I said finally. "We'll see how this goes. If anything goes wrong—anything at all—we leave. No arguments."

She nodded.

"Rose?"

We both looked up at Dimitri's looming form. I hoped he hadn't heard the part about us leaving.

"You're late for practice," he said evenly. Seeing Lissa, he gave a polite nod. "Princess."

As he and I walked away, I worried about Lissa and wondered if staying here was the right thing to do. I felt nothing alarming through the bond, but her emotions spiked all over the place. Confusion. Nostalgia. Fear. Anticipation. Strong and powerful, they flooded into me.

I felt the pull just before it happened. It was exactly like what had happened on the plane: her emotions grew so strong that they "sucked" me into her head before I could stop them. I could now see and feel what she did.

She walked slowly around the commons, toward the small Russian Orthodox chapel that served most of the school's religious needs. Lissa had always attended mass regularly. Not me.

I had a standing arrangement with God: I'd agree to believe in him—barely—so long as he let me sleep in on Sundays.

But as she went inside, I could feel that she wasn't there to pray. She had another purpose, one I didn't know about. Glancing around, she verified that neither the priest nor any worshippers were close by. The place was empty.

Slipping through a doorway in the back of the chapel, she climbed a narrow set of creaky stairs up into the attic. Here it was dark and dusty. The only light came through a large stained-glass window that fractured the faint glow of sunrise into tiny, multicolored gems across the floor.

I hadn't known until that moment that this room was a regular retreat for Lissa. But now I could feel it, feel her memories of how she used to escape here to be alone and to think. The anxiety in her ebbed away ever so slightly as she took in the familiar surroundings. She climbed up into the window seat and leaned her head back against its side, momentarily entranced by the silence and the light.

Moroi could stand some sunlight, unlike the Strigoi, but they had to limit their exposure. Sitting here, she could almost pretend she was in the sun, protected by the glass's dilution of the rays.

Breathe, just breathe, she told herself. *It'll be okay. Rose will take care of everything.*

She believed that passionately, like always, and relaxed further.

Then a low voice spoke from the darkness.

"You can have the Academy but not the window seat."

She sprang up, heart pounding. I shared her anxiety, and my own pulse quickened. "Who's there?"

A moment later, a shape rose from behind a stack of crates, just outside her field of vision. The figure stepped forward, and in the poor lighting, familiar features materialized. Messy black hair. Pale blue eyes. A perpetually sardonic smirk.

Christian Ozera.

"Don't worry," he said. "I won't bite. Well, at least not in the way you're afraid of." He chuckled at his own joke.

She didn't find it funny. She had completely forgotten about Christian. So had I.

No matter what happened in our world, a few basic truths about vampires remained the same. Moroi were alive; Strigoi were undead. Moroi were mortal; Strigoi were immortal. Moroi were born; Strigoi were *made*.

And there were two ways to make a Strigoi. Strigoi could forcibly turn humans, dhampirs, or Moroi with a single bite. Moroi tempted by the promise of immortality could become Strigoi by choice if they purposely killed another person while feeding. Doing that was considered dark and twisted, the greatest of all sins, both against the Moroi way of life and nature itself. Moroi who chose this dark path lost their ability to connect with elemental magic and other powers of the world. That was why they could no longer go into the sun.

This is what had happened to Christian's parents. They were Strigoi.

FIVE

OR RATHER, THEY *HAD* BEEN Strigoi. A regiment of guardians had hunted them down and killed them. If rumors were true, Christian had witnessed it all when he was very young. And although he wasn't Strigoi himself, some people thought he wasn't far off, with the way he always wore black and kept to himself.

Strigoi or not, I didn't trust him. He was a jerk, and I silently screamed at Lissa to get out of there—not that my screaming did much good. Stupid one-way bond.

"What are you doing here?" she asked.

"Taking in the sights, of course. That chair with the tarp on it is particularly lovely this time of year. Over there, we have an old box full of the writings of the blessed and crazy St. Vladimir. And let's not forget that beautiful table with no legs in the corner."

"Whatever." She rolled her eyes and moved toward the door, wanting to leave, but he blocked her way.

"Well, what about *you*?" he taunted. "Why are you up here? Don't you have parties to go to or lives to destroy?"

Some of Lissa's old spark returned. "Wow, that's hilarious. Am I like a rite of passage now? Go and see if you can piss off Lissa to prove how cool you are? Some girl I don't even know yelled at me today, and now I've got to deal with you? What does it take to be left alone?"

"Oh. So that's why you're up here. For a pity party."

"This isn't a joke. I'm serious." I could tell Lissa was getting angry. It was trumping her earlier distress.

He shrugged and leaned casually against the sloping wall. "So am I. I love pity parties. I wish I'd brought the hats. What do you want to mope about first? How it's going to take you a whole day to be popular and loved again? How you'll have to wait a couple weeks before Hollister can ship out some new clothes? If you spring for rush shipping, it might not be so long."

"Let me leave," she said angrily, this time pushing him aside.

"Wait," he said, as she reached the door. The sarcasm disappeared from his voice. "What . . . um, what was it like?"

"What was *what* like?" she snapped.

"Being out there. Away from the Academy."

She hesitated for a moment before answering, caught off guard by what seemed like a genuine attempt at conversation. "It was great. No one knew who I was. I was just another face. Not Moroi. Not royal. Not anything." She looked down at the floor. "Everyone here thinks they know who I am."

"Yeah. It's kind of hard to outlive your past," he said bitterly.

It occurred to Lissa at that moment—and me to by default—just how hard it might be to be Christian. Most of the time, people treated him like he didn't exist. Like he was a ghost. They didn't talk to or about him. They just didn't notice him. The stigma of his parents' crime was too strong, casting its shadow onto the entire Ozera family.

Still, he'd pissed her off, and she wasn't about to feel sorry for him.

"Wait—is this your pity party now?"

He laughed, almost approvingly. "This room has been my pity party for a year now."

"Sorry," said Lissa snarkily. "I was coming here before I left. I've got a longer claim."

"Squatters' rights. Besides, I have to make sure I stay near the chapel as much as possible so people know I haven't gone Strigoi . . . yet." Again, the bitter tone rang out.

"I used to always see you at mass. Is that the only reason you go? To look good?" Strigoi couldn't enter holy ground. More of that sinning-against-the-world thing.

"Sure," he said. "Why else go? For the good of your *soul*?"

"Whatever," said Lissa, who clearly had a different opinion. "I'll leave you alone then."

"Wait," he said again. He didn't seem to want her to go. "I'll make you a deal. You can hang out here too if you tell me one thing."

"What?" She glanced back at him.

He leaned forward. "Of all the rumors I heard about you today—and believe me, I heard plenty, even if no one actually told them to me—there was one that didn't come up very much.

They dissected everything else: why you left, what you did out there, why you came back, the specialization, what Rose said to Mia, blah, blah, blah. And in all of that, no one, no one ever questioned that stupid story that Rose told about there being all sorts of fringe humans who let you take blood."

She looked away, and I could feel her cheeks starting to burn. "It's not stupid. Or a story."

He laughed softly. "I've lived with humans. My aunt and I stayed away after my parents . . . died. It's not that easy to find blood." When she didn't answer, he laughed again. "It was Rose, wasn't it? She fed you."

A renewed fear shot through both her and me. No one at school could know about that. Kirova and the guardians on the scene knew, but they'd kept that knowledge to themselves.

"Well. If that's not friendship, I don't know what it is," he said.

"You can't tell anyone," she blurted out.

This was all we needed. As I'd just been reminded, feeders were vampire-bite addicts. We accepted that as part of life but still looked down on them for it. For anyone else—*especially* a dhampir—letting a Moroi take blood from you was almost, well, dirty. In fact, one of the kinkiest, practically pornographic things a dhampir could do was let a Moroi drink blood during sex.

Lissa and I hadn't had sex, of course, but we'd both known what others would think of me feeding her.

"Don't tell anyone," Lissa repeated.

He stuffed his hands in his coat pockets and sat down on one of the crates. "Who am I going to tell? Look, go grab the window seat. You can have it today and hang out for a while. If you're not still afraid of me."

She hesitated, studying him. He looked dark and surly, lips curled in a sort of I'm-such-a-rebel smirk. But he didn't look too dangerous. He didn't look Strigoi. Gingerly, she sat back down in the window seat, unconsciously rubbing her arms against the cold.

Christian watched her, and a moment later, the air warmed up considerably.

Lissa met Christian's eyes and smiled, surprised she'd never noticed how icy blue they were before. "You specialized in fire?"

He nodded and pulled up a broken chair. "Now we have luxury accommodations."

I snapped out of the vision.

"Rose? Rose?"

Blinking, I focused on Dimitri's face. He was leaning toward me, his hands gripping my shoulders. I'd stopped walking; we stood in the middle of the quad separating the upper school buildings.

"Are you all right?"

"I . . . yeah. I was . . . I was with Lissa. . . ." I put a hand to my forehead. I'd never had such a long or clear experience like that. "I was in her head."

"Her . . . head?"

"Yeah. It's part of the bond." I didn't really feel like elaborating.

"Is she all right?"

"Yeah, she's . . ." I hesitated. *Was* she all right? Christian Ozera had just invited her to hang out with him. Not good. There was "coasting through the middle," and then there was turning to the dark side. But the feelings humming through our bond were no longer scared or upset. She was almost content, though still a little nervous. "She's not in danger," I finally said. I hoped.

"Can you keep going?"

The hard, stoic warrior I'd met earlier was gone—just for a moment—and he actually looked concerned. Truly concerned. Feeling his eyes on me like that made something flutter inside of me—which was stupid, of course. I had no reason to get all goofy, just because the man was too good-looking for his own good. After all, he was an antisocial god, according to Mason. One who was supposedly going to leave me in all sorts of pain.

"Yeah. I'm fine."

I went into the gym's dressing room and changed into the workout clothes someone had finally thought to give me after a day of practicing in jeans and a T-shirt. Gross. Lissa hanging out with Christian troubled me, but I shoved that thought away for later as my muscles informed me they did not want to go through any more exercise today.

So I suggested to Dimitri that maybe he should let me off this time.

He laughed, and I was pretty sure it was *at* me and not *with* me.

"Why is that funny?"

"Oh," he said, his smile dropping. "You were serious."

"Of course I was! Look, I've technically been awake for *two* days. Why do we have to start this training now? Let me go to bed," I whined. "It's just one hour."

He crossed his arms and looked down at me. His earlier concern was gone. He was all business now. Tough love. "How do you feel right now? After the training you've done so far?"

"I hurt like hell."

"You'll feel worse tomorrow."

"So?"

"So, better to jump in now while you still feel . . . not as bad."

"What kind of logic is that?" I retorted.

But I didn't argue anymore as he led me into the weight room. He showed me the weights and reps he wanted me to do, then sprawled in a corner with a battered Western novel. Some god.

When I finished, he stood beside me and demonstrated a few cool-down stretches.

"How'd you end up as Lissa's guardian?" I asked. "You weren't here a few years ago. Were you even trained at this school?"

He didn't answer right away. I got the feeling he didn't talk about himself very often. "No. I attended the one in Siberia."

"Whoa. That's got to be the only place worse than Montana."

A glint of something—maybe amusement—sparked in his eyes, but he didn't acknowledge the joke. "After I graduated, I was a guardian for a Zeklos lord. He was killed recently." His smile dropped, his face grew dark. "They sent me here because they needed extras on campus. When the princess turned up, they assigned me to her, since I'd already be around. Not that it matters until she leaves campus."

I thought about what he'd said before. Some Strigoi killed the guy he was supposed to have been guarding? "Did this lord die on your watch?"

"No. He was with his other guardian. I was away."

He fell silent, his mind obviously somewhere else. The Moroi expected a lot from us, but they did recognize that the guardians were—more or less—only human. So, guardians got pay and time off like you'd get in any other job. Some hard-core guardians—like my mom—refused vacations, vowing never to leave their Moroi's sides. Looking at Dimitri now, I had a feeling he might very well turn into one of those. If he'd been away on legitimate leave, he could hardly blame himself for what happened to that guy. Still, he probably did anyway. I'd blame myself too if something happened to Lissa.

"Hey," I said, suddenly wanting to cheer him up, "did you

help come up with the plan to get us back? Because it was pretty good. Brute force and all that."

He arched an eyebrow curiously. Cool. I'd always wished I could do that. "You're complimenting me on that?"

"Well, it was a hell of a lot better than the last one they tried."

"Last one?"

"Yeah. In Chicago. With the pack of psi-hounds."

"This was the first time we found you. In Portland."

I sat up from my stretches and crossed my legs. "Um, I don't think I imagined psi-hounds. Who else could have sent them? They only answer to Moroi. Maybe no one told you about it."

"Maybe," he said dismissively. I could tell by his face he didn't believe that.

I returned to the novices' dorm after that. The Moroi students lived on the other side of the quad, closer to the commons. The living arrangements were partly based on convenience. Being here kept us novices closer to the gym and training grounds. But we also lived separately to accommodate the differences in Moroi and dhampir lifestyles. Their dorm had almost no windows, aside from tinted ones that dimmed sunlight. They also had a special section where feeders always stayed on hand. The novices' dorm was built in a more open way, allowing for more light.

I had my own room because there were so few novices, let alone girls. The room they'd given me was small and plain,

with a twin bed and a desk with a computer. My few belong-
ings had been spirited out of Portland and now sat in boxes
around the room. I rummaged through them, pulling out a
T-shirt to sleep in. I found a couple of pictures as I did, one of
Lissa and me at a football game in Portland and another taken
when I'd gone on vacation with her family, a year before the
accident.

I set them on my desk and booted up the computer. Someone from tech support had helpfully given me a sheet with
instructions for renewing my e-mail account and setting up a
password. I did both, happy to discover no one had realized
that this would serve as a way for me to communicate with
Lissa. Too tired to write to her now, I was about to turn everything off when I noticed I already had a message. From Janine
Hathaway. It was short:

I'm glad you're back. What you did was inexcusable.

"Love you too, Mom," I muttered, shutting it all down.

When I went to bed afterward, I passed out before even
hitting the pillow, and just as Dimitri had predicted, I felt ten
times worse when I woke up the next morning. Lying there in
bed, I reconsidered the perks of running away. Then I remembered getting my ass kicked and figured the only way to pre-
vent that from happening again was to go endure some more
of it this morning.

My soreness made it all that much worse, but I survived
the before-school practice with Dimitri and my subsequent
classes without passing out or fainting.

At lunch, I dragged Lissa away from Natalie's table early and gave her a Kirova-worthy lecture about Christian—particularly chastising her for letting him know about our blood arrangement. If that got out, it'd kill both of us socially, and I didn't trust him not to tell.

Lissa had other concerns.

"You were in my head again?" she exclaimed. "For *that* long?"

"I didn't do it on purpose," I argued. "It just happened. And that's not the point. How long did you hang out with him afterward?"

"Not that long. It was kind of . . . fun."

"Well, you can't do it again. If people find out you're hanging out with him, they'll crucify you." I eyed her warily. "You aren't, like, into him, are you?"

She scoffed. "No. Of course not.

"Good. Because if you're going to go after a guy, steal Aaron back." He was boring, yes, but safe. Just like Natalie. How come all the harmless people were so lame? Maybe that was the definition of safe.

She laughed. "Mia would claw my eyes out."

"We can take her. Besides, he deserves someone who doesn't shop at Gap Kids."

"Rose, you've got to stop saying things like that."

"I'm just saying what you won't."

"She's only a year younger," said Lissa. She laughed. "I can't believe you think *I'm* the one who's going to get us in trouble."

Smiling as we strolled toward class, I gave her a sidelong glance. "Aaron does look pretty good though, huh?"

She smiled back and avoided my eyes. "Yeah. Pretty good."

"Ooh. You see? You should go after him."

"Whatever. I'm fine being friends now."

"Friends who used to stick their tongues down each other's throats."

She rolled her eyes.

"Fine." I let my teasing go. "Let Aaron stay in the nursery school. Just so long as you stay away from Christian. He's dangerous."

"You're overreacting. He's not going Strigoi."

"He's a bad influence."

She laughed. "You think *I'm* in danger of going Strigoi?"

She didn't wait for my answer, instead pushing ahead to open the door to our science class. Standing there, I uneasily replayed her words and then followed a moment later. When I did, I got to see royal power in action. A few guys—with giggling, watching girls—were messing with a gangly-looking Moroi. I didn't know him very well, but I knew he was poor and certainly not royal. A couple of his tormentors were air-magic users, and they'd blown the papers off his desk and were pushing them around the room on currents of air while the guy tried to catch them.

My instincts urged me to do something, maybe go smack one of the air users. But I couldn't pick a fight with everyone who annoyed me, and certainly not a group of royals—especially when Lissa needed to stay off their radar. So I could only give them a look of disgust as I walked to my desk. As I did, a hand caught my arm. Jesse.

"Hey," I said jokingly. Fortunately, he didn't appear to be participating in the torture session. "Hands off the merchandise."

He flashed me a smile but kept his hand on me. "Rose, tell Paul about the time you started the fight in Ms. Karp's class."

I cocked my head toward him, giving him a playful smile. "I started a lot of fights in her class."

"The one with the hermit crab. And the gerbil."

I laughed, recalling it. "Oh yeah. It was a hamster, I think. I just dropped it into the crab's tank, and they were both worked up from being so close to me, so they went at it."

Paul, a guy sitting nearby whom I didn't really know, chuckled too. He'd transferred last year, apparently, and hadn't heard of this. "Who won?"

I looked at Jesse quizzically. "I don't remember. Do you?"

"No. I just remember Karp freaking out." He turned toward Paul. "Man, you should have seen this messed-up teacher we used to have. Used to think people were after her and would go off on stuff that didn't make any sense. She was nuts. Used to wander campus while everyone was asleep."

I smiled tightly, like I thought it was funny. Instead, I thought back to Ms. Karp again, surprised to be thinking about her for the second time in two days. Jesse was right—

she *had* wandered campus a lot when she still worked here. It was pretty creepy. I'd run into her once—unexpectedly.

I'd been climbing out of my dorm window to go hang out with some people. It was after hours, and we were all supposed to be in our rooms, fast asleep. Such escape tactics were a regular practice for me. I was good at them.

But I fell that time. I had a second-floor room, and I lost my grip about halfway down. Sensing the ground rush up toward me, I tried desperately to grab hold of something and slow my fall. The building's rough stone tore into my skin, causing cuts I was too preoccupied to feel. I slammed into the grassy earth, back first, getting the wind knocked out of me.

"Bad form, Rosemarie. You should be more careful. Your instructors would be disappointed."

Peering through the tangle of my hair, I saw Ms. Karp looking down at me, a bemused look on her face. Pain, in the meantime, shot through every part of my body.

Ignoring it as best I could, I clambered to my feet. Being in class with Crazy Karp while surrounded by other students was one thing. Standing outside alone with her was an entirely different matter. She always had an eerie, distracted gleam in her eye that made my skin break out in goose bumps.

There was also now a high likelihood she'd drag me off to Kirova for a detention. Scarier still.

Instead, she just smiled and reached for my hands. I flinched but let her take them. She *tsk*ed when she saw the scrapes. Tightening her grip on them, she frowned slightly. A tingle burned my skin, laced with a sort of pleasant buzz, and then the wounds closed up. I had a brief sense of dizziness. My temperature spiked. The blood disappeared, as did the pain in my hip and leg.

Gasping, I jerked my hands away. I'd seen a lot of Moroi magic, but never anything like that.

"What . . . what did you do?"

She gave me that weird smile again. "Go back to your dorm, Rose. There are bad things out here. You never know what's following you."

I was still staring at my hands. "But . . ."

I looked back up at her and for the first time noticed scars on the sides of her forehead. Like nails had dug into them. She winked. "I won't tell on you if you don't tell on me."

I jumped back to the present, unsettled by the memory of that bizarre night. Jesse, in the meantime, was telling me about a party.

"You've got to slip your leash tonight. We're going up to that spot in the woods around eight thirty. Mark got some weed."

I sighed wistfully, regret replacing the chill I'd felt over the memory of Ms. Karp. "Can't slip that leash. I'm with my Russian jailer."

He let go of my arm, looking disappointed, and ran a hand through his bronze-colored hair. Yeah. Not being able to hang out with him was a damned shame. I really would have to fix that someday. "Can't you ever get off for good behavior?" he joked.

I gave him what I hoped was a seductive smile as I found my seat. "Sure," I called over my shoulder. "If I was ever good."

SIX

As MUCH AS LISSA AND Christian's meeting bothered me, it gave me an idea the next day.

"Hey, Kirova—er, Ms. Kirova." I stood in the doorway of her office, not having bothered to make an appointment. She raised her eyes from some paperwork, clearly annoyed to see me.

"Yes, Miss Hathaway?"

"Does my house arrest mean I can't go to church?"

"I beg your pardon?"

"You said that whenever I'm not in class or practice, I have to stay in the dorm. But what about church on Sundays? I don't think it's really fair to keep me away from my religious . . . um, needs." Or deprive me of another chance— no matter how short and boring—to hang out with Lissa.

She pushed her glasses up the bridge of her nose. "I wasn't aware you had any religious needs."

"I found Jesus while I was gone."

"Isn't your mother an atheist?" she asked skeptically.

"And my dad's probably Muslim. But I've moved on to my own path. You shouldn't keep me from it."

She made a noise that sort of sounded like a snicker. "No, Miss Hathaway, I should not. Very well. You may attend services on Sundays."

The victory was short-lived, however, because church was every bit as lame as I remembered when I attended a few days later. I did get to sit next to Lissa, though, which made me feel like I was getting away with something. Mostly I just people-watched. Church was optional for students, but with so many Eastern European families, a lot of students were Eastern Orthodox Christians and attended either because they believed or because their parents made them.

Christian sat on the opposite side of the aisle, pretending to be just as holy as he'd said. As much as I didn't like him, his fake faith still made me smile. Dimitri sat in the back, face lined with shadows, and, like me, didn't take communion. As thoughtful as he looked, I wondered if he even listened to the service. I tuned in and out.

"Following God's path is never easy," the priest was saying. "Even St. Vladimir, this school's own patron saint, had a difficult time. He was so filled with spirit that people often flocked around him, enthralled just to listen and be in his presence. So great was his spirit, the old texts say, that he could heal the sick. Yet despite these gifts, many did not respect him. They mocked him, claiming he was misguided and confused."

Which was a nice way of saying Vladimir was insane. Everyone knew it. He was one of a handful of Moroi saints, so the priest liked to talk about him a lot. I'd heard all about him, many times over, before we left. Great. It looked like I had an eternity of Sundays to hear his story over and over again.

". . . and so it was with shadow-kissed Anna."

I jerked my head up. I had no idea what the priest was talking about now, because I hadn't been listening for some time. But those words burned into me. *Shadow-kissed*. It had been a while since I heard them, but I'd never forgotten them. I waited, hoping he'd continue, but he'd already moved on to the next part of the service. The sermon was over.

Church concluded, and as Lissa turned to go, I shook my head at her. "Wait for me. I'll be right there."

I pushed my way through the crowd, up to the front, where the priest was speaking with a few people. I waited impatiently while he finished. Natalie was there, asking him about volunteer work she could do. Ugh. When she finished, she left, greeting me as she passed.

The priest raised his eyebrows when he saw me. "Hello, Rose. It's nice to see you again."

"Yeah . . . you too," I said. "I heard you talking about Anna. About how she was 'shadow-kissed.' What does that mean?"

He frowned. "I'm not entirely sure. She lived a very long time ago. It was often common to refer to people by titles that reflected some of their traits. It might have been given to make her sound fierce."

I tried to hide my disappointment. "Oh. So who was she?"

This time his frown was disapproving rather than thoughtful. "I mentioned it a number of times."

"Oh. I must have, um, missed that."

His disapproval grew, and he turned around. "Wait just a moment."

He disappeared through the door near the altar, the one Lissa had taken to the attic. I considered fleeing but thought God might strike me down for that. Less than a minute later, the priest returned with a book. He handed it to me. *Moroi Saints*.

"You can learn about her in here. The next time I see you, I'd like to hear what you've learned."

I scowled as I walked away. Great. Homework from the priest.

In the chapel's entryway, I found Lissa talking to Aaron. She smiled as she spoke, and the feelings coming off her were happy, though certainly not infatuated.

"You're kidding," she exclaimed.

He shook his head. "Nope."

Seeing me stroll over, she turned to me. "Rose, you're never going to believe this. "You know Abby Badica? And Xander? Their guardian wants to resign. And marry *another* guardian."

Now t*his* was exciting gossip. A scandal, actually. "Seriously? Are they, like, going to run off together?"

She nodded. "They're getting a house. Going to get jobs with humans, I guess."

I glanced at Aaron, who had suddenly turned shy with me there. "How are Abby and Xander dealing with that?"

"Okay. Embarrassed. They think it's stupid." Then he realized who he was speaking to. "Oh. I didn't mean—"

"Whatever." I gave him a tight smile. "It *is* stupid."

Wow. I was stunned. The rebellious part me of loved any

story where people "fought the system." Only, in this case, they were fighting *my* system, the one I'd been trained to believe in my entire life.

Dhampirs and Moroi had a strange arrangement. Dhampirs had originally been born from Moroi mixing with humans. Unfortunately, dhampirs couldn't reproduce with each other—or with humans. It was a weird genetic thing. Mules were the same way, I'd been told, though that wasn't a comparison I really liked hearing. Dhampirs and full Moroi *could* have children together, and, through another genetic oddity, their kids came out as standard dhampirs, with half human genes, half vampire genes.

With Moroi being the only ones with whom dhampirs could reproduce, we had to stay close to them and intermingle with them. Likewise, it became important to us that the Moroi simply *survived*. Without them, we were done. And with the way Strigoi loved picking off Moroi, their survival became a legitimate concern for us.

That was how the guardian system developed. Dhampirs couldn't work magic, but we made great warriors. We'd inherited enhanced senses and reflexes from our vampire genes and better strength and endurance from our human genes. We also weren't limited by a need for blood or trouble with sunlight. Sure, we weren't as powerful as the Strigoi, but we trained hard, and guardians did a kick-ass job at keeping Moroi safe. Most dhampirs felt it was worth risking their own lives to make sure our kind could still keep having children.

Since Moroi usually wanted to have and raise Moroi children, you didn't find a lot of long-term Moroi-dhampir romances. You especially didn't find a lot of Moroi women hooking up with dhampir guys. But plenty of young Moroi men liked fooling around with dhampir women, although those guys usually went on to marry Moroi women. That left a lot of single dhampir mothers, but we were tough and could handle it.

However, many dhampir mothers chose not to become guardians in order to raise their children. These women sometimes worked "regular" jobs with Moroi or humans; some of them lived together in communities. These communities had a bad reputation. I don't know how much of it was true, but rumors said Moroi men visited *all the time* for sex. and that some dhampir women let them drink blood while doing it. Blood whores.

Regardless, almost all guardians were men, which meant there were a lot more Moroi than guardians. Most dhampir guys accepted that they wouldn't have kids. They knew it was their job to protect Moroi while their sisters and cousins had babies.

Some dhampir women, like my mother, still felt it was their duty to become guardians—even if it meant not raising their own kids. After I'd been born, she'd handed me over to be raised by Moroi. Moroi and dhampirs start school pretty young, and the Academy had essentially taken over as my parent by the time I was four.

Between her example and my life at the Academy, I believed wholeheartedly that it was a dhampir's job to protect Moroi. It was part of our heritage, *and* it was the only way we'd keep going. It was that simple.

And that was what made what the Badicas' guardian had done so shocking. He'd abandoned his Moroi and run off with another guardian, which meant she'd abandoned *her* Moroi. They couldn't even have children together, and now two families were unprotected. What was the point? No one cared if teenage dhampirs dated or if adult dhampirs had flings. But a long-term relationship? Particularly one that involved them running away? A complete waste. And a disgrace.

After a little more speculation on the Badicas, Lissa and I left Aaron. As we stepped outside, I heard a funny shifting sound and then something sliding. Too late, I realized what was happening, just as a pile of slush slid off the chapel's roof and onto us. It was early October, and we'd had early snow last night that had started melting almost immediately. As a result, the stuff that fell on us was very wet and very cold.

Lissa took the brunt of it, but I still yelped as icy water landed on my hair and neck. A few others squealed nearby too, having caught the edge of the mini-avalanche.

"You okay?" I asked her. Her coat was drenched, and her platinum hair clung to the sides of her face.

"Y-yeah," she said through chattering teeth.

I pulled off my coat and handed it to her. It had a slick surface and had repelled most of the water. "Take yours off."

"But you'll be—"

"Take this."

She did, and as she slipped on my coat, I finally tuned into the laughter that always follows these situations. I avoided the eyes, instead focusing on holding Lissa's wet jacket while she changed.

"Wish you hadn't been wearing a coat, Rose," said Ralf Sarcozy, an unusually bulky and plump Moroi. I hated him. "That shirt would have looked good wet."

"That shirt's so ugly it should be burned. Did you get that from a homeless person?"

I glanced up as Mia walked over and looped her arm through Aaron's. Her blond curls were arranged perfectly, and she had on an awesome pair of black heels that would have looked much better on me. At least they made her look taller, I'd give her that. Aaron had been a few steps behind us but had miraculously avoided being nailed by the slush. Seeing how smug she looked, I decided there'd been no miracles involved.

"I suppose you want to offer to burn it, huh?" I asked, refusing to let her know how much that insult bugged me. I knew perfectly well my fashion sense had slipped over the last two years. "Oh, wait—fire isn't your element, is it? You work with water. What a coincidence that a bunch just fell on us."

Mia looked as if she'd been insulted, but the gleam in her eyes showed that she was enjoying this way too much to be an innocent bystander. "What's that supposed to mean?"

"Nothing to me. But Ms. Kirova will probably have something to say when she finds out you used magic against another student."

"That wasn't an attack," she scoffed. "And it wasn't me. It was an act of God."

A few others laughed, much to her delight. In my imagination, I responded with, *So is this*, and then slammed her into the side of the church. In real life, Lissa simply nudged me and said, "Let's go."

She and I walked off toward our respective dorms, leaving behind laughter and jokes about our wet states and how Lissa wouldn't know anything about specialization. Inside, I seethed. I had to do something about Mia, I realized. In addition to the general irritation of Mia's bitchiness, I didn't want Lissa to have to deal with any more stress than she had to. We'd been okay this first week, and I wanted to keep it that way.

"You know," I said, "I'm thinking more and more that you stealing Aaron back is a good thing. It'll teach Bitch Doll a lesson. I bet it'd be easy, too. He's still crazy about you."

"I don't want to teach anyone a lesson," said Lissa. "And *I'm* not crazy about him."

"Come on, she picks fights and talks about us behind our backs. She accused me of getting jeans from the Salvation Army yesterday."

"Your jeans *are* from the Salvation Army."

"Well, yeah," I snorted, "but she has no right making fun of them when she's wearing stuff from Target."

"Hey, there's nothing wrong with Target. I like Target."

"So do I. That's not the point. She's trying to pass her stuff off like it's freaking Stella McCartney."

"And that's a crime?"

I affected a solemn face. "Absolutely. You've gotta take revenge."

"I told you, I'm not interested in revenge." Lissa cut me a sidelong look. "And you shouldn't be either."

I smiled as innocently as I could, and when we parted ways, I felt relieved again that she couldn't read my thoughts.

"So when's the big catfight going to happen?"

Mason was waiting for me outside our dorm after I'd parted ways with Lissa. He looked lazy and cute, leaning against the wall with crossed arms as he watched me.

"I'm sure I don't know what you mean."

He unfolded himself and walked with me into the building, handing me his coat, since I'd let Lissa go off with my dry one. "I saw you guys sparring outside the chapel. Have you no respect for the house of God?"

I snorted. "You've got about as much respect for it as I do, you heathen. You didn't even go. Besides, as you said, we were *outside*."

"And you still didn't answer the question."

I just grinned and slipped on his coat.

We stood in the common area of our dorm, a well-supervised

lounge and study area where male and female students could mingle, along with Moroi guests. Being Sunday, it was pretty crowded with those cramming for last-minute assignments due tomorrow. Spying a small, empty table, I grabbed Mason's arm and pulled him toward it.

"Aren't you supposed to go straight to your room?"

I hunkered down in my seat, glancing around warily. "There are so many people here today, it'll take them a while to notice me. God, I'm so sick of being locked away. And it's only been a week."

"I'm sick of it too. We missed you last night. A bunch of us went and shot pool in the rec room. Eddie was on fire."

I groaned. "Don't tell me that. I don't want to hear about your glamorous social life."

"All right." He propped his elbow up on the table and rested his chin in his hand. "Then tell me about Mia. You're just going to turn around and punch her one day, aren't you? I think I remember you doing that at least ten times with people that pissed you off."

"I'm a new, reformed Rose," I said, doing my best impression of demure. Which wasn't very good. He emitted a choking sort of laugh. "Besides, if I do that, I'll have broken my probation with Kirova. Gotta walk the straight and narrow."

"In other words, find some way to get back at Mia that you won't get in trouble for."

I felt a smile tug at the corners of my lips. "You know what I like about you, Mase? You think just like I do."

"Frightening concept," he replied drily. "So tell me what you think of this: I might know something about her, but I probably shouldn't tell you. . . ."

I leaned forward. "Oh, you already tipped me off. You've *got* to tell me now."

"It'd be wrong," he teased. "How do I know you'd use this knowledge for good instead of evil?"

I batted my eyelashes. "Can you resist this face?"

He took a moment to study me. "No. I can't, actually. Okay, here you go: Mia isn't royal."

I slouched back in my chair. "No kidding. I already knew that. I've known who's royal since I was two."

"Yeah, but there's more than just that. Her parents work for one of the Drozdov lords." I waved my hand impatiently. A lot of Moroi worked out in the human world, but Moroi society had plenty of jobs for its own kind too. Someone had to fill them. "Cleaning stuff. Practically servants. Her dad cuts grass, and her mom's a maid."

I actually had a healthy respect for anyone who pulled a full day's work, regardless of the job. People everywhere had to do crappy stuff to make a living. But, much like with Target, it became another matter altogether when someone was trying to pass herself off as something else. And in the week that I'd been here, I'd picked up on how desperately Mia wanted to fit in with the school elite.

"No one knows," I said thoughtfully.

"And she doesn't want them to. You know how the royals

are." He paused. "Well, except for Lissa, of course. They'd give Mia a hard time over it."

"How do you know all this?"

"My uncle's a guardian for the Drozdovs."

"And you've just been sitting on this secret, huh?"

"Until you broke me. So which path will you choose: good or evil?"

"I think I'll give her a grace—"

"Miss Hathaway, you know you aren't supposed to be here."

One of the dorm matrons stood over us, disapproval all over her face.

I hadn't been joking when I said Mason thought like me. He could bullshit as well as I could. "We have a group project to do for our humanities class. How are we supposed to do it if Rose is in isolation?"

The matron narrowed her eyes. "You don't look like you're doing work."

I slid over the priest's book and opened it at random. I'd placed it on the table when we sat down. "We're, um, working on this."

She still looked suspicious. "One hour. I'll give you one more hour down here, and I'd better actually see you working."

"Yes, ma'am," said Mason straight-faced. "Absolutely."

She wandered off, still eyeing us. "My hero," I declared.

He pointed at the book. "What is this?"

"Something the priest gave me. I had a question about the service."

He stared at me, astonished.

"Oh, stop it and look interested." I skimmed the index. "I'm trying to find some woman named Anna."

Mason slid his chair over so that he was sitting right beside me. "All right. Let's 'study.'"

I found a page number, and it took me to the section on St. Vladimir, not surprisingly. We read through the chapter, scanning for Anna's name. When we found it, the author didn't have much to say about her. He did include an excerpt written by some guy who had apparently lived at the same time as St. Vladimir:

And with Vladimir always is Anna, the daughter of Fyodor. Their love is as chaste and pure as that of brother and sister, and many times has she defended him from Strigoi who would seek to destroy him and his holiness. Likewise, it is she who comforts him when the spirit becomes too much to bear, and Satan's darkness tries to smother him and weaken his own health and body. This too she defends against, for they have been bound together ever since he saved her life as a child. It is a sign of God's love that He has sent the blessed Vladimir a guardian such as her, one who is shadow-kissed and always knows what is in his heart and mind.

"There you go," Mason said. "She was his guardian."

"It doesn't say what 'shadow-kissed' means."

"Probably doesn't mean anything."

Something in me didn't believe that. I read it again, trying to make sense of the old-fashioned language. Mason watched me curiously, looking like he very much wanted to help.

"Maybe they were hooking up," he suggested.

I laughed. "He was a *saint*."

"So? Saints probably like sex too. That 'brother and sister' stuff is probably a cover." He pointed to one of the lines. "See? They were 'bound' together." He winked. "It's code."

Bound. It was a weird word choice, but that didn't necessarily mean Anna and Vladimir were ripping each other's clothes off.

"I don't think so. They're just close. Guys and girls can just be friends." I said it pointedly, and he gave me a dry look.

"Yeah? *We're* friends, and I don't know what's in your 'heart and mind.'" Mason put on a fake philosopher's look. "Of course, some might argue that one can never know what's in the heart of a woman—"

"Oh, shut up," I groaned, punching him in the arm.

"For they are strange and mysterious creatures," he continued in his scholarly voice, "and a man must be a mind reader if he ever wishes to make them happy."

I started giggling uncontrollably and knew I'd probably get in trouble again. "Well, try to read my mind and stop being such a—"

I stopped laughing and looked back down at the book.

Bound together and *always knows what is in his heart and mind*.

They had a bond, I realized. I would have bet everything I owned—which wasn't much—on it. The revelation was astonishing. There were lots of vague stories and myths about how guardians and Moroi 'used to have bonds.' But this was the first I'd ever heard of anyone specific that it had happened to.

Mason had noticed my startled reaction. "You okay? You look kind of weird."

I shrugged it off. "Yeah. Fine."

SEVEN

A COUPLE WEEKS PASSED AFTER that, and I soon forgot about the Anna thing as life at the Academy wrapped around me. The shock of our return had worn off a little, and we began to fall into a semi-comfortable routine. My days revolved around church, lunch with Lissa, and whatever sort of social life I could scrape together outside of that. Denied any real free time, I didn't have too hard a time staying out of the spotlight, although I did manage to steal a little attention here and there, despite my noble speech to her about 'coasting through the middle.' I couldn't help it. I liked flirting, I liked groups, and I liked making smartass comments in class.

Her new, incognito role attracted attention simply because it was so different than before we'd left, back when she'd been so active with the royals. Most people soon let that go, accepting that the Dragomir princess was fading off the social radar and content to run with Natalie and her group. Natalie's rambling still made me want to beat my head against a wall sometimes, but she was really nice—nicer than almost any of the other royals—and I enjoyed hanging around her most of the time.

And, just as Kirova had warned, I was indeed training and working out all the time. But as more time passed, my body stopped hating me. My muscles grew tougher, and my stamina increased. I still got my ass kicked in practice but not quite as badly as I used to, which was something. The biggest toll now seemed to be on my skin. Being outside in the cold so much was chapping my face, and only Lissa's constant supply of skin-care lotions kept me from aging before my time. She couldn't do much for the blisters on my hands and feet.

A routine also developed with Dimitri and me. Mason had been right about him being antisocial. Dimitri didn't hang out much with the other guardians, though it was clear they all respected him. And the more I worked with him, the more I respected him too, though I didn't really understand his training methods. They didn't seem very badass. We always started by stretching in the gym, and lately he'd been sending me outside to run, braving the increasingly cold Montana autumn.

Three weeks after my return to the Academy, I walked into the gym before school one day and found him sprawled on a mat, reading a Louis L'Amour book. Someone had brought in a portable CD player, and while that cheered me up at first, the song coming from it did not: "When Doves Cry" by Prince. It was embarrassing to know the title, but one of our former housemates had been obsessed with the '80s.

"Whoa, Dimitri," I said, tossing my bag on the floor. "I realize this is actually a current hit in Eastern Europe right now, but do you think we could maybe listen to something that wasn't recorded before I was born?"

Only his eyes flicked toward me; the rest of his posture

remained the same. "What does it matter to you? I'm the one who's going to be listening to it. You'll be outside running."

I made a face as I set my foot up on one of the bars and stretched my hamstrings. All things considered, Dimitri had a good-natured tolerance for my snarkiness. So long as I didn't slack in my training, he didn't mind my running commentary.

"Hey," I asked, moving on to the next set of stretches, "what's with all the running, anyway? I mean, I realize the importance of stamina and all that, but shouldn't I be moving on to something with a little hitting? They're still killing me in group practice."

"Maybe you should hit harder," he replied drily.

"I'm serious."

"Hard to tell the difference." He set the book down but didn't move from his sprawl. "My job is to get you ready to defend the princess and fight dark creatures, right?"

"Yup."

"So tell me this: suppose you manage to kidnap her again and take her off to the mall. While you're there, a Strigoi comes at you. What will you do?"

"Depends on what store we're in."

He looked at me.

"Fine. I'll stab him with a silver stake."

Dimitri sat up now, crossing his long legs in one fluid motion. I still couldn't figure out how someone so tall could be so graceful. "Oh?" He raised his dark eyebrows. "Do you have a silver stake? Do you even know how to use one?"

I dragged my eyes away from his body and scowled. Made with elemental magic, silver stakes were a guardian's deadliest weapon. Stabbing a Strigoi through the heart with one meant instant death. The blades were also lethal to Moroi, so they weren't given out lightly to novices. My classmates had just started learning how to use them. I'd trained with a gun before, but no one would let me near a stake yet. Fortunately, there were two other ways to kill a Strigoi.

"Okay. I'll cut his head off."

"Ignoring the fact that you don't have a weapon to do that, how will you compensate for the fact that he may be a foot taller than you?"

I straightened up from touching my toes, annoyed. "Fine, then I'll set him on fire."

"Again, with what?"

"All right, I give up. You've already got the answer. You're just messing with me. I'm at the mall and I see a Strigoi. What do I do?"

He looked at me and didn't blink. "You run."

I repressed the urge to throw something at him. When I finished my stretches, he told me he'd run with me. That was a first. Maybe running would give me some insight into his killer reputation.

We set out into the chilly October evening. Being back on a vampiric schedule still felt weird to me. With school about to start in an hour, I expected the sun to be coming up, not down. But it was sinking on the western horizon, lighting up the snow-capped mountains with an orange glow. It didn't really warm things up, and I soon felt the cold pierce my lungs as my need for oxygen deepened. We didn't speak. He slowed his pace to match mine, so we stayed together.

Something about that bothered me; I suddenly very much wanted his approval. So I picked up my own pace, working my lungs and muscles harder. Twelve laps around the track made three miles; we had nine more to go.

When we reached the third-to-last loop, a couple of other novices passed by, preparing to go to the group practice I'd soon be at as well. Seeing me, Mason cheered. "Good form, Rose!"

I smiled and waved back.

"You're slowing down," Dimitri snapped, jerking my gaze from the boys. The harshness in his voice startled me. "Is this why your times aren't getting any faster? You're easily distracted?"

Embarrassed, I increased my speed once more, despite the fact that my body started screaming obscenities at me. We finished the twelve laps, and when he checked, he found we'd shaved two minutes off my best time.

"Not bad, huh?" I crowed when we headed back inside for cool-down stretches. "Looks like I could get as far as the Limited before the Strigoi got me at the mall. Not sure how Lissa would do."

"If she was with you, she'd be okay."

I looked up in surprise. It was the first real compliment

he'd paid me since I started training with him. His brown eyes watched me, both approving and amused.

And that's when it happened.

I felt like someone had shot me. Sharp and biting, terror exploded in my body and in my head. Small razors of pain. My vision blurred, and for a moment, I wasn't standing there. I was running down a flight of stairs, scared and desperate, needing to get out of there, needing to find . . . me.

My vision cleared, leaving me back on the track and out of Lissa's head. Without a word to Dimitri, I tore off, running as fast as I could toward the Moroi dorm. It didn't matter that I'd just put my legs through a mini-marathon. They ran hard and fast, like they were shiny and new. Distantly, I was aware of Dimitri catching up to me, asking me what was wrong. But I couldn't answer him. I had one task and one alone: get to the dorm.

Its looming, ivy-covered form was just coming into view when Lissa met up with us, her face streaked with tears. I came to a jarring stop, my lungs ready to burst.

"What's wrong? What happened?" I demanded, clutching her arms, forcing her to look into my eyes.

But she couldn't answer. She just flung her arms around me, sobbing into my chest. I held her there, stroking her sleek, silky hair while I told her it was going to be all right—whatever 'it' was. And honestly, I didn't care what it was just then. She was here, and she was safe, which was all that mattered. Dimitri hovered over us, alert and ready for any threat, his body coiled to attack. I felt safe with him beside us.

A half hour later, we were crammed inside Lissa's dorm room with three other guardians, Ms. Kirova, and the hall matron. This was the first time I'd seen Lissa's room. Natalie had indeed managed to get her as a roommate, and the two sides of the room were a study in contrasts. Natalie's looked lived in, with pictures on the wall and a frilly bedspread that wasn't dorm-issue. Lissa had as few possessions as I did, making her half noticeably bare. She did have one picture taped to the wall, a picture taken from last Halloween, when we'd dressed up like fairies, complete with wings and glittery makeup. Seeing that picture and remembering how things used to be made a dull pain form in my chest.

With all the excitement, no one seemed to remember that I wasn't supposed to be in there. Outside in the hall, other Moroi girls crowded together, trying to figure out what was going on. Natalie pushed her way through them, wondering what the commotion in her room was. When she discovered it, she came to a screeching halt.

Shock and disgust showed on almost everyone's faces as we stared at Lissa's bed. There was a fox on the pillow. Its coat was reddish-orange, tinged in white. It looked so soft and cuddly that it could have been a pet, perhaps a cat, something you'd hold in your arms and snuggle with.

Aside from the fact that its throat had been slit.

The inside of the throat looked pink and jellylike. Blood stained that soft coat and had run down onto the yellow bedspread, forming a dark pool that spread across the fabric. The fox's eyes stared upward, glazed, over with a sort of shocked look about them, like the fox couldn't believe this was happening.

Nausea built up in my stomach, but I forced myself to keep looking. I couldn't afford to be squeamish. I'd be killing Strigoi someday. If I couldn't handle a fox, I'd never survive major kills.

What had happened to the fox was sick and twisted, obviously done by someone too fucked up for words. Lissa stared at it, her face death-pale, and took a few steps toward it, hand involuntarily reaching out. This gross act hit her hard, I knew, digging at her love of animals. She loved them, they loved her. While on our own, she'd often begged me for a pet, but I'd always refused and reminded her we couldn't take care of one when we might have to flee at a moment's notice. Plus, they hated me. So she'd contented herself with helping and patching up strays she found and making friends with other people's pets, like Oscar the cat.

She couldn't patch this fox up, though. There was no coming back for it, but I saw in her face she wanted to help it, like she helped everything. I took her hand and steered her away, suddenly recalling a conversation from two years ago.

"What is that? Is it a crow?"

"Too big. It's a raven."

"Is it dead?"

"Yeah. Definitely dead. Don't touch it."

She hadn't listened to me back then. I hoped she would now.

"It was still alive when I got back," Lissa whispered to me, clutching my arm. "Barely. Oh God, it was twitching. It must have suffered so much."

I felt bile rise in my throat now. Under no circumstances would I throw up. "Did you—?"

"No. I wanted to. . . . I started to. . . ."

"Then forget about it," I said sharply. "It's stupid. Somebody's stupid joke. They'll clean it up. Probably even give you a new room if you want."

She turned to me, eyes almost wild. "Rose . . . do you remember . . . that one time. . . ."

"Stop it," I said. "Forget about it. This isn't the same thing."

"What if someone saw? What if someone knows? . . ."

I tightened my grip on her arm, digging my nails in to get her attention. She flinched. "No. It's not the same. It has nothing to do with that. Do you hear me?" I could feel both Natalie and Dimitri's eyes on us. "It's going to be okay. Everything's going to be okay."

Not looking like she believed me at all, Lissa nodded.

"Get this cleaned up," Kirova snapped to the matron. "And find out if anyone saw anything."

Someone finally realized I was there and ordered Dimitri to take me away, no matter how much I begged them to let me stay with Lissa. He walked me back to the novices' dorm. He didn't speak until we were almost there. "You know something. Something about what happened. Is this what you meant when you told Headmistress Kirova that Lissa was in danger?"

"I don't know anything. It's just some sick joke."

"Do you have any idea who'd do it? Or why?"

I considered this. Before we'd left, it could have been any number of people. That was the way it was when you were popular. People loved you, people hated you. But now? Lissa had faded off to a certain extent. The only person who really and truly despised her was Mia, but Mia seemed to fight her battles with words, not actions. And even if she did decide to do something more aggressive, why do this? She didn't seem like the type. There were a million other ways to get back at a person.

"No," I told him. "No clue."

"Rose, if you know something, tell me. We're on the same side. We both want to protect her. This is serious."

I spun around, taking my anger over the fox out on him. "Yeah, it *is* serious. It's all serious. And you have me doing laps every day when I should be learning to fight and defend her! If you want to help her, then teach me something! *Teach me how to fight.* I already know how to run away."

I didn't realize until that moment how badly I did want to learn, how I wanted to prove myself to him, to Lissa, and to everyone else. The fox incident had made me feel powerless, and I didn't like that. I wanted to do something, *anything*.

Dimitri watched my outburst calmly, with no change in his expression. When I finished, he simply beckoned me forward like I hadn't said anything. "Come on. You're late for practice."

EIGHT

BURNING WITH ANGER, I FOUGHT harder and better that day than I ever had in any of my classes with the novices. So much so that I finally won my first hand-to-hand pairing, annihilating Shane Reyes. We'd always gotten along, and he took it good-naturedly, applauding my performance, as did a few others.

"The comeback's starting," observed Mason after class.

"So it would seem."

He gently touched my arm. "How's Lissa?"

It didn't surprise me that he knew. Gossip spread so fast around here sometimes, it felt like everyone had a psychic bond.

"Okay. Coping." I didn't elaborate on how I knew that. Our bond was a secret from the student body. "Mase, you claim to know about Mia. You think she might have done that?"

"Whoa, hey, I'm not an expert on her or anything. But honestly? No. Mia won't even do dissections in biology. I can't picture her actually catching a fox, let alone, um, killing it."

"Any friends who might do it for her?"

He shook his head. "Not really. They're not really the types to get their hands dirty either. But who knows?"

Lissa was still shaken when I met her for lunch later, her

mood made worse when Natalie and her crew wouldn't shut up about the fox. Apparently Natalie had overcome her disgust enough to enjoy the attention the spectacle had brought her. Maybe she wasn't as content with her fringe status as I'd always believed.

"And it was just *there*," she explained, waving her hands for emphasis. "Right in the middle of the bed. There was blood *everywhere*."

Lissa looked as green as the sweater she wore, and I pulled her away before I even finished my food and immediately launched into a string of obscenities about Natalie's social skills.

"She's nice," Lissa said automatically. "You were just telling me the other day how much you liked her."

"I do like her, but she's just incompetent about certain things."

We stood outside our animal behavior class, and I noticed people giving us curious looks and whispering as they passed. I sighed.

"How are you doing with all this?"

A half-smile crossed her face. "Can't you already feel it?"

"Yeah, but I want to hear it from you."

"I don't know. I'll be okay. I wish everyone wouldn't keep staring at me like I'm some kind of freak."

My anger exploded again. The fox was bad. People upsetting her made it worse, but at least I could do something about them. "Who's bothering you?"

"Rose, you can't beat up everyone we have a problem with."

"Mia?" I guessed.

"And others," she said evasively. "Look, it doesn't matter. What I want to know is how this could have . . . that is, I can't stop thinking about that time—"

"Don't," I warned.

"Why do you keep pretending that didn't happen? You of all people. You made fun of Natalie for going on and on, but it's not like you've got a good grip on your control switch. You'll normally talk about anything."

"But not *that*. We need to forget about it. It was a long time ago. We don't even really know what happened."

She stared at me with those big green eyes, calculating her next argument.

"Hey, Rose."

Our conversation dropped as Jesse strolled up to us. I turned on my best smile.

"Hey."

He nodded cordially to Lissa. "So hey, I'm going to be in your dorm tonight for a study group. You think . . . maybe . . ."

Momentarily forgetting Lissa, I focused my full attention on Jesse. Suddenly, I *so* needed to do something wild and bad. Too much had happened today. "Sure."

He told me when he'd be there, and I told him I'd meet him in one of the common areas with "further instructions."

Lissa stared at me when he left. "You're under house arrest. They won't let you hang out and talk to him."

"I don't really want to 'talk' to him. We'll slip away."

She groaned. "I just don't know about you sometimes."

"That's because you're the cautious one, and I'm the reckless one."

Once animal behavior started, I pondered the likelihood of Mia being responsible. From the smug look on her psycho-angel face, she certainly seemed to be enjoying the sensation caused by the bloody fox. But that didn't mean she was the culprit, and after observing her over the last couple of weeks, I knew she'd enjoy anything that upset Lissa and me. She didn't need to be the one who had done it.

"Wolves, like many other species, differentiate their packs into alpha males and alpha females whom the others defer to. Alphas are almost always the strongest physically, though many times, confrontations turn out to be more a matter of willpower and personality. When an alpha is challenged and replaced, that wolf may find himself ostracized from the group or even attacked."

I looked up from my daydreams and focused on Ms. Meissner.

"Most challenges are likely to occur during mating season," she continued. This, naturally, brought snickers from the class. "In most packs, the alpha pair are the *only* ones who mate. If the alpha male is an older, seasoned wolf, a younger competitor may think he has a shot. Whether that is true works on a case-by-case basis. The young often don't realize how seriously outclassed they are by the more experienced."

The old-and-young-wolf thing notwithstanding, I thought the rest was pretty relevant. Certainly in the Academy's social structure, I decided bitterly, there seemed to be a lot of alphas and challenges.

Mia raised her hand. "What about foxes? Do *they* have alphas too?"

There was a collective intake of breath from the class, followed by a few nervous giggles. No one could believe Mia had gone there.

Ms. Meissner flushed with what I suspected was anger. "We're discussing wolves today, Miss Rinaldi."

Mia didn't seem to mind the subtle chastising, and when the class paired off to work on an assignment, she spent more time looking over at us and giggling. Through the bond, I could feel Lissa growing more and more upset as images of the fox kept flashing through her mind.

"Don't worry," I told her. "I've got a way—"

"Hey, Lissa," someone interrupted.

We both looked up as Ralf Sarcozy stopped by our desks. He wore his trademark stupid grin, and I had a feeling he'd come over here on a dare from his friends.

"So, admit it," he said. "You killed the fox. You're trying to convince Kirova you're crazy so that you can get out of here again."

"Screw you," I told him in a low voice.

"Are you offering?"

"From what I've heard, there isn't much to screw," I shot back.

"Wow," he said mockingly. "You *have* changed. Last I remembered, you weren't too picky about who you got naked with."

"And the last *I* remember, the only people you ever saw naked were on the Internet."

He cocked his head in an overly dramatic fashion. "Hey, I just got it: it was you, wasn't it?" He looked at Lissa, the back at me. "She got *you* to kill the fox, didn't she? Some weird kind of lesbian voo—ahhh!"

Ralf burst into flames.

I jumped up and pushed Lissa out of the way—not easy to do, since we were sitting at our desks. We both ended up on the floor as screams—Ralf's in particular—filled the classroom and Ms. Meissner sprinted for the fire extinguisher.

And then, just like that, the flames disappeared. Ralf was still screaming and patting himself down, but he didn't have a single singe mark on him. The only indication of what had happened was the lingering smell of smoke in the air.

For several seconds, the entire classroom froze. Then, slowly, everyone put the pieces together. Moroi magical specializations were well known, and after scanning the room, I deduced three fire users: Ralf, his friend Jacob, and—

Christian Ozera.

Since neither Jacob nor Ralf would have set Ralf on fire, it sort of made the culprit obvious. The fact that Christian was laughing hysterically sort of gave it away too.

Ms. Meissner changed from red to deep purple. "Mr. Ozera!" she screamed. "How dare you—do you have any idea—report to Headmistress Kirova's office now!"

Christian, completely unfazed, stood up and slung his backpack over one shoulder. That smirk stayed on his face. "Sure thing, Ms. Meissner."

He went out of his way to walk past Ralf, who quickly backed away as he passed. The rest of the class stared, open-mouthed.

After that, Ms. Meissner attempted to return the class to normal, but it was a lost cause. No one could stop talking about what had happened. It was shocking on a few different levels. First, no one had ever seen that kind of spell: a massive fire that didn't actually burn anything. Second, Christian had used it offensively. He had attacked another person. Moroi never did that. They believed magic was meant to take care of the earth, to help people live better lives. It was never, ever used as a weapon. Magic instructors never taught those kinds of spells; I don't think they even knew any. Finally, craziest of all, *Christian* had done it. Christian, whom no one ever noticed or gave a damn about. Well, they'd noticed him now.

It appeared someone still knew offensive spells after all, and as much as I had enjoyed the look of terror on Ralf's face, it suddenly occurred to me that Christian might really and truly be a psycho.

"Liss," I said as we walked out of class, "please tell me you haven't hung out with him again."

The guilt that flickered through the bond told me more than any explanation could.

"Liss!" I grabbed her arm.

"Not that much," she said uneasily. "He's really okay—"

"Okay? *Okay*?" People in the hall stared at us. I realized I was practically shouting. "He's out of his mind. *He set Ralf on fire.* I thought we decided you weren't going to see him anymore."

"*You* decided, Rose. Not me." There was an edge in her voice I hadn't heard in a while.

"What's going on here? Are you guys . . . you know? . . ."

"No!" she insisted. "I told you that already. God." She shot me a look of disgust. "Not everyone thinks—and acts—like you."

I flinched at the words. Then we noticed that Mia was passing by. She hadn't heard the conversation but had caught the tone. A snide smile spread over her face. "Trouble in paradise?"

"Go find your pacifier, and shut the hell up," I told her, not waiting to hear her response. Her mouth dropped open, then tightened into a scowl.

Lissa and I walked on in silence, and then Lissa burst out laughing. Like that, our fight diffused.

"Rose . . ." Her tone was softer now.

"Lissa, he's dangerous. I don't like him. Please be careful."

She touched my arm. "I am. I'm the cautious one, remember? You're the reckless one."

I hoped that was still true.

But later, after school, I had my doubts. I was in my room doing homework when I felt a trickle of what could only be called sneakiness coming from Lissa. Losing track of my work, I stared off into space, trying to get a more detailed understanding of what was happening to her. If ever there was a time for me to slip into her mind, it was now, but I didn't know how to control that.

Frowning, I tried to think what normally made that connection occur. Usually she was experiencing some strong emotion, an emotion so powerful it tried to blast into my mind. I had to work hard to fight against that; I always sort of kept a mental wall up.

Focusing on her now, I tried to remove the wall. I steadied my breathing and cleared my mind. My thoughts didn't matter, only hers did. I needed to open myself to her and let us connect.

I'd never done anything like this before; I didn't have the patience for meditation. My need was so strong, however, that I forced myself into an intense, focused relaxation. I needed to know what was going on with her, and after a few more moments, my effort paid off.

I was in.

NINE

I SNAPPED INTO HER MIND, once again seeing and directly experiencing what went on around her.

She was sneaking into the chapel's attic again, confirming my worst fears. Like last time, she met no resistance. *Good God,* I thought, *could that priest be any worse about securing his own chapel?*

Sunrise lit up the stained-glass window, and Christian's silhouette was framed against it: he was sitting in the window seat.

"You're late," he told her. "Been waiting a while."

Lissa pulled up one of the rickety chairs, brushing dust off it. "I figured you'd be tied up with Headmistress Kirova."

He shook his head. "Not much to it. They suspended me for a week, that's all. Not like it's hard to sneak out." He waved his hands around. "As you can see."

"I'm surprised you didn't get more time."

A patch of sunlight lit up his crystal-blue eyes. "Disappointed?"

She looked shocked. "You set someone on fire!"

"No, I didn't. Did you see any burns on him?"

"He was covered in flames."

"I had them under control. I kept them off of him."

She sighed. "You shouldn't have done that."

Straightening out of his lounging position, he sat up and leaned toward her. "I did it for you."

"You attacked someone for me?"

"Sure. He was giving you and Rose a hard time. She was doing an okay job against him, I guess, but I figured she could use the backup. Besides, this'll shut anyone else up about the whole fox thing, too."

"You shouldn't have done that," she repeated, looking away. She didn't know how to feel about this "generosity." "And don't act like it was all for me. You *liked* doing it. Part of you wanted to—just because."

Christian's smug expression dropped, replaced by one of uncharacteristic surprise. Lissa might not be psychic, but she had a startling ability to read people.

Seeing him off guard, she continued. "Attacking someone else with magic is forbidden—and that's *exactly* why you wanted to do it. You got a thrill out of it."

"Those rules are stupid. If we used magic as a weapon instead of just for warm and fuzzy shit, Strigoi wouldn't keep killing so many of us."

"It's wrong," she said firmly. "Magic is a gift. It's peaceful."

"Only because they say it is. You're repeating the party line we've been fed our whole lives." He stood up and paced the small space of the attic. "It wasn't always that way, you know. We used to fight, right along with the guardians—centuries ago. Then people started getting scared and stopped. Figured it was safer to just hide. They forgot the attack spells."

"Then how did you know that one?"

He crooked her a smile. "Not everyone forgot."

"Like your family? Like your parents?"

The smile disappeared. "You don't know anything about my parents."

His face darkened, his eyes grew hard. To most people, he might have appeared scary and intimidating, but as Lissa studied and admired his features, he suddenly seemed very, very vulnerable.

"You're right," she admitted softly, after a moment. "I don't. I'm sorry."

For the second time in this meeting, Christian looked astonished. Probably no one apologized to him that often. Hell, no one even talked to him that often. Certainly no one ever listened. Like usual, he quickly turned into his cocky self.

"Forget it." Abruptly, he stopped pacing and knelt in front of her so they could look each other in the eye. Feeling him so close made her hold her breath. A dangerous smile curled his lips. "And really, I don't get why *you* of all people should act so outraged that I used 'forbidden' magic."

"Me 'of all people'? What's that supposed to mean?"

"You can play all innocent if you want—and you do a pretty good job—but I know the truth."

"What truth is that?" She couldn't hide her uneasiness from me or Christian.

He leaned even closer. "That you use compulsion. All the time."

"No, I don't," she said immediately.

"Of course you do. I've been lying awake at night, trying to figure out how in the world you two were able to rent out a place and go to high school without anyone ever wanting to meet your parents. Then I figured it out. You had to be using compulsion. That's probably how you broke out of here in the first place."

"I see. You just figured it out. Without any proof."

"I've got all the proof I need, just from watching you."

"You've been watching me—spying on me—to prove I'm using compulsion?"

He shrugged. "No. Actually, I've been watching you just because I like it. The compulsion thing was a bonus. I saw you use it the other day to get an extension on that math assignment. And you used it on Ms. Carmack when she wanted to make you go through more testing."

"So you assume it's compulsion? Maybe I'm just really good at convincing people." There was a defiant note in her voice: understandable, considering her fear and anger. Only she delivered it with a toss of her hair which—if I didn't know any better—might have been considered flirtatious. And I did know better . . . right? Suddenly, I wasn't sure.

He went on, but something in his eyes told me he'd noticed the hair, that he always noticed everything about her. "People get these goofy looks on their faces when you talk to them. And not just any people—you're able to do it to Moroi. Probably dhampirs, too. Now *that's* crazy. I didn't even know that was possible. You're some kind of superstar. Some kind of evil, compulsion-abusing superstar." It was an accusation, but his tone and presence radiated the same flirtatiousness she had.

Lissa didn't know what to say. He was right. Everything he'd said was right. Her compulsion was what had allowed us to dodge authority and get along in the world without adult help. It was what had allowed us to convince the bank to let her tap into her inheritance.

And it was considered every bit as wrong as using magic as a weapon. Why not? It *was* a weapon. A powerful one, one that could be abused very easily. Moroi children had it drilled into them from an early age that compulsion was very, very wrong. No one was taught to use it, though every Moroi technically had the ability. Lissa had just sort of stumbled into it—deeply—and, as Christian had pointed out, she could wield it over Moroi, as well as humans and dhampirs.

"What are you going to do then?" she asked. "You going to turn me in?"

He shook his head and smiled. "No. I think it's hot."

She stared, eyes widening and heart racing. Something about the shape of his lips intrigued her. "Rose thinks you're dangerous," she blurted out nervously. "She thinks you might have killed the fox."

I didn't know how I felt about being dragged into this

bizarre conversation. Some people were scared of me. Maybe he was too.

Judging from the amusement in his voice when he spoke, it appeared he wasn't. "People think I'm unstable, but I tell you, Rose is ten times worse. Of course, that makes it harder for people to fuck with *you*, so I'm all for it." Leaning back on his heels, he finally broke the intimate space between them. "And I sure as hell didn't do *that*. Find out who did, though . . . and what I did to Ralf won't seem like anything."

His gallant offer of creepy vengeance didn't exactly reassure Lissa . . . but it did thrill her a little. "I don't want you doing anything like that. And I still don't know who did it."

He leaned back toward her and caught her wrists in his hands. He started to say something, then stopped and looked down in surprise, running his thumbs over faint, barely there scars. Looking back up at her, he had a strange—for him—kindness in his face.

"You might not know who did it. But you know something. Something you aren't talking about."

She stared at him, a swirl of emotions playing in her chest. "You can't know all my secrets," she murmured.

He glanced back down at her wrists and then released them, that dry smile of his back on his face. "No. I guess not."

A feeling of peace settled over her, a feeling I thought only I could bring. Returning to my own head and my room, I sat on the floor staring at my math book. Then, for reasons I didn't really get, I slammed it shut and threw it against the wall.

I spent the rest of the night brooding until the time I was supposed to meet Jesse came around. Slipping downstairs, I went into the kitchen—a place I could visit so long as I kept things brief—and caught his eye when I cut through the main visiting area.

Moving past him, I paused and whispered, "There's a lounge on the fourth floor that nobody uses. Take the stairs on the other side of the bathrooms and meet me there in five minutes. The lock on the door is broken."

He complied to the second, and we found the lounge dark, dusty, and deserted. The drop in guardian numbers over the years meant a lot of the dorm stayed empty, a sad sign for Moroi society but terribly convenient right now.

He sat down on the couch, and I lay back on it, putting my feet in his lap. I was still annoyed after Lissa and Christian's bizarre attic romance and wanted nothing more than to forget about it for a while.

"You really here to study, or was it just an excuse?" I asked.

"No. It was real. Had to do an assignment with Meredith." The tone in his voice indicated he wasn't happy about that.

"Oooh," I teased. "Is working with a dhampir beneath your royal blood? Should I be offended?"

He smiled, showing a mouth full of perfect white teeth and fangs. "You're a lot hotter than she is."

"Glad I make the cut." There was a sort of a heat in his eyes that was turning me on, as was his hand sliding up my leg. But I needed to do something first. It was time for some vengeance. "Mia must too, since you guys let her hang out with you. She's not royal."

His finger playfully poked me in the calf. "She's with Aaron. And I've got lots of friends who aren't royal. And friends who are dhamps. I'm not a total asshole."

"Yeah, but did you know her parents are practically custodians for the Drozdovs?"

The hand on my leg stopped. I'd exaggerated, but he was a sucker for gossip—and he was notorious for spreading it.

"Seriously?"

"Yeah. Scrubbing floors and stuff like that."

"Huh."

I could see the wheels turning in his dark blue eyes and had to hide a smile. The seed was planted.

Sitting up, I moved closer to him and draped a leg over his lap. I wrapped my arms around him, and without further delay, thoughts of Mia disappeared as his testosterone kicked in. He kissed me eagerly—sloppily, even—pushing me against the back of the couch, and I relaxed into what had to be the first enjoyable physical activity I'd had in weeks.

We kissed like that for a long time, and I didn't stop him when he pulled off my shirt.

"I'm not having sex," I warned between kisses. I had no intention of losing my virginity on a couch in a lounge.

He paused, thinking about this, and finally decided not to push it. "Okay."

But he pushed me onto the couch, lying over me, still kissing with that same fierceness. His lips traveled down to my neck, and when the sharp points of his fangs brushed against my skin, I couldn't help an excited gasp.

He raised himself up, looking into my face with open surprise. For a moment, I could barely breathe, recalling that rush of pleasure that a vampire bite could fill me with, wondering what it'd be like to feel that while making out. Then the old taboos kicked in. Even if we didn't have sex, giving blood while we did *this* was still wrong, still dirty.

"Don't," I warned.

"You want to." His voice held excited wonder. "I can tell."

"No, I don't."

His eyes lit up. "You do. How—hey, have you done it before?"

"No," I scoffed. "Of course not."

Those gorgeous blue eyes watched me, and I could see the wheels spinning behind them. Jesse might flirt a lot and have a big mouth, but he wasn't stupid.

"You act like you have. You got excited when I was by your neck."

"You're a good kisser," I countered, though it wasn't entirely true. He drooled a little more than I would have preferred. "Don't you think everyone would know if I was giving blood?"

The realization seized him. "Unless you weren't doing it before you left. You did it while you were gone, didn't you? You fed Lissa."

"Of course not," I repeated.

But he was on to something, and he knew it. "It was the only way. You didn't have feeders. Oh, man."

"She found some," I lied. It was the same line we'd fed Natalie, the one she'd spread around and that no one—except Christian—had ever questioned. "Plenty of humans are into it."

"Sure," he said with a smile. He leaned his mouth back to my neck.

"I'm not a blood whore," I snapped, pulling away from him.

"But you *want* to. You like it. All you dhamp girls do." His teeth were on my skin again. Sharp. Wonderful.

I had a feeling hostility would only make things worse, so I defused the situation with teasing. "Stop it," I said gently, running a fingertip over his lips. "I told you, I'm not like that. But if you want something to do with your mouth, I can give you some ideas."

That peaked his interest. "Yeah? Like wha—?"

And that was when the door opened.

We sprang apart. I was ready to handle a fellow student or even possibly the matron. What I was not ready for was Dimitri.

He burst in the door like he'd expected to find us, and in

that horrible moment, with him raging like a storm, I knew why Mason had called him a god. In the blink of an eye, he crossed the room and jerked Jesse up by his shirt, nearly holding the Moroi off the ground.

"What's your name?" barked Dimitri.

"J-Jesse, sir. Jesse Zeklos, sir."

"Mr. Zeklos, do you have permission to be in this part of the dorm?"

"No, sir."

"Do you know the rules about male and female interactions around here?"

"Yes, sir."

"Then I suggest you get out of here as fast as you can before I turn you over to someone who will punish you accordingly. If I ever see you like this again"—Dimitri pointed to where I cowered, half-dressed, on the couch—"*I* will be the one to punish you. And it will hurt. A lot. Do you understand?"

Jesse swallowed, eyes wide. None of the bravado he usually showed was there. I guess there was "usually" and then there was being held in the grip of a really ripped, really tall, and really pissed-off Russian guy. "Yes, sir!"

"Then *go*." Dimitri released him, and, if possible, Jesse got out of there faster than Dimitri had burst in. My mentor then turned to me, a dangerous glint in his eyes. He didn't say anything, but the angry, disapproving message came through loud and clear.

And then it shifted.

It was almost like he'd been taken by surprise, like he'd never noticed me before. Had it been any other guy, I would have said he was checking me out. As it was, he was definitely studying me. Studying my face, my body. And I suddenly realized I was only in jeans and a bra—a black bra at that. I knew perfectly well that there weren't a lot of girls at this school who looked as good in a bra as I did. Even a guy like Dimitri, one who seemed so focused on duty and training and all of that, had to appreciate that.

And, finally, I noticed that a hot flush was spreading over me, and that the look in his eyes was doing more to me than Jesse's kisses had. Dimitri was quiet and distant sometimes, but he also had a dedication and an intensity that I'd never seen in any other person. I wondered how that kind of power and strength translated into . . . well, sex. I wondered what it'd be like for him to touch me and—shit!

What was I thinking? Was I out of my mind? Embarrassed, I covered my feelings with attitude.

"You see something you like?" I asked.

"Get dressed."

The set of his mouth hardened, and whatever he'd just felt was gone. That fierceness sobered me up and made me forget about my own troubling reaction. I immediately pulled my shirt back on, uneasy at seeing his badass side.

"How'd you find me? You following me to make sure I don't run away?"

"Be quiet," he snapped, leaning down so that we were at

eye level. "A janitor saw you and reported it. Do you have any idea how stupid this was?"

"I know, I know, the whole probation thing, right?"

"Not just that. I'm talking about the stupidity of getting in *that* kind of situation in the first place."

"I get in *that* kind of situation all the time, Comrade. It's not a big deal." Anger replaced my fear. I didn't like being treated like a child.

"Stop calling me that. You don't know even know what you're talking about."

"Sure I do. I had to do a report on Russia and the R.S.S.R. last year."

"*U.*S.S.R. And it *is* a big deal for a Moroi to be with a dhampir girl. They like to brag."

"So?"

"*So?*" he looked disgusted. "So don't you have any respect? Think about Lissa. You make yourself look cheap. You live up to what a lot of people already think about dhampir girls, and it reflects back on her. And me."

"Oh, I see. Is that what this is about? Am I hurting your big, bad male pride? Are you afraid I'll ruin your reputation?"

"My reputation is already made, Rose. I set my standards and lived up to them long ago. What you do with yours remains to be seen." His voice hardened again. "Now get back to your room—if you can manage it without throwing yourself at someone else."

"Is that your subtle way of calling me a slut?"

"I hear the stories you guys tell. I've heard stories about you."

Ouch. I wanted to yell back that it was none of his business what I did with my body, but something about the anger and disappointment on his face made me falter. I didn't know what it was. "Disappointing" someone like Kirova was a non-event, but Dimitri? . . . I remembered how proud I'd felt when he praised me the last few times in our practices. Seeing that disappear from him . . . well, it suddenly made me feel as cheap as he'd implied I was.

Something broke inside of me. Blinking back tears, I said, "Why is it wrong to . . . I don't know, have fun? I'm seventeen, you know. I should be able to enjoy it."

"You're seventeen, and in less than a year, someone's life and death will be in your hands." His voice still sounded firm, but there was a gentleness there too. "If you were human or Moroi, you could have fun. You could do things other girls could."

"But you're saying I can't."

He glanced away, and his dark eyes went unfocused. He was thinking about something far away from here. "When I was seventeen, I met Ivan Zeklos. We weren't like you and Lissa, but we became friends, and he requested me as his guardian when I graduated. I was the top student in my school. I paid attention to everything in my classes, but in the end, it wasn't enough. That's how it is in this life. One slip, one distraction . . . " He sighed. "And it's too late."

A lump formed in my throat as I thought about one slip or one distraction costing Lissa her life.

"Jesse's a Zeklos," I said, suddenly realizing Dimitri had just thrown around a relative of his former friend and charge.

"I know."

"Does it bother you? Does he remind you of Ivan?"

"It doesn't matter how I feel. It doesn't matter how any of us feel."

"But it does bother you." It suddenly became very obvious to me. I could read his pain, though he clearly worked hard to hide it. "You hurt. Every day. Don't you? You miss him."

Dimitri looked surprised, like he didn't want me to know that, like I'd uncovered some secret part of him. I'd been thinking he was some aloof, antisocial tough guy, but maybe he kept himself apart from other people so he wouldn't get hurt if he lost them. Ivan's death had clearly left a permanent mark.

I wondered if Dimitri was lonely.

The surprised look vanished, and his standard serious one returned. "It doesn't matter how I feel. *They* come first. Protecting them."

I thought about Lissa again. "Yeah. They do."

A long silence fell before he spoke again.

"You told me you want to fight, to *really* fight. Is that still true?"

"Yes. Absolutely."

"Rose . . . I can teach you, but I have to believe you're

dedicated. Really dedicated. I can't have you distracted by things like this." He gestured around the lounge. "Can I trust you?"

Again, I felt like crying under that gaze, under the seriousness of what he asked. I didn't get how he could have such a powerful effect on me. I'd never cared so much about what one person thought. "Yes. I promise."

"All right. I'll teach you, but I need you strong. I know you hate the running, but it really is necessary. You have no idea what Strigoi are like. The school tries to prepare you, but until you've seen how strong they are and how fast . . . well, you can't even imagine. So I can't stop the running and the conditioning. If you want to learn more about fighting, we need to add more trainings. It'll take up more of your time. You won't have much left for your homework or anything else. You'll be tired. A lot."

I thought about it, about him, and about Lissa. "It doesn't matter. If you tell me to do it, I'll do it."

He studied me hard, like he was still trying to decide if he could believe me. Finally satisfied, he gave me a sharp nod. "We'll start tomorrow."

TEN

"EXCUSE ME, MR. NAGY? I CAN'T really concentrate with Lissa and Rose passing notes over there."

Mia was attempting to distract attention from herself—as well as from her inability to answer Mr. Nagy's question—and it was ruining what had otherwise been a promising day. A few of the fox rumors still circulated, but most people wanted to talk about Christian attacking Ralf. I still hadn't cleared Christian of the fox incident—I was pretty sure he was psycho enough to have done it as some crazy sign of affection for Lissa—but whatever his motives, he had shifted the attention off her, just as he'd said.

Mr. Nagy, legendary for his ability to humiliate students by reading notes aloud, homed in on us like a missile. He snatched the note away, and the excited class settled in for a full reading. I swallowed my groan, trying to look as blank and unconcerned as possible. Beside me, Lissa looked like she wanted to die.

"My, my," he said, looking the note over. "If only students would write this much in their essays. One of you has considerably worse writing than the other, so forgive me if I get anything wrong here." He cleared his throat. "'*So, I saw J last night*,' begins the person with bad handwriting, to which the response is, *'What happened,'* followed by no fewer than five question marks. Understandable, since sometimes one—let alone four—just won't get the point across, eh?" The class laughed, and I noticed Mia throwing me a particularly mean smile. "The first speaker responds: *'What do you think happened? We hooked up in one of the empty lounges.'*"

Mr. Nagy glanced up after hearing some more giggles in the room. His British accent only added to the hilarity.

"May I assume by this reaction that the use of 'hook up' pertains to the more recent, shall we say, *carnal* application of the term than the tamer one I grew up with?"

More snickers ensued. Straightening up, I said boldly, "Yes, sir, Mr. Nagy. That would be correct, sir." A number of people in the class laughed outright.

"Thank you for that confirmation, Miss Hathaway. Now, where was I? Ah yes, the other speaker then asks, *'How was it?'* The response is, *'Good,'* punctuated with a smiley face to confirm said adjective. Well. I suppose kudos are in order for the mysterious J, hmmm? *'So, like, how far did you guys go?'* Uh, ladies," said Mr. Nagy, "I do hope this doesn't surpass a PG rating. *'Not very. We got caught.'* And again, we are shown the severity of the situation, this time through the use of a not-smiling face. *'What happened?'* *'Dimitri showed up. He threw Jesse out and then bitched me out.'*"

The class lost it, both from hearing Mr. Nagy say "bitched" and from finally getting some participants named.

"Why, Mr. Zeklos, are you the aforementioned J? The one

who earned a smiley face from the sloppy writer?" Jesse's face turned beet red, but he didn't look entirely displeased at having his exploits made known in front of his friends. He'd kept what had happened a secret thus far—including the blood talk—because I suspected Dimitri had scared the hell out of him. "Well, while I applaud a good misadventure as much as the next teacher whose time is utterly wasted, do remind your 'friends' in the future that my class is not a chat room." He tossed the paper back on to Lissa's desk. "Miss Hathaway, it seems there's no feasible way to punish you, since you're already maxed out on penalties around here. Ergo, you, Miss Dragomir, will serve two detentions instead of one on behalf of your friend. Stay here when the bell rings, please."

After class, Jesse found me, an uneasy look on his face. "Hey, um, about that note . . . you know I didn't have anything to do with that. If Belikov finds out about it . . . you'll tell him? I mean, you'll let him know I didn't—"

"Yeah, yeah," I interrupted him. "Don't worry, you're safe."

Standing with me, Lissa watched him walk out of the room. Thinking of how easily Dimitri had thrown him around—and of his apparent cowardice—I couldn't help but remark, "You know, Jesse's suddenly not as hot as I used to think."

She only laughed. "You'd better go. I've got desks to wash."

I left her, heading back for my dorm. As I did, I passed

a number of students gathered in small clusters outside the building. I regarded them wistfully, wishing I had the free time to socialize.

"No, it's true," I heard a confident voice say. Camille Conta. Beautiful and popular, from one of the most prestigious families in the Conta clan. She and Lissa had sort of been friends before we left, in the uneasy way two powerful forces keep an eye on each other. "They, like, clean toilets or something."

"Oh my God," her friend said. "I'd die if I was Mia."

I smiled. Apparently Jesse had spread some of the stories I'd told him last night. Unfortunately, the next overheard conversation shattered my victory.

"—heard it was still *alive*. Like, twitching on her bed."

"That is so gross. Why would they just leave it there?"

"I don't know. Why kill it in the first place?"

"You think Ralf was right? That she and Rose did it to get kicked—"

They saw me and shut up.

Scowling, I skulked off across the quadrangle. *Still alive, still alive.*

I'd refused to let Lissa talk about the similarities between the fox and what had happened two years ago. I didn't want to believe they were connected, and I certainly didn't want her to either.

But I hadn't been able to stop thinking about that incident, not only because it was chilling, but because it really did remind me of what had just happened in her room.

We had been out in the woods near campus one evening, having skipped out on our last class. I'd traded a pair of cute, rhinestone-studded sandals to Abby Badica for a bottle of peach schnapps—desperate, yes, but you did what you had to in Montana—which she'd somehow gotten hold of. Lissa had shaken her head in disapproval when I suggested cutting class to go put the bottle out of its misery, but she'd come along anyway. Like always.

We found an old log to sit on near a scummy green marsh. A half-moon cast a tiny sliver of light on us, but it was more than enough for vampires and half-vampires to see by. Passing the bottle back and forth, I grilled her on Aaron. She'd fessed up that the two of them had had sex the weekend before, and I felt a surge of jealousy that she'd been the one to have sex first.

"So what was it like?"

She shrugged and took another drink. "I don't know. It wasn't anything."

"What do you mean it wasn't anything? Didn't the earth move or the planets align or something?"

"No," she said, smothering a laugh. "Of course not."

I didn't really get why that should be funny, but I could tell she didn't want to talk about it. This was around the time the bond had begun forming, and her emotions were starting to creep into me now and then. I held up the bottle and glared at it.

"I don't think this stuff is working."

"That's because there's barely any alcohol in—"

The sound of something moving in the brush came from nearby. I immediately shot up, putting my body between her and the noise.

"It's some animal," she said when a minute went by in silence.

That didn't mean it wasn't dangerous. The school's wards kept out Strigoi, but wild animals often wandered into the outskirts of campus, posing their own threats. Bears. Cougars.

"Come on," I told her. "Let's head back."

We hadn't gone very far when I heard something moving again, and someone stepped out into our path. "Ladies."

Ms. Karp.

We froze, and whatever quick reactions I'd shown back by the marsh disappeared as I delayed a few moments in hiding the bottle behind my back.

A half-smile crossed her face, and she held out her hand.

Sheepishly, I gave the bottle to her, and she tucked it under her arm. She turned without another word, and we followed, knowing there would be consequences to deal with.

"You think no one notices when half a class is gone?" she asked after a little while.

"Half a class?"

"A few of you apparently chose today to skip. Must be the nice weather. Spring fever."

Lissa and I trudged along. I'd never been comfortable around Ms. Karp since the time she'd healed my hands. Her weird, paranoid behavior had taken on a strange quality to me—a lot stranger than before. Scary, even. And lately I couldn't look at her without seeing those marks by her forehead. Her deep red hair usually covered them but not always. Sometimes there were new marks; sometimes the old ones faded to nothing.

A weird fluttering noise sounded to my right. We all stopped.

"One of your classmates, I imagine," murmured Ms. Karp, turning toward the sound.

But when we reached the spot, we found a large black bird lying on the on the ground. Birds—and most animals—didn't do anything for me, but even I had to admire its sleek feathers and fierce beak. It could probably peck someone's eyes out in thirty seconds—if it weren't obviously dying. With a last, half-hearted shake, the bird finally went still.

"What is that? Is it a crow?" I asked.

"Too big," said Ms. Karp. "It's a raven."

"Is it dead?" asked Lissa.

I peered at it. "Yeah. Definitely dead. Don't touch it."

"Probably attacked by another bird," observed Ms. Karp. "They fight over territory and resources sometimes."

Lissa knelt down, compassion on her face. I wasn't surprised, since she'd always had a thing for animals. She'd lectured me for days after I'd instigated the infamous hamster-and-hermit-crab fight. I'd viewed the fight as a testing of worthy opponents. She'd seen it as animal cruelty.

Transfixed, she reached toward the raven.

"Liss!" I exclaimed, horrified. "It's probably got a disease."

But her hand moved out like she hadn't even heard me. Ms. Karp stood there like a statue, her white face looking like a ghost's. Lissa's fingers stroked the raven's wings.

"Liss," I repeated, starting to move toward her, to pull her back. Suddenly, a strange sensation flooded through my head, a sweetness that was beautiful and full of life. The feeling was so intense, it stopped me in my tracks.

Then the raven moved.

Lissa gave a small scream and snatched her hand back. We both stared wide-eyed.

The raven flapped its wings, slowly trying to right itself and stand up. When it managed to do so, it turned toward us, fixing Lissa with a look that seemed too intelligent for a bird. Its eyes held hers, and I couldn't read her reaction through the bond. At long last, the raven broke the gaze and lifted into the air, strong wings carrying it away.

Wind stirring the leaves was the only sound left.

"Oh my God," breathed Lissa. "What just happened?"

"Hell if I know," I said, hiding my stark terror.

Ms. Karp strode forward and grabbed Lissa's arm, forcefully turning her so that they faced each other. I was there in a flash, ready to take action if Crazy Karp tried anything, though even I had qualms about taking down a teacher.

"Nothing happened," said Ms. Karp in an urgent voice, her eyes wild-looking. "Do you hear me? Nothing. And you can't tell anyone—*anyone*—about what you saw. Both of you. Promise me. Promise me you won't ever talk about this again."

Lissa and I exchanged uneasy glances. "Okay," she croaked out.

Ms. Karp's grip relaxed a little. "And don't ever do it again. If you do, they'll find out. They'll try to find you." She turned to me. "You can't let her do it. Not ever again."

On the quad, outside my dorm, someone was saying my name.

"Hey, Rose? I've called you, like, a hundred times."

I forgot about Ms. Karp and the raven and glanced over at Mason, who had apparently started walking with me toward the dorm while I was off in la-la land.

"Sorry," I mumbled. "I'm out of it. Just . . . um, tired."

"Too much excitement last night?"

I gave him a narrow-eyed look. "Nothing I couldn't handle."

"I guess," he laughed, though he didn't exactly sound amused. "Sounds like Jesse couldn't handle it."

"He did okay."

"If you say so. But personally, I think you've got bad taste."

I stopped walking. "And *I* don't think it's any of your business."

He looked away angrily. "You made it the whole class's business."

"Hey, I didn't do that on purpose."

"Would've happened anyway. Jesse's got a big mouth."

"He wouldn't have told."

"Yeah," said Mason. "Because he's so cute and has such an important family."

"Stop being an idiot," I snapped. "And why do you even care? Jealous I'm not doing it with you?"

His flush grew, going all the way to the roots of his red hair. "I just don't like hearing people talk shit about you, that's all. There are a lot of nasty jokes going around. They're calling you a slut."

"I don't care what they call me."

"Oh, yeah. You're really tough. You don't need anyone."

I stopped. "I don't. I'm one of the best novices in this fucking place. I don't need you acting all gallant and coming to my defense. Don't treat me like I'm some helpless girl."

I turned around and kept walking, but he caught up to me easily. The woes of being five-seven.

"Look . . . I didn't mean to upset you. I'm just worried about you."

I gave a harsh laugh.

"I'm serious. Wait . . ." he began. "I, uh, did something for you. Sort of. I went to the library last night and tried to look up St. Vladimir."

I stopped again. "You did?"

"Yeah, but there wasn't much on Anna. All the books were kind of generic. Just talked about him healing people, bringing them back from the edge of death."

That last part hit a nerve.

"Was . . . was there anything else?" I stammered.

He shook his head. "No. You probably need some primary sources, but we don't have any here."

"Primary what?"

He scoffed, a smile breaking over his face. "Do you do anything but pass notes? We just talked about them the other day in Andrews' class. They're books from the actual time period you want to study. Secondary ones are written by people living today. You'll get better information if you find something written by the guy himself. Or someone who actually knew him."

"Huh. Okay. What are you, like, a boy genius now?"

Mason gave me a light punch in the arm. "I pay attention, that's all. You're so oblivious. You miss all sorts of things." He smiled nervously. "And look . . . I really am sorry about what I said. I was just—"

Jealous, I realized. I could see it in his eyes. How had I never noticed this before? He was crazy about me. I guess I really was oblivious.

"It's all right, Mase. Forget about it." I smiled. "And thanks for looking that stuff up."

He smiled back, and I went inside, sad that I didn't feel the same way about him.

ELEVEN

"YOU NEED SOMETHING TO WEAR?" Lissa asked.

"Hmm?"

I glanced over at her. We were waiting for Mr. Nagy's Slavic art class to start, and I was preoccupied with listening to Mia adamantly deny the claims about her parents to one of her friends.

"It's not like they're servants or anything," she exclaimed, clearly flustered. Straightening her face, she tried for haughtiness. "They're practically advisors. The Drozdovs don't decide *anything* without them."

I choked on a laugh, and Lissa shook her head.

"You're enjoying this way too much."

"Because it's awesome. What'd you just ask me?" I dug through my bag, messily looking for my lip gloss. I made a face when I found it. It was almost empty; I didn't know where I was going to score some more.

"I asked if you need something to wear tonight," she said.

"Well, *yeah*, of course I do. But none of your stuff fits me."

"What are you going to do?"

I shrugged my shoulders. "Improvise, like always. I don't really care anyway. I'm just glad Kirova's letting me go."

We had an assembly tonight. It was November 1, All Saints'

Day—which also meant we'd been back almost a month now. A royal group was visiting the school, including Queen Tatiana herself. Honestly, that wasn't what excited me. She'd visited the Academy before. It was pretty common and a lot less cool than it sounded. Besides, after living among humans and elected leaders, I didn't think much of stiff royals. Still, I'd gotten permission to go because everyone else would be there. It was a chance to hang out with actual people for a change and not stay locked in my dorm room. A little freedom was definitely worth the pain of sitting through a few boring speeches.

I didn't stay to chat with Lissa after school like I usually did. Dimitri had stuck to his promise about extra trainings, and I was trying to stick to mine. I now had two additional hours of practice with him, one before *and* one after school. The more I watched him in action, the more I understood the badass-god reputation. He clearly knew a lot—his six *molnija* marks proved as much—and I burned to have him teach me what he knew.

When I arrived at the gym, I noticed he was wearing a T-shirt and loose running pants, as opposed to his usual jeans. It was a good look for him. Really good. *Stop looking,* I immediately told myself.

He positioned me so that we stood facing each other on the mat and crossed his arms. "What's the first problem you'll run into when facing a Strigoi?"

"They're immortal?"

"Think of something more basic."

More basic than that? I considered. "They could be bigger than me. And stronger."

Most Strigoi—unless they'd been human first—had the same height as their Moroi cousins. Strigoi also had better strength, reflexes, and senses than dhampirs. That's why guardians trained so hard; we had a "learning curve" to compensate for.

Dimitri nodded. "That makes it difficult but not impossible. You can usually use a person's extra height and weight against them."

He turned and demonstrated several maneuvers, pointing out where to move and how to strike someone. Going through the motions with him, I gained some insight into why I took such a regular beating in group practice. I absorbed his techniques quickly and couldn't wait to actually use them. Near the end of our time together, he let me try.

"Go ahead," he said. "Try to hit me."

I didn't need to be told twice. Lunging forward, I tried to land a blow and was promptly blocked and knocked down onto the mat. Pain surged through my body, but I refused to give in to it. I jumped up again, hoping to catch him off guard. I didn't.

After several more failed attempts, I stood up and held out my hands in a gesture of truce. "Okay, what am I doing wrong?"

"Nothing."

I wasn't as convinced. "If I wasn't doing anything wrong, I'd have rendered you unconscious by now."

"Unlikely. Your moves are all correct, but this is the first time you've really tried. I've done it for years."

I shook my head and rolled my eyes at his older-and-wiser manner. He'd once told me he was twenty-four. "Whatever you say, Grandpa. Can we try it again?"

"We're out of time. Don't you want to get ready?"

I looked at the dusty clock on the wall and perked up. Almost time for the banquet. The thought made me giddy. I felt like Cinderella, but without the clothes.

"Hell, yeah, I do."

He walked off ahead of me. Studying him carefully, I realized I couldn't let the opportunity go by. I leapt at his back, positioning myself exactly the way he'd taught me. I had the element of surprise. Everything was perfect, and he wouldn't even see me coming.

Before I could make contact, he spun around at a ridiculously high speed. In one deft motion, he grabbed me like I weighed nothing and threw me to the ground, pinning me there.

I groaned. "I didn't do anything wrong!"

His eyes looked levelly into mine as he held my wrists, but he didn't look as serious as he had during the lesson. He seemed to find this funny. "The battle cry sort of gave you away. Try not to yell next time."

"Would it have really made a difference if I'd been quiet?"

He thought about it. "No. Probably not."

I sighed loudly, still in too much of a good mood to really let this disappointment get me down. There were some advantages to having such a kick-ass mentor—one who also happened to have a foot of height on me and outweighed me considerably. And that wasn't even considering his strength. He wasn't bulky, but his body had a lot of hard, lean muscle. If I could ever beat *him*, I could beat anyone.

All of a sudden, it occurred to me that he was still holding me down. The skin on his fingers was warm as he clutched my wrists. His face hovered inches from my own, and his legs and torso were actually pressing against mine. Some of his long brown hair hung around his face, and he appeared to be noticing me too, almost like he had that night in the lounge. And oh *God*, did he smell good. Breathing became difficult for me, and it had nothing to do with the workout or my lungs being crushed.

I would have given anything to be able to read his mind right then. Ever since that night in the lounge, I'd noticed him watching me with this same, studious expression. He never actually did it during the trainings themselves—those were *business*. But before and after, he would sometimes lighten up just a little, and I'd see him look at me in a way that was almost admiring. And sometimes, if I was really, really lucky, he'd smile at me. A real smile, too—not the dry one that accompanied the sarcasm we tossed around so often. I didn't want to admit it to anyone—not to Lissa, not even to myself—

but some days, I lived for those smiles. They lit up his face. "Gorgeous" no longer adequately describrd him.

Hoping to appear calm, I tried to think of something professional and guardian-related to say. Instead, I said, "So um . . . you got any other moves to show me?"

His lips twitched, and for a moment, I thought I was going to get one of those smiles. My heart leapt. Then, with visible effort, he pushed the smile back and once more became my tough-love mentor. He shifted off me, leaned back on his heels, and rose. "Come on. We should go."

I scrambled to my own feet and followed him out of the gym. He didn't look back as he walked, and I mentally kicked myself on the way back to my room.

I was crushing on my mentor. Crushing on my *older* mentor. I had to be out of my mind. He was seven years older than me. Old enough to be my . . . well, okay, nothing. But still older than me. Seven years was a lot. He'd been learning to write when I was born. When I'd been learning to write and throw books at my teachers, he'd probably been kissing girls. Probably lots of girls, considering how he looked.

I *so* did not need this complication in my life right now.

I found a passable sweater back in my room and after a quick shower, I headed off across campus to the reception.

Despite the looming stone walls, fancy statues, and turrets on the outsides of the buildings, the Academy's insides were quite modern. We had Wi-Fi, fluorescent lights, and just about anything else technological you could imagine. The commons in particular looked pretty much like the cafeterias I'd eaten in while in Portland and Chicago, with simple rectangular tables, soothing taupe walls, and a little room off to the side where our dubiously prepared meals were served. Someone had at least hung framed black-and-white photos along the walls in an effort to decorate it, but I didn't really consider pictures of vases and leafless trees "art."

Tonight, however, someone had managed to transform the normally boring commons into a bona fide dining room. Vases spilling over with crimson roses and delicate white lilies. Glowing candles. Tablecloths made of—wait for it—bloodred linen. The effect was gorgeous. It was hard to believe this was the same place I usually ate chicken patty sandwiches in. It looked fit for, well, a queen.

The tables had been arranged in straight lines, creating an aisle down the middle of the room. We had assigned seating, and naturally, I couldn't sit anywhere near Lissa. She sat in the front with the other Moroi; I was in the back with the novices. But she did catch my eye when I entered and flashed me a smile. She'd borrowed a dress from Natalie—blue, silky, and strapless—that looked amazing with her pale features. Who'd known Natalie owned anything so good? It made my sweater lose a few cool points.

They always conducted these formal banquets in the same way. A head table sat on a dais at the front of the room, where we could all ooh and ahh and watch Queen Tatiana and other royals eat dinner. Guardians lined the walls, as stiff and formal as statues. Dimitri stood among them, and a weird feeling twisted my stomach as I recalled what had happened in the gym. His eyes stared straight ahead, as if focusing on nothing and everything in the room at once.

When the time came for the royals' entrance, we all stood up respectfully and watched as they walked down the aisle. I recognized a few, mostly those who had children attending the Academy. Victor Dashkov was among them, walking slowly and with a cane. While I was happy to see him, I cringed to watch each agonizing step he took toward the front of the room.

Once that group had passed, four solemn guardians with red-and-black-pin-striped jackets entered the commons. Everyone but the guardians along the walls sank to our knees in a silly show of loyalty.

What a lot of ceremony and posturing, I thought wearily. Moroi monarchs were chosen by the previous monarch from within the royal families. The king or queen couldn't choose one of his or her own direct descendents, and a council from the noble and royal families could dispute the choice with enough cause. That almost never happened, though.

Queen Tatiana followed her guards, wearing a red silk dress and matching jacket. She was in her early sixties and had dark gray hair bobbed to her chin and crowned with a Miss America–type tiara. She moved into the room slowly, like she was taking a stroll, four more guardians at her back.

She moved through the novices' section fairly quickly, though she did nod and smile here and there. Dhampirs might just be the half-human, illegitimate children of the Moroi, but we trained and dedicated our lives to serving and protecting them. The likelihood was strong that many of us gathered here would die young, and the queen had to show her respect for that.

When she got to the Moroi section, she paused longer and actually spoke to a few students. It was a big deal to be acknowledged, mostly a sign that someone's parents had gotten in good with her. Naturally, the royals got the most attention. She didn't really say much to them that was all that interesting, mostly just a lot of fancy words.

"Vasilisa Dragomir."

My head shot up. Alarm coursed through the bond at the sound of her name. Breaking protocol, I pushed out of my position and wiggled over to get a better view, knowing no one would notice me when the queen herself had personally singled out the last of the Dragomirs. Everyone was eager to see what the monarch had to say to Lissa the runaway princess.

"We heard you had returned. We are glad to have the Dragomirs back, even though only one remains. We deeply regret the loss of your parents and your brother; they were among the finest of the Moroi, their deaths a true tragedy."

I'd never really understood the royal "we" thing, but otherwise, everything sounded okay.

"You have an interesting name," she continued. "Many heroines in Russian fairy tales are named Vasilisa. Vasilisa the Brave, Vasilisa the Beautiful. They are different young women, all having the same name and the same excellent qualities: strength, intelligence, discipline, and virtue. All accomplish great things, triumphing over their adversaries.

"Likewise, the Dragomir name commands its own respect. Dragomir kings and queens have ruled wisely and justly in our history. They have used their powers for miraculous ends. They have slain Strigoi, fighting right alongside their guardians. They are *royal* for a reason."

She waited a moment, letting the weight of her words sink in. I could feel the mood changing in the room, as well as the surprise and shy pleasure creeping out from Lissa. This would shake the social balance. We could probably expect a few wannabes trying to get in good with Lissa tomorrow.

"Yes," Tatiana continued, "you are doubly named with power. Your names represent the finest qualities people have to offer and hearken back in time to deeds of greatness and valor." She paused a moment. "But, as you have demonstrated, names do *not* make a person. Nor do they have any bearing on how that person turns out."

And with that verbal slap in the face, she turned away and continued her procession.

A collective shock filled the room. I briefly contemplated and then dismissed any attempts at jumping into the aisle and tackling the queen. Half a dozen guardians would have me down on the floor before I'd even taken five steps. So I sat impatiently through dinner, all the while feeling Lissa's absolute mortification.

When the post-dinner reception followed, Lissa made a beeline for the doors leading out to the courtyard. I followed, but got delayed having to weave around and avoid the mingling, socializing people.

She'd wandered outside to an adjacent courtyard, one that matched the Academy's grand external style. A roof of carved, twisting wood covered the garden, with little holes here and there to let in some light, but not enough to cause damage to Moroi. Trees, leaves now gone for the winter, lined the area and guarded paths leading out to other gardens, courtyards, and the main quadrangle. A pond, also emptied for the winter, lay in a corner, and standing over it was an imposing statue of St. Vladimir himself. Carved of gray rock, he wore long robes and had a beard and mustache.

Rounding a corner, I stopped when I saw Natalie had beaten me to Lissa. I considered interrupting but stepped back before they could see me. Spying might be bad, but I was suddenly very curious to hear what Natalie had to say to Lissa.

"She shouldn't have said that," Natalie said. She wore a yellow dress similar in cut to Lissa's, but somehow lacked the grace and poise to make it look as good. Yellow was also a terrible color on her. It clashed with her black hair, which she'd put up into an off-center bun. "It wasn't right," she went on. "Don't let it bother you."

"Kind of late for that." Lissa's eyes were locked firmly on the stone walkway below.

"She was wrong."

"She's *right*," Lissa exclaimed. "My parents . . . and Andre . . . they would have hated me for what I did."

"No, they wouldn't have." Natalie spoke in a gentle voice.

"It was stupid to run away. Irresponsible."

"So what? You made a mistake. I make mistakes all the time. The other day, I was doing this assignment in science, and it was for chapter ten, and I'd actually read chapter elev—" Natalie stopped herself and, in a remarkable show of restraint, got herself back on track. "People change. We're always changing, right? You aren't the same as you were then. I'm not the same as I was then."

Actually, Natalie seemed *exactly* the same to me, but that didn't bother me so much anymore. She'd grown on me.

"Besides," she added, "was running away really a mistake? You must have done it for a reason. You must have gotten something out of it, right? There was a lot of bad stuff going on with you, wasn't there? With your parents and your brother. I mean, maybe it was the right thing to do."

Lissa hid a smile. Both of us were pretty sure Natalie was trying to find out why we had left—just like everyone else in the school. She sort of sucked at being sneaky.

"I don't know if it was, no," Lissa answered. "I was weak.

Andre wouldn't have run away. He was so good. Good at everything. Good at getting along with people and all that royal crap."

"You're good at that too."

"I guess. But I don't like it. I mean, I like people . . . but most of what they do is so fake. That's what I don't like."

"Then don't feel bad about not getting involved," Natalie said. "I don't hang out with all those people either, and look at *me*. I'm just fine. Daddy says he doesn't care if I hang out with the royals or not. He just wants me to be happy."

"And that," I said, finally making my appearance, "is why *he* should be ruling instead of that bitch of a queen. He got robbed."

Natalie nearly jumped ten feet. I felt pretty confident her vocabulary of swear words mostly consisted of "golly" and "darn."

"I wondered where you were," said Lissa.

Natalie looked back and forth between us, suddenly seeming a little embarrassed to be right between the best-friends dream team. She shifted uncomfortably and tucked some messy hair behind her ear. "Well . . . I should go find Daddy. I'll see you back in the room."

"See you," said Lissa. "And thanks."

Natalie hurried off.

"Does she really call him '*Daddy*'?"

Lissa cut me a look. "Leave her alone. She's nice."

"She is, actually. I heard what she said, and as much as I

hate to admit it, there was nothing there I could really make fun of. It was all true." I paused. "I'll kill her, you know. The queen, not Natalie. Screw the guardians. I'll do it. She can't get away with that."

"God, Rose! Don't say that. They'll arrest you for treason. Just let it go."

"Let it go? After what she said to you? In front of everyone?"

She didn't answer or even look at me. Instead, she toyed absentmindedly with the branches of a scraggly bush that had gone dormant for the winter. There was a vulnerable look about her that I recognized—and feared.

"Hey." I lowered my voice. "Don't look like that. She doesn't know what she's talking about, okay? Don't let this get you down. Don't do anything you shouldn't."

She glanced back up at me. "It's going to happen again, isn't it?" she whispered. Her hand, still clutching the tree, began to tremble.

"Not if you don't let it." I tried to look at her wrists without being too obvious. "You haven't? . . ."

"No." She shook her head and blinked back tears. "I haven't wanted to. I was upset after the fox, but it's been okay. I like the coasting thing. I miss seeing you, but everything's been all right. I like . . ." She paused.

I could hear the word forming in her mind.

"Christian."

"I wish you couldn't do that. Or wouldn't."

"Sorry. Do I need to give you the Christian's-a-psycho-pathic-loser talk again?"

"I think I've got it memorized after the last ten times," she muttered.

I started to launch into number eleven when I heard the sound of laughter and the clatter of high heels on stone. Mia walked toward us with a few friends in tow but no Aaron. Immediately, my defenses snapped on.

Internally, Lissa was still shaken over the queen's comments. Sorrow and humiliation were swirling inside of her. She felt embarrassed over what others must think of her now and kept thinking about how her family would have hated her for running away. I didn't believe that, but it felt real to her, and her dark emotions churned and churned. She was *not* okay, no matter how casual she'd just tried to act, and I was worried she might do something reckless. Mia was the last person she needed to see right now.

"What do you want?" I demanded.

Mia smiled haughtily at Lissa and ignored me, taking a few steps forward. "Just wanted to know what it's like to be *so* important and *so* royal. You must be so excited that the queen talked to you." Giggles surfaced from the gathering group.

"You're standing too close." I stepped between them, and Mia flinched a little, possibly still worried I might break her arm. "And hey, at least the queen knew her name, which is more than I can say for you and your wannabe-royal act. *Or* your parents."

I could see the pain that caused her. Man, she wanted to be royal so badly. "At least I *see* my parents," she retorted. "At least I know who they both are. God only knows who your father is. And your mom's one of the most famous guardians around, but she couldn't care less about you either. Everyone knows she never visits. Probably was glad when you were gone. If she even *noticed*."

That hurt. I clenched my teeth. "Yeah, well, at least she's famous. She really does advise royals and nobles. She doesn't clean up after them."

I heard one of her friends snicker behind her. Mia opened her mouth, no doubt to unleash one of the many retorts she'd had to accumulate since the story started going around, when the lightbulb suddenly went off in her head.

"It was *you*," she said, eyes wide. "Someone told me Jesse'd started it, but he couldn't have known anything about me. He got it from you. When you *slept* with him."

Now she was really starting to piss me off. "I didn't sleep with him."

Mia pointed at Lissa and glared back at me. "So that's it, huh? You do her dirty work because she's too pathetic to do it herself. You aren't always going to be able to protect her," she warned. "*You* aren't safe either."

Empty threats. I leaned forward, making my voice as menacing as possible. In my current mood, it wasn't difficult. "Yeah? Try and touch me now and find out."

I hoped she would. I wanted her to. We didn't need her

messed-up vendetta in our lives just now. She was a distraction—one I very much wanted to punch right now.

Looking past her, I saw Dimitri move out into the garden, eyes searching for something—or someone. I had a pretty good idea who it was. When he saw me, he strode forward, shifting his attention when he noticed the crowd gathered around us. Guardians can smell a fight a mile away. Of course, a six-year-old could have smelled this fight.

Dimitri stood beside me and crossed his arms. "Everything all right?"

"Sure thing, Guardian Belikov." I smiled as I said it, but I was furious. Raging, even. This whole Mia confrontation had only made Lissa feel worse. "We were just swapping family stories. Ever heard Mia's? It's *fascinating*."

"Come on," said Mia to her followers. She led them off, but not before she'd given me one last, chilling look. I didn't need to read her mind to know what it said. This wasn't over. She was going to try to get one or both of us back. Fine. Bring it on, Mia.

"I'm supposed to take you back to your dorm," Dimitri told me drily. "You weren't about to just start a fight, were you?"

"Of course not," I said, my eyes still staring at the empty doorway Mia had disappeared through. "I don't start fights where people can see them."

"Rose," groaned Lissa.

"Let's go. Good night, Princess."

He turned, but I didn't move. "You going to be okay, Liss?"

She nodded. "I'm fine."

It was such a lie, I couldn't believe she had the nerve to try to put it past me. I didn't need the bond to see tears shining in her eyes. We should never have come back to this place, I realized bleakly.

"Liss . . ."

She gave me a small, sad smile and nodded in Dimitri's direction. "I told you, I'm fine. You've got to go."

Reluctantly, I followed him. He led me out toward the other side of the garden. "We may need to add an extra training on self-control," he noted.

"I have plenty of self contr—hey!"

I stopped talking as I saw Christian slip past us, moving down the path we'd just come from. I hadn't seen him at the reception, but if Kirova had released me to come tonight, I suppose she would have done the same for him.

"You going to see Lissa?" I demanded, shifting my Mia rage to him.

He stuffed his hands into his pockets and gave me that look of bad-boy indifference. "What if I am?"

"Rose, this isn't the time," said Dimitri.

But it was *so* the time. Lissa had ignored my warnings about Christian for weeks. It was time to go to the source and stop their ridiculous flirtation once and for all.

"Why don't you just leave her alone? Are you so messed

up and desperate for attention that you can't tell when someone doesn't like you?" He scowled. "You're some crazy stalker, and she knows it. She's told me all about your weird obsession—how you're always hanging out in the attic together, how you set Ralf on fire to impress her. She thinks you're a freak, but she's too nice to say anything."

His face had paled, and something dark churned in his eyes. "But *you* aren't too nice?"

"No. Not when I feel sorry for someone."

"Enough," said Dimitri, steering me away.

"Thanks for 'helping,' then," snapped Christian, his voice dripping with animosity.

"No problem," I called back over my shoulder.

When we'd gone a little ways, I stole a glance behind me and saw Christian standing just outside the garden. He'd stopped walking and now stood staring down the path that led to Lissa in the courtyard. Shadows covered his face as he thought, and then, after a few moments, he turned around and headed back toward the Moroi dorms.

TWELVE

SLEEP CAME RELUCTANTLY THAT NIGHT, and I tossed and turned for a long time before finally going under.

An hour or so later, I sat up in bed, trying to relax and sort out the emotions coming to me. Lissa. Scared and upset. Unstable. The night's events suddenly came rushing back to me as I went through what could be bothering her. The queen humiliating her. Mia. Maybe even Christian—he could have found her for all I knew.

Yet . . . none of those was the problem right now. Buried within her, there was something else. Something terribly wrong.

I climbed out of bed, dressed hastily, and considered my options. I had a third-floor room now—way too high to climb down from, particularly since I had no Ms. Karp to patch me up this time. I would never be able to sneak out of the main hall. That only left going through the "appropriate" channels.

"Where do you think you're going?"

One of the matrons who supervised my hall looked up from her chair. She sat stationed at the end of the hall, near the stairs going down. During the day, that stairwell had loose supervision. At night, we might as well have been in jail.

I crossed my arms. "I need to see Dim—Guardian Belikov."

"It's late."

"It's an emergency."

She looked me up and down. "You seem okay to me."

"You're going to be in so much trouble tomorrow when everyone finds out you stopped me from reporting what I know."

"Tell me."

"It's private guardian stuff."

I gave her as hard a stare as I could manage. It must have worked, because she finally stood up and pulled out a cell phone. She called someone—Dimitri, I hoped—but murmured too low for me to hear. We waited several minutes, and then the door leading to the stairs opened. Dimitri appeared, fully dressed and alert, though I felt pretty sure we'd pulled him out of bed.

He took one look at me. "Lissa."

I nodded.

Without another word, he turned around and started back down the stairs. I followed. We walked across the quad in silence, toward the imposing Moroi dorm. It was "night" for the vampires, which meant it was daytime for the rest of the world. Mid-afternoon sun shone with a cold, golden light on us. The human genes in me welcomed it and always sort of regretted how Moroi light sensitivity forced us to live in darkness most of the time.

Lissa's hall matron gaped when we appeared, but Dimitri was too intimidating to oppose. "She's in the bathroom,"

I told them. When the matron started to follow me inside, I wouldn't let her. "She's too upset. Let me talk to her alone first."

Dimitri considered. "Yes. Give them a minute."

I pushed the door open.

"Liss?"

A soft sound, like a sob, came from within. I walked down five stalls and found the only one closed. I knocked softly.

"Let me in," I said, hoping I sounded calm and strong.

I heard a sniffle, and a few moments later, the door unlatched. I wasn't prepared for what I saw. Lissa stood before me . . .

. . . covered in blood.

Horrified, I squelched a scream and almost called for help. Looking more closely, I saw that a lot of the blood wasn't actually coming from her. It was smeared on her, like it had been on her hands and she'd rubbed her face. She sank to the floor, and I followed, kneeling before her.

"Are you okay?" I whispered. "What happened?"

She only shook her head, but I saw her face crumple as more tears spilled from her eyes. I took her hands.

"Come on. Let's get you cleaned—"

I stopped. She *was* bleeding after all. Perfect lines crossed her wrists, not near any crucial veins, but enough to leave wet, red tracks across her skin. She hadn't hit her veins when she did this; death hadn't been her goal. She met my eyes.

"I'm sorry. . . . I didn't mean . . . Please don't let them

know . . ." she sobbed. "When I saw *it*, I freaked out." She nodded toward her wrists. "This just happened before I could stop. I was upset. . . ."

"It's okay," I said automatically, wondering what "it" was. "Come on."

I heard a knock on the door. "Rose?"

"Just a sec," I called back.

I took her to the sink and rinsed the blood off her wrists. Grabbing the first-aid kit, I hastily put some Band-Aids on the cuts. The bleeding had already slowed.

"We're coming in," the matron called.

I jerked off my hoodie sweatshirt and quickly handed it to Lissa. She had just pulled it on when Dimitri and the matron entered. He raced to our sides in an instant, and I realized that in hiding Lissa's wrists, I'd forgotten the blood on her face.

"It's not mine," she said quickly, seeing his expression. "It . . . it's the rabbit. . . ."

Dimitri assessed her, and I hoped he wouldn't look at her wrists. When he seemed satisfied she had no gaping wounds, he asked, "What rabbit?" I was wondering the same thing.

With shaking hands, she pointed at the trash can. "I cleaned it up. So Natalie wouldn't see."

Dimitri and I both walked over and peered into the can. I pulled myself away immediately, swallowing back my stomach's need to throw up. I don't know how Lissa knew it was a rabbit. All I could see was blood. Blood and blood-soaked paper towels. Globs of gore I couldn't identify. The smell was horrible.

Dimitri shifted closer to Lissa, bending down until they were at eye level. "Tell me what happened." He handed her several tissues.

"I came back about an hour ago. And it was there. Right there in the middle of the floor. Torn apart. It was like it had . . . exploded." She sniffed. "I didn't want Natalie to find it, didn't want to scare her . . . so I—I cleaned it up. Then I just couldn't . . . I couldn't go back. . . ." She began to cry, and her shoulders shook.

I could figure out the rest, the part she didn't tell Dimitri. She'd found the rabbit, cleaned up, and freaked out. Then she'd cut herself, but it was the weird way she coped with things that upset her.

"No one should be able to get into those rooms!" exclaimed the matron. "How is this happening?"

"Do you know who did it?" Dimitri's voice was gentle.

Lissa reached into her pajama pocket and pulled out a crumpled piece of paper. It had so much blood soaked into it, I could barely read it as he held it and smoothed it out.

I know what you are. You won't survive being here. I'll make sure of it. Leave now. It's the only way you might live through this.

The matron's shock transformed into something more determined, and she headed for the door. "I'm getting Ellen." It took me a second to remember that was Kirova's first name.

"Tell her we'll be at the clinic," said Dimitri. When she left, he turned to Lissa. "You should lie down."

When she didn't move, I linked my arm through hers. "Come on, Liss. Let's get you out of here."

Slowly, she put one foot in front of the other and let us lead her to the Academy's medical clinic. It was normally staffed by a couple of doctors, but at this time of night, only a nurse stayed on duty. She offered to wake one of the doctors, but Dimitri declined. "She just needs to rest."

Lissa had no sooner stretched out on a narrow bed than Kirova and a few others showed up and started questioning her.

I thrust myself in front of them, blocking her. "Leave her alone! Can't you see she doesn't want to talk about it? Let her get some sleep first!"

"Miss Hathaway," declared Kirova, "you're out of line as usual. I don't even know what you're doing here."

Dimitri asked if he could speak with her privately and led her into the hall. I heard angry whispers from her, calm and firm ones from him. When they returned, she said stiffly, "You may stay with her for a little while. We'll have janitors do further cleaning and investigation in the bathroom and your room, Miss Dragomir, and then discuss the situation in detail in the morning."

"Don't wake Natalie," whispered Lissa. "I don't want to scare her. I cleaned up everything in the room anyway."

Kirova looked doubtful. The group retreated but not before the nurse asked if Lissa wanted anything to eat or drink. She declined. Once we were alone, I lay down beside her and put my arm around her.

"I won't let them find out," I told her, sensing her worry about her wrists. "But I wish you'd told me before I left the reception. You'd said you'd always come to me first."

"I wasn't going to do it then," she said, her eyes staring blankly off. "I swear, I wasn't going to. I mean, I was upset . . . but I thought . . . I thought I could handle it. I was trying so hard . . . really, Rose. I was. But then I got back to my room, and I saw *it*, and I . . . just lost it. It was like the last straw, you know? And I knew I had to clean it up. Had to clean it up before they saw, before they found out, but there was so much blood . . . and afterward, after it was done, it was too much, and I felt like I was going to . . . I don't know . . . explode, and it was just too much, I had to let it out, you know? I had to—"

I interrupted her hysteria. "It's okay, I understand."

That was a lie. I didn't get her cutting at all. She'd done it sporadically, ever since the accident, and it scared me each time. She'd try to explain it to me, how she didn't want to die—she just needed to get *it* out somehow. She felt so much emotionally, she would say, that a physical outlet—physical pain—was the only way to make the internal pain go away. It was the only way she could control it.

"Why is this happening?" she cried into her pillow. "Why am I a freak?"

"You aren't a freak."

"No one else has this happen to them. No one else does magic like I can."

"Did you try to do magic?" No answer. "Liss? Did you try to heal the rabbit?"

"I reached out, just to see if I could maybe fix it, but there was just too much blood. . . . I couldn't."

The more she uses it, the worse it'll get. Stop her, Rose.

Lissa was right. Moroi magic could conjure fire and water, move rocks and other pieces of earth. But no one could heal or bring animals back from the dead. No one except Ms. Karp.

Stop her before they notice, before they notice and take her away too. Get her out of here.

I hated carrying this secret, mostly because I didn't know what to do about it. I didn't like feeling powerless. I needed to protect her from this—and from herself. And yet, at the same time, I needed to protect her from *them*, too.

"We should go," I said abruptly. "We're going to leave."

"Rose—"

"It's happening again. And it's worse. Worse than last time."

"You're afraid of the note."

"I'm not afraid of any note. But this place isn't safe."

I suddenly longed for Portland again. It might be dirtier and more crowded than the rugged Montana landscape, but at least you knew what to expect—not like here. Here at the Academy, past and present warred with each other. It might have its beautiful old walls and gardens, but inside, modern things were creeping in. People didn't know how to handle that. It was just like the Moroi themselves. Their archaic royal families still held the power on the surface, but people were growing discontent. Dhampirs who wanted more to their lives. Moroi like Christian who wanted to fight the Strigoi. The royals still clung to their traditions, still touted their power over everyone else, just as the Academy's elaborate iron gates put on a show of tradition and invincibility.

And, oh, the lies and secrets. They ran through the halls and hid in the corners. Someone here hated Lissa, someone who was probably smiling right to her face and pretending to be her friend. I couldn't let them destroy her.

"You need to get some sleep," I told her.

"I can't sleep."

"Yes, you can. I'm right here. You won't be alone."

Anxiety and fear and other troubled emotions coursed through her. But in the end, her body's needs won out. After a while, I saw her eyes close. Her breathing became even, and the bond grew quiet.

I watched her sleep, too keyed up with adrenaline to allow myself any rest. I think maybe an hour had passed when the nurse returned and told me I had to leave.

"I can't go," I said. "I promised her she wouldn't be alone."

The nurse was tall, even for a Moroi, with kind brown eyes. "She won't be. I'll stay with her."

I regarded her skeptically.

"I promise."

Back in my room, I had my own crash. The fear and excitement had worn me out too, and for an instant, I wished I could have a normal life and a normal best friend. Immediately, I cast that thought out. No one was normal, not really. And I'd never have a better friend than Lissa . . . but man, it was so hard sometimes.

I slept heavily until morning. I went to my first class tentatively, nervous that word about last night had gotten around. As it turned out, people *were* talking about last night, but their attention was still focused on the queen and the reception. They knew nothing about the rabbit. As hard as it was to believe, I'd nearly forgotten about that other stuff. Still, it suddenly seemed like a small thing compared to someone causing a bloody explosion in Lissa's room.

Yet, as the day went on, I noticed something weird. People stopped looking at Lissa so much. The started looking at *me*. Whatever. Ignoring them, I hunted around and found Lissa finishing up with a feeder. That funny feeling I always got came over me as I watched her mouth work against the feeder's neck, drinking his blood. A trickle of it ran down his throat, standing out against his pale skin. Feeders, though human, were nearly as pale as Moroi from all the blood loss. He didn't seem to notice; he was long gone on the high of the bite. Drowning in jealousy, I decided I needed therapy.

"You okay?" I asked her later, on our way to class. She wore long sleeves, purposefully obscuring her wrists.

"Yeah . . . I still can't stop thinking about that rabbit. . . . It was so horrible. I keep seeing it in my head. And then what I did." She squeezed her eyes shut, just for a moment, and then opened them again. "People are talking about us."

"I know. Ignore them."

"I *hate* it," she said angrily. A surge of darkness shot up into her and through the bond. It made me cringe. My best friend was lighthearted and kind. She didn't have feelings like that. "I hate all the gossip. It's so stupid. How can they all be so shallow?"

"Ignore them," I repeated soothingly. "You were smart not to hang out with them anymore."

Ignoring them grew harder and harder, though. The whispers and looks increased. In animal behavior, it became so bad, I couldn't even concentrate on my now-favorite subject. Ms. Meissner had started talking about evolution and survival of the fittest and how animals sought mates with good genes. It fascinated me, but even she had a hard time staying on task, since she had to keep yelling at people to quiet down and pay attention.

"Something's going on," I told Lissa between classes. "I don't know what, but they're all over something new."

"Something else? Other than the queen hating me? What more could there be?"

"Wish I knew."

Things finally came to a head in our last class of the day, Slavic art. It started when a guy I barely knew made a very explicit and nearly obscene suggestion to me while we all worked on individual projects. I replied in kind, letting him know exactly what he could do with his request.

He only laughed. "Come on, Rose. I *bleed* for you."

Loud giggles ensued, and Mia cut us a taunting look. "Wait, it's Rose who does the bleeding, right?"

More laughter. Understanding slapped me in the face. I jerked Lissa away. "They know."

"Know what?"

"About us. About how you . . . you know, how I fed you while we were gone."

She gaped. "How?"

"How do you think? Your 'friend' Christian."

"No," she said adamantly. "He wouldn't have."

"Who else knew?"

Faith in Christian flashed in her eyes and in our bond. But she didn't know what I knew. She didn't know how I'd bitched him out last night, how I'd made him think she hated him. The guy was unstable. Spreading our biggest secret—well, one of them—would be an adequate revenge. Maybe he'd killed the rabbit, too. After all, it had died only a couple hours after I'd told him off.

Not waiting around to hear her protests, I stalked off to the other side of the room where Christian was working by himself, as usual. Lissa followed in my wake. Not caring if people saw us, I leaned across the table toward him, putting my face inches from his.

"I'm going to kill you."

His eyes darted to Lissa, the faintest glimmer of longing in them, and then a scowl spread over his face. "Why? Is it like guardian extra credit?"

"Stop with the attitude," I warned, pitching my voice low. "You told. You told how Lissa had to feed off me."

"Tell her," said Lissa desperately. "Tell her she's wrong."

Christian dragged his eyes from me to her, and as they regarded each other, I felt such a powerful wave of attraction, it was a wonder it didn't knock me over. Her heart was in her eyes. It was obvious to me he felt the same way about her, but she couldn't see it, particularly since he was still glaring at her.

"You can stop it, you know," he said. "You don't have to pretend anymore."

Lissa's giddy attraction vanished, replaced by hurt and shock over his tone. "I . . . what? Pretend what? . . ."

"You *know* what. Just stop. Stop with the act."

Lissa stared at him, her eyes wide and wounded. She had no clue I'd gone off on him last night. She had no clue that he believed she hated him.

"Get over feeling sorry for yourself, and tell us what's going on," I snapped at him. "Did you or didn't you tell them?"

He fixed me with a defiant look. "No. I didn't."

"I don't believe you."

"I do," said Lissa.

"I know it's impossible to believe a *freak* like me could keep his mouth shut—especially since neither of you can—but I have better things to do than spread stupid rumors. You want someone to blame? Blame your golden boy over there."

I followed his gaze to where Jesse was laughing about something with that idiot Ralf.

"Jesse doesn't know," said Lissa defiantly.

Christian's eyes were glued to me. "He *does*, though. Doesn't he, Rose? He knows."

My stomach sank out of me. Yes. Jesse did know. He'd figured it out that night in the lounge. "I didn't think . . . I didn't think he'd tell. He was too afraid of Dimitri."

"You *told* him?" exclaimed Lissa.

"No, he guessed." I was starting to feel sick.

"He apparently did more than guess," muttered Christian.

I turned on him. "What's that supposed to mean?"

"Oh. You don't know."

"I swear to God, Christian, I'm going to break your neck after class."

"Man, you really are unstable." He said it almost happily, but his next words were more serious. He still wore that sneer, still glowed with anger, but when he spoke, I could hear the faintest uneasiness in his voice. "He sort of elaborated on what was in your note. Got into a little more detail."

"Oh, I get it. He said we had sex." I didn't need to mince words. Christian nodded. So. Jesse was trying to boost his own reputation. Okay. That I could deal with. Not like my reputation was that stellar to begin with. Everyone already believed I had sex all the time.

"And uh, Ralf too. That you and he—"

Ralf? No amount of alcohol or any illegal substance would

make me touch him. "I—what? That I had sex with Ralf too?"

Christian nodded.

"That asshole! I'm going to—"

"There's more."

"How? Did I sleep with the basketball team?"

"He said—they both said—you let them . . . well, you let them drink your blood."

That stopped even me. Drinking blood during sex. The dirtiest of the dirty. Sleazy. Beyond being easy or a slut. A gazillion times worse than Lissa drinking from me for survival. Blood-whore territory.

"That's crazy!" Lissa cried. "Rose would never—Rose?"

But I wasn't listening anymore. I was in my own world, a world that took me across the classroom to where Jesse and Ralf sat. They both looked up, faces half smug and half . . . nervous, if I had to guess. Not unexpected, since they were both lying through their teeth.

The entire class came to a standstill. Apparently they'd been expecting some type of showdown. My unstable reputation in action.

"What the hell do you think you're doing?" I asked in a low, dangerous voice.

Jesse's nervous look turned to one of terror. He might have been taller than me, but we both knew who would win if I turned violent. Ralf, however, gave me a cocky smile.

"We didn't do anything you didn't want us to do." His smiled turned cruel. "And don't even think about laying a hand on us. You start a fight, and Kirova'll kick you out to go live with the other blood whores."

The rest of the students were holding their breaths, waiting to see what we'd do. I don't know how Mr. Nagy could have been oblivious to the drama occurring in his class.

I wanted to punch both of them, hit them so hard that it'd make Dimitri's brawl with Jesse look like a pat on the back. I wanted to wipe that smirk off Ralf's face.

But asshole or not, he was right. If I touched them, Kirova would expel me in the blink of an eye. And if I got kicked out, Lissa would be alone. Taking a deep breath, I made one of the hardest decisions of my life.

I walked away.

The rest of the day was miserable. In backing down from the fight, I opened myself up to mockery from everyone else. The rumors and whispers grew louder. People stared at me openly. People laughed. Lissa kept trying to talk to me, to console me, but I ignored even her. I went through the rest of my classes like a zombie, and then I headed off to practice with Dimitri as fast I could. He gave me a puzzled look but didn't ask any questions.

Alone in my room later on, I cried for the first time in years.

Once I got that out of my system, I was about to put on my pajamas when I heard a knock at my door. Dimitri. He studied my face and then glanced away, obviously aware I'd been crying. I could tell, too, that the rumors had finally reached him. He knew.

"Are you okay?"

"It doesn't matter if I am, remember?" I looked up at him. "Is Lissa okay? This'll be hard on her."

A funny look crossed his face. I think it astonished him that I'd still be worried about her at a time like this. He beckoned me to follow and led me out to a back stairwell, one that usually stayed locked to students. But it was open tonight, and he gestured me outside. "Five minutes," he warned.

More curious than ever, I stepped outside. Lissa stood there. I should have sensed she was close, but my own out-of-control feelings had obscured hers. Without a word, she put her arms around me and held me for several moments. I had to hold back more tears. When we broke apart, she looked at me with calm, level eyes.

"I'm sorry," she said.

"Not your fault. It'll pass."

She clearly doubted that. So did I.

"It *is* my fault," she said. "She did it to get back at me."

"She?"

"Mia. Jesse and Ralf aren't smart enough to think of something like that on their own. You said it yourself: Jesse was too scared of Dimitri to talk much about what happened. And why wait until now? It happened a while ago. If he'd wanted to spread stuff around, he would have done it back then. Mia's doing this as retaliation for you talking about her parents. I don't know how she managed it, but she's the one who got them to say those things."

In my gut, I realized Lissa was right. Jesse and Ralf were the tools; Mia had been the mastermind.

"Nothing to be done now," I sighed.

"Rose—"

"Forget it, Liss. It's done, okay?"

She studied me quietly for a few seconds. "I haven't seen you cry in a long time."

"I wasn't crying."

A feeling of heartache and sympathy beat through to me from the bond.

"She can't do this to you," she argued.

I laughed bitterly, half surprised at my own hopelessness. "She already did. She said she'd get back at me, that I wouldn't be able to protect you. She did it. When I go back to classes . . ." A sickening feeling settled in my stomach. I thought about the friends and respect I'd managed to eke out, despite our low profile. That would be gone. You couldn't come back from something like this. Not among the Moroi. Once a blood whore, always a blood whore. What made it worse was that some dark, secret part of me did like being bitten.

"You shouldn't have to keep protecting me," she said.

I laughed. "That's my job. I'm going to be your guardian."

"I know, but I meant like this. You shouldn't suffer because of me. You shouldn't always have to look after me. And yet you always do. You got me out of here. You took care of everything when we were on our own. Even since coming back . . . you've always been the one who does all the work. Every time I break down—like last night—you're always there. Me, I'm *weak*. I'm not like you."

I shook my head. "That doesn't matter. It's what I do. I don't mind."

"Yeah, but look what happened. I'm the one she really has a grudge against—even though I still don't know why. Whatever. It's going to stop. I'm going to protect *you* from now on."

There was a determination in her expression, a wonderful confidence radiating off of her that reminded me of the Lissa I'd known before the accident. At the same time, I could feel something else in her—something darker, a sense of deeply buried anger. I'd seen this side of her before too, and I didn't like it. I didn't want her tapping into it. I just wanted her to be safe.

"Lissa, you can't protect me."

"I can," she said fiercely. "There's one thing Mia wants more than to destroy you and me. She wants to be accepted. She wants to hang out with the royals and feel like she's one of them. I can take that away from her." She smiled. "I can turn them against her."

"How?"

"By *telling* them." Her eyes flashed.

My mind was moving too slowly tonight. It took me a while to catch on. "Liss—no. You can't use compulsion. Not around here."

"I might as well get some use out of these stupid powers."

The more she uses it, the worse it'll get. Stop her, Rose. Stop her before they notice, before they notice and take her away too. Get her out of here.

"Liss, if you get caught—"

Dimitri stuck his head out. "You've got to get back inside, Rose, before someone finds you."

I shot a panicked look at Lissa, but she was already retreating. "I'll take care of everything this time, Rose. *Everything.*"

THIRTEEN

THE AFTERMATH OF JESSE AND Ralf's lies was about as horrible as I'd expected. The only way I survived was by putting blinders on, by ignoring everyone and everything. It kept me sane—barely—but I hated it. I felt like crying all the time. I lost my appetite and didn't sleep well.

Yet, no matter how bad it got for me, I didn't worry about myself as much as I did Lissa. She stood by her promise to change things. It was slow at first, but gradually, I would see a royal or two come up to her at lunch or in class and say hello. She'd turn on a brilliant smile, laughing and talking to them like they were all best friends.

At first, I didn't understand how she was pulling it off. She'd told me she would use compulsion to win the other royals over and turn them against Mia. But I didn't *see* it happening. It was possible, of course, that she was winning people over without compulsion. After all, she was funny, smart, and nice. Anyone would like her. Something told me she wasn't winning friends the old-fashioned way, and I finally figured it out.

She was using compulsion when I wasn't around. I only saw her for a small part of the day, and since she knew I didn't approve, she only worked her power when I was away.

After a few days of this secret compulsion, I knew what I needed to do: I had to get back in her head again. By choice. I'd done it before; I could do it again.

At least, that's what I told myself, sitting and spacing out in Stan's class one day. But it wasn't as easy as I'd thought it would be, partly because I felt too keyed up to relax and open myself to her thoughts. I also had trouble because I picked a time when she felt relatively calm. She came through the "loudest" when her emotions were running strong.

Still, I tried to do what I'd done before, back when I'd spied on her and Christian. The meditation thing. Slow breathing. Eyes closed. Mental focus like that still wasn't easy for me, but at long last I managed the transition, slipping into her head and experiencing the world as hers. She stood in her American lit class, during project-work time, but, like most of the students, she wasn't working. She and Camille Conta leaned against a wall on the far side of the room, talking in hushed voices.

"It's gross," said Camille firmly, a frown crossing her pretty face. She had on a blue skirt made of velvetlike fabric, short enough to show off her long legs and possibly raise eyes about the dress code. "If you guys were doing it, I'm not surprised she got addicted and did it with Jesse."

"She *didn't* do it with Jesse," insisted Lissa. "And it's not like we had *sex*. We just didn't have any feeders, that's all." Lissa focused her full attention on Camille and smiled. "It's no big deal. Everyone's overreacting."

Camille looked like she seriously doubted this, and then,

the more she stared at Lissa, the more unfocused her eyes became. A blank look fell over her.

"Right?" asked Lissa, voice like silk. "It's not a big deal."

The frown returned. Camille tried to shake the compulsion. That fact that it'd even gotten this far was incredible. As Christian had observed, using it on Moroi was unheard of.

Camille, although strong-willed, lost the battle. "Yeah," she said slowly. "It's really not that big a deal."

"And Jesse's lying."

She nodded. "Definitely lying."

A mental strain burned inside of Lissa as she held onto the compulsion. It took a lot of effort, and she wasn't finished.

"What are you guys doing tonight?"

"Carly and I are going to study for Mattheson's test in her room."

"Invite me."

Camille thought about it. "Hey, you want to study with us?"

"Sure," said Lissa, smiling at her. Camille smiled back.

Lissa dropped the compulsion, and a wave of dizziness swept over her. She felt weak. Camille glanced around, momentarily surprised, then shook off the weirdness. "See you after dinner then."

"See you," murmured Lissa, watching her walk away. When Camille was gone, Lissa reached up to tie her hair up in a ponytail. Her fingers couldn't quite get all the hair through, and suddenly, another pair of hands caught hold and helped her. She spun around and found herself staring into Christian's ice-blue eyes. She jerked away from him.

"Don't do that!" she exclaimed, shivering at the realization that it had been *his* fingers touching her.

He gave her his lazy, slightly twisted smile and brushed a few pieces of unruly black hair out of his face. "Are you asking me or *ordering* me?"

"Shut up." She glanced around, both to avoid his eyes and make sure no one saw them together.

"What's the matter? Worried about what your slaves'll think if they see you talking to me?"

"They're my *friends*," she retorted.

"Oh. Right. Of course they are. I mean, from what I saw, Camille would probably *do anything* for you, right? Friends till the end." He crossed his arms over his chest, and in spite of her anger, she couldn't help but notice how the silvery gray of his shirt set off his black hair and blue eyes.

"At least she isn't like you. She doesn't pretend to be my friend one day and then ignore me for no reason."

An uncertain look flickered across his features. Tension and anger had built up between them in the last week, ever since I'd yelled at Christian after the royal reception. Believing what I'd told him, Christian had stopped talking to her and had treated her rudely every time she'd tried to start a conversation. Now, hurt and confused, she'd given up attempts at being nice. The situation just kept getting worse and worse.

Looking out through Lissa's eyes, I could see that he still

cared about her and still wanted her. His pride had been hurt, however, and he wasn't about to show weakness.

"Yeah?" he said in a low, cruel voice. "I thought that was the way all royals were supposed to act. You certainly seem to be doing a good job with it. Or maybe you're just using compulsion on me to make me think you're a two-faced bitch. Maybe you really aren't. But I doubt it."

Lissa flushed at the word *compulsion*—and cast another worried look around—but decided not to give him the satisfaction of arguing anymore. She simply gave him one last glare before storming off to join a group of royals huddled over an assignment

Returning to myself, I stared blankly around the classroom, processing what I'd seen. Some tiny, tiny part of me was starting to feel sorry for Christian. It was only a tiny part, though, and very easy to ignore.

At the beginning of the next day, I headed out to meet Dimitri. These practices were my favorite part of the day now, partly because of my stupid crush on him and partly because I didn't have to be around the others.

He and I started with running as usual, and he ran with me, quiet and almost gentle in his instructions, probably worried about causing some sort of breakdown. He knew about the rumors somehow, but he never mentioned them.

When we finished, he led me through an offensive exercise where I could use any makeshift weapons I could find to attack him. To my surprise, I managed to land a few blows on him, although they seemed to do me more damage than him. The impacts always made *me* stagger back, but he never budged. It still didn't stop me from attacking and attacking, fighting with an almost blind rage. I didn't know who I really fought in those moments: Mia or Jesse or Ralf. Maybe all of them.

Dimitri finally called a break. We carried the equipment we'd used on the field and returned everything to the supply room. While putting it away, he glanced at me and did a double take.

"Your hands." He swore in Russian. I could recognize it by now, but he refused to teach me what any of it meant. "Where are your gloves?"

I looked down at my hands. They'd suffered for weeks, and today had only made them worse. The cold had turned the skin raw and chapped, and some parts were actually bleeding a little. My blisters swelled. "Don't have any. Never needed them in Portland."

He swore again and beckoned me to a chair while he retrieved a first-aid kit. Wiping away the blood with a wet cloth, he told me gruffly, "We'll get you some."

I looked down at my destroyed hands as he worked. "This is only the start, isn't it?"

"Of what?"

"Me. Turning into Alberta. Her . . . and all the other female guardians. They're all leathery and stuff. Fighting and training and always being outdoors—they aren't pretty anymore." I paused. "This . . . this life. It destroys them. Their looks, I mean."

He hesitated for a moment and looked up from my hands. Those warm brown eyes surveyed me, and something tightened in my chest. Damn it. I had to stop feeling this way around him. "It won't happen to *you*. You're too . . ." He groped for the right word, and I mentally substituted all sorts of possibilities. *Goddesslike. Scorchingly sexy.* Giving up, he simply said, "It won't happen to you."

He turned his attention back to my hands. Did he . . . did he think I was *pretty*? I never doubted the reaction I caused among guys my own age, but with him, I didn't know. The tightening in my chest increased.

"It happened to my mom. She used to be beautiful. I guess she still is, sort of. But not the way she used to be." Bitterly, I added, "Haven't seen her in a while. She could look completely different for all I know."

"You don't like your mother," he observed.

"You noticed that, huh?"

"You barely know her."

"That's the point. She abandoned me. She left me to be raised by the Academy."

When he finished cleaning my open wounds, he found a jar of salve and began rubbing it into the rough parts of my skin. I sort of got lost in the feel of his hands massaging mine.

"You say that . . . but what else should she have done? I know you want to be a guardian. I know how much it means to you. Do you think she feels any differently? Do you think

she should have quit to raise you when you'd spend most of
your life here anyway?"

I didn't like having reasonable arguments thrown at me.
"Are you saying I'm a hypocrite?"

"I'm just saying maybe you shouldn't be so hard on her.
She's a very respected dhampir woman. She's set you on the
path to be the same."

"It wouldn't kill her to visit more," I muttered. "But I guess
you're right. A little. It could have been worse, I suppose. I
could have been raised with blood whores."

Dimitri looked up. "I was raised in a dhampir commune.
They aren't as bad as you think."

"Oh." I suddenly felt stupid. "I didn't mean—"

"It's all right." He focused his attention back on my hands.

"So, did you, like, have family there? Grow up with them?"

He nodded. "My mother and two sisters. I didn't see them
much after I went to school, but we still keep in touch. Mostly,
the communities are about family. There's a lot of love there,
no matter what stories you've heard."

My bitterness returned, and I glanced down to hide my glare.
Dimitri had had a happier family life with his disgraced mother
and relatives than I'd had with my "respected" guardian mother.
He most certainly knew his mother better than I knew mine.

"Yeah, but . . . isn't it weird? Aren't there a lot of Moroi
men visiting to, you know? . . ."

His hands rubbed circles into mine. "Sometimes."

There was something dangerous in his tone, something

that told me this was an unwelcome topic. "I—I'm sorry. I didn't mean to bring up something bad. . . ."

"Actually . . . you probably wouldn't think it's bad," he said after almost a minute had passed. A tight smile formed on his lips. "You don't know your father, do you?"

I shook my head. "No. All I know he is he must have had wicked cool hair."

Dimitri glanced up, and his eyes swept me. "Yes. He must have." Returning to my hands, he said carefully, "I knew mine."

I froze. "Really? Most Moroi guys don't stay—I mean, some do, but you know, usually they just—"

"Well, he liked my mother." He didn't say "liked" in a nice way. "And he visited her a lot. He's my sisters' father too. But when he came . . . well, he didn't treat my mother very well. He did some horrible things."

"Like . . ." I hesitated. This was Dimitri's mother we were talking about. I didn't know how far I could go. "Blood-whore things?"

"Like beating-her-up kinds of things," he replied flatly.

He'd finished the bandages but was still holding my hands. I don't even know if he noticed. I certainly did. His were warm and large, with long and graceful fingers. Fingers that might have played the piano in another life.

"Oh God," I said. How horrible. I tightened my hands in his. He squeezed back. "That's horrible. And she . . . she just let it happen?"

"She did." The corner of his mouth turned up into a sly, sad smile. "But I didn't."

Excitement surged through me. "Tell me, *tell me* you beat the crap out of him."

His smile grew. "I did."

"Wow." I hadn't thought Dimitri could be any cooler, but I was wrong. "You beat up your dad. I mean, that's really horrible . . . what happened. But, *wow.* You really are a god."

He blinked. "What?"

"Uh, nothing." Hastily, I tried to change the subject. "How old were you?"

He still seemed to be puzzling out the god comment. "Thirteen."

Whoa. Definitely a god. "You beat up your dad when you were *thirteen*?"

"It wasn't that hard. I was stronger than he was, almost as tall. I couldn't let him keep doing that. He had to learn that being royal and Moroi doesn't mean you can do anything you want to other people—even blood whores."

I stared. I couldn't believe he'd just said that about his mother. "I'm sorry."

"It's all right."

Pieces clicked into place for me. "That's why you got so upset about Jesse, isn't it? He was another royal, trying to take advantage of a dhampir girl."

Dimitri averted his eyes. "I got upset over that for a lot of reasons. After all, you were breaking the rules, and . . ."

He didn't finish, but he looked back into my eyes in a way that made warmth build between us.

Thinking about Jesse soon darkened my mood, unfortunately. I looked down. "I know you heard what people are saying, that I—"

"I know it's not true," he interrupted.

His immediate, certain answer surprised me, and I stupidly found myself questioning it. "Yeah, but how do you—"

"Because I know you," he replied firmly. "I know your character. I know you're going to be a great guardian."

His confidence made that warm feeling return. "I'm glad someone does. Everyone else thinks I'm totally irresponsible."

"With the way you worry more about Lissa than yourself . . ." He shook his head. "No. You understand your responsibilities better than guardians twice your age. You'll do what you have to do to succeed."

I thought about that. "I don't know if I can do everything I have to do."

He did that cool one-eyebrow thing.

"I don't want to cut my hair," I explained.

He looked puzzled. "You don't have to cut your hair. It's not required."

"All the other guardian women do. They show off their tattoos."

Unexpectedly, he released my hands and leaned forward. Slowly, he reached out and held a lock of my hair, twisting it around one finger thoughtfully. I froze, and for a moment, there was nothing going on in the world except him touching my hair. He let my hair go, looking a little surprised—and embarrassed—at what he'd done.

"Don't cut it," he said gruffly.

Somehow, I remembered how to talk again. "But no one'll see my tattoos if I don't."

He moved toward the doorway, a small smile playing over his lips. "Wear it up."

FOURTEEN

I CONTINUED SPYING ON LISSA over the next couple of days, feeling mildly guilty each time. She'd always hated it when I did by accident, and now I did it on purpose.

Steadily, I watched as she reintegrated herself into the royal power players one by one. She couldn't do group compulsion, but catching one person alone was just as effective, if slower. And really, a lot didn't need to be compelled to start hanging out with her again. Many weren't as shallow as they seemed; they remembered Lissa and liked her for who she was. They flocked to her, and now, a month and a half after our return to the Academy, it was like she'd never left at all. And during this rise to fame, she advocated for me and rallied against Mia and Jesse.

One morning, I tuned into her while she was getting ready for breakfast. She'd spent the last twenty minutes blow-drying and straightening her hair, something she hadn't done in a while. Natalie, sitting on the bed in their room, watched the process with curiosity. When Lissa moved on to makeup, Natalie finally spoke.

"Hey, we're going to watch a movie in Erin's room after school. You going to come?" I'd always made jokes about Natalie being boring, but her friend Erin had the personality of dry wall.

"Can't. I'm going to help Camille bleach Carly's hair."

"You sure spend a lot of time with them now."

"Yeah, I guess." Lissa dabbed mascara across her lashes, instantly making her eyes look bigger.

"I thought you didn't like them anymore."

"I changed my mind."

"They sure seem to like you a lot now. I mean, not that anyone wouldn't like you, but once you came back and didn't talk to them, they seemed okay ignoring you too. I heard them talking about you a lot. I guess that's not surprising, because they're Mia's friends too, but isn't it weird how much they like you now? Like, I hear them always waiting to see what you want to do before they make plans and stuff. And a bunch of them are defending Rose now, which is *really* crazy. Not that I believe any of that stuff about her, but I never would have thought it was possible—"

Underneath Natalie's rambling was the seed of suspicion, and Lissa picked up on it. Natalie probably never would have dreamed of compulsion, but Lissa couldn't risk innocent questions turning into something more. "You know what?" she interrupted. "Maybe I will swing by Erin's after all. I bet Carly's hair won't take that long."

The offer derailed Natalie's train of thought. "Really? Oh wow, that would be great. She was telling me how sad she was that you're not around as much anymore, and I told her . . ."

On it went. Lissa continued her compulsion and return to popularity. I watched it all quietly, always worrying, even though her efforts were starting to reduce the stares and gossip about me.

"This is going to backfire," I whispered to her in church one day. "Someone's going to start wondering and asking questions."

"Stop being so melodramatic. Power shifts all the time around here."

"Not like this."

"You don't think my winning personality could do this on its own?"

"Of course I do, but if Christian spotted *it* right away, then someone else will—"

My words were interrupted when two guys farther down the pew suddenly exploded into snickers. Glancing up, I saw them looking right at me, not even bothering to hide their smirks.

Looking away, I tried to ignore them, suddenly hoping the priest would start up soon. But Lissa returned their looks, and a sudden fierceness flashed across her face. She didn't say a word, but their smiles grew smaller under her heavy gaze.

"Tell her you're sorry," she told them. "And make sure she believes it."

A moment later, they practically fell all over themselves apologizing to me and begging for forgiveness. I couldn't believe it. She'd used compulsion in public—in church, of all places. *And* on two people at the same time.

They finally exhausted their supply of apologies, but Lissa wasn't finished.

"That's the *best* you can do?" she snapped.

Their eyes widened in alarm, both terrified that they'd angered her.

"Liss," I said quickly, touching her arm. "It's okay. I, uh, accept their apologies."

Her face still radiated disapproval, but she finally nodded. The guys slumped in relief.

Yikes. I'd never felt so relieved to have a service start. Through the bond, I felt a sort of dark satisfaction coming from Lissa. It was uncharacteristic for her, and I didn't like it.

Needing to distract myself from her troubling behavior, I studied other people as I so often did. Nearby, Christian openly watched Lissa, a troubled look on his face. When he saw me, he scowled and turned away.

Dimitri sat in the back as usual, for once not scanning every corner for danger. His attention was turned inward, his expression almost pained. I still didn't know why he came to church. He always seemed to be wrestling with something.

In the front, the priest was talking about St. Vladimir again.

"His spirit was strong, and he was truly gifted by God. When he touched them, the crippled walked, and the blind could see. Where he walked, flowers bloomed."

Man, the Moroi needed to get more saints—

Healing cripples and blind people?

I'd forgotten all about St. Vladimir. Mason had mentioned Vladimir bringing people back from the dead, and it had reminded me of Lissa at the time. Then other things had distracted me. I hadn't thought about the saint or his "shadow-kissed" guardian—and their bond—in a while. How could I have overlooked this? Ms. Karp, I realized, wasn't the only other Moroi who could heal like Lissa. Vladimir could too.

"And all the while, the masses gathered to him, loving him, eager to follow his teachings and hear him preach the word of God. . . ."

Turning, I stared at Lissa. She gave me a puzzled look. "What?"

I didn't get a chance to elaborate—I don't even know if I could have formed the words—because I was whisked back to my prison almost as soon as I stood up at the end of the service.

Back in my room, I went online to research St. Vladimir but turned up nothing useful. Damn it. Mason had skimmed the books in the library and said there was little there. What did that leave me with? I had no way of learning more about that dusty old saint.

Or did I? What had Christian said that first day with Lissa?

Over there, we have an old box full of the writings of the blessed and crazy St. Vladimir.

The storage room above the chapel. It had the writings. Christian had pointed them out. I needed to look at them, but how? I couldn't ask the priest. How would he react if he found out students were going up there? It'd put an end to Christian's lair. But maybe . . . maybe Christian himself could help.

It was Sunday, though, and I wouldn't see him until tomorrow afternoon. Even then, I didn't know if I'd get a chance to talk to him alone.

While heading out to practice later, I stopped in the dorm's kitchen to grab a granola bar. As I did, I passed a couple of novice guys, Miles and Anthony. Miles whistled when he saw me.

"How's it been going, Rose? You getting lonely? Want some company?"

Anthony laughed. "I can't bite you, but I can give you something else you want."

I had to pass through the doorway they stood in to get outside. Glaring, I pushed past, but Miles caught me around the waist, his hand sliding down to my butt.

"Get your hands off my ass before I break your face," I told him, jerking away. In doing so, I only bumped into Anthony.

"Come on," Anthony said, "I thought you didn't have a problem taking on two guys at the same time."

A new voice spoke up. "If you guys don't walk away right now, *I'll* take both of you on." Mason. My hero.

"You're so full of it, Ashford," said Miles. He was the bigger of the two and left me to go square off with Mason. Anthony backed off from me, more interested in whether or not there'd be a fight. There was so much testosterone in the air, I felt like I needed a gas mask.

"Are you doing her too?" Miles asked Mason. "You don't want to share?"

"Say one more word about her, and I'll rip your head off."

"Why? She's just a cheap blood—"

Mason punched him. It didn't rip Miles' head off or even cause anything to break or bleed, but it looked like it hurt. His eyes widened, and he lunged toward Mason. The sound of doors opening in the hall caused everyone to freeze. Novices got in a lot of trouble for fighting.

"Probably some guardians coming." Mason grinned. "You want them to know you were beating up on a girl?"

Miles and Anthony exchanged glances. "Come on," Anthony said. "Let's go. We don't have time for this."

Miles reluctantly followed. "I'll find you later, Ashford."

When they were gone, I turned on Mason. "'Beat up on a girl'?"

"You're welcome," he said drily.

"I didn't need your help."

"Sure. You were doing just fine on your own."

"They caught me off guard, that's all. I could have dealt with them eventually."

"Look, don't take being pissed off at them out on me."

"I just don't like being treated like . . . a girl."

"You *are* a girl. And I was just trying to help."

I looked at him and saw the earnestness on his face. He meant well. No point in being a bitch to him when I had so many other people to hate lately.

"Well . . . thanks. Sorry I snapped at you."

We talked a little bit, and I managed to get him to spill some more school gossip. He had noticed Lissa's rise in status but didn't seem to find it strange. As I talked to him, I noticed the adoring look he always got around me spread across his face. It made me sad to have him feel that way about me. Guilty, even.

How hard would it be, I wondered, to go out with him? He was nice, funny, and reasonably good-looking. We got along. Why did I get caught up in so many messes with other guys when I had a perfectly sweet one here who wanted me? Why couldn't I just return his feelings?

The answer came to me before I'd even finished asking myself the question. I couldn't be Mason's girlfriend because when I imagined someone holding me and whispering dirty things in my ear, he had a Russian accent.

Mason continued watching me admiringly, oblivious to what was going on in my head. And seeing that adoration, I suddenly realized how I could use it to my advantage.

Feeling a little guilty, I shifted my conversation to a more flirty style and watched Mason's glow increase.

I leaned beside him on the wall so our arms just touched and gave him a lazy smile. "You know, I still don't approve of your whole hero thing, but you did scare them. That was almost worth it."

"But you don't approve?"

I trailed fingers up his arm. "No. I mean, it's hot in principle but not in practice."

He laughed. "The hell it isn't." He caught hold of my hand and gave me a knowing look. "Sometimes you need to be saved.

I think you like being saved sometimes and just can't admit it."

"And I think *you* get off on saving people and just can't admit it."

"I don't think you know what gets me off. Saving damsels like you is just the honorable thing to do," he declared loftily.

I repressed the urge to smack him over the use of *damsels*. "Then prove it. Do me a favor just because it's 'the right thing to do.'"

"Sure," he said immediately. "Name it."

"I need you to get a message to Christian Ozera."

His eagerness faltered. "What the—? You aren't serious."

"Yes. Completely."

"Rose . . . I can't talk to him. You know that."

"I thought you said you'd help. I thought you said helping 'damsels' is the honorable thing to do."

"I don't really see how honor's involved here." I gave him the most smoldering look I could manage. He caved. "What do you want me to tell him?"

"Tell him I need St. Vladimir's books. The ones in storage. He needs to sneak them to me soon. Tell him it's for Lissa. And tell him . . . tell him I lied the night of the reception." I hesitated. "Tell him I'm sorry."

"That doesn't make any sense."

"It doesn't have to. Just do it. Please?" I turned on the beauty queen smile again.

With hasty assurances that he'd see what he could do, he left for lunch, and I went off to practice.

FIFTEEN

MASON DELIVERED.

He found me the next day before school. He was carrying a box of books.

"I got them," he said. "Hurry and take them before you get in trouble for talking to me."

He handed them over, and I grunted. They were heavy. "Christian gave you these?"

"Yeah. Managed to talk to him without anyone noticing. He's got kind of an attitude, did you ever notice that?"

"Yeah, I noticed." I rewarded Mason with a smile that he ate up. "Thanks. This means a lot."

I hauled the loot up to my room, fully aware of how weird it was that someone who hated to study as much as I did was about to get buried in dusty crap from the fourteenth century. When I opened the first book, though, I saw that these must be reprints of reprints of reprints, probably because anything that old would have long since fallen apart.

Sifting through the books, I discovered they fell into three categories: books written by people after St. Vladimir had died, books written by other people when he was still alive, and one diary of sorts written by him. What had Mason said about primary and secondary sources? Those last two groups were the ones I wanted.

Whoever had reprinted these had reworded the books enough so that I didn't have to read Ye Olde English or anything. Or rather, Russian, I supposed. St. Vladimir had lived in the old country.

Today I healed the mother of Sava who has long since suffered from sharp pains within her stomach. Her malady is now gone, but God has not allowed me to do such a thing lightly. I am weak and dizzy, and the madness is trying to leak into my head. I thank God every day for shadow-kissed Anna, for without her, I would surely not be able to endure.

Anna again. And "shadow-kissed." He talked about her a lot, among other things. Most of the time he wrote long sermons, just like what I'd hear in church. Super boring. But other times, the book read just like a diary, recapping what he did each day. And if it really wasn't just a load of crap, he healed all the time. Sick people. Injured people. Even plants. He brought dead crops back to life when people were starving. Sometimes he would make flowers bloom just for the hell of it.

Reading on, I found out that it was a good thing old Vlad had Anna around, because he was pretty messed up. The more he used his powers, the more they started to get to him. He'd get irrationally angry and sad. He blamed it on demons and stupid stuff like that, but it was obvious he suffered from depression. Once, he admitted in his diary, he tried to kill himself. Anna stopped him.

Later, browsing through the book written by the guy who knew Vladimir, I read:

And many think it miraculous too, the power the blessed Vladimir shows over others. Moroi and dhampirs flock to him and listen to his words, happy just to be near him. Some say it is madness that touches him and not spirit, but most adore him and would do anything he asked. Such is the way God marks his favorites, and if such moments are followed by hallucinations and despair, it is a small sacrifice for the amount of good and leadership he can show among the people.

It sounded a lot like what the priest had said, but I sensed more than just a "winning personality." People adored him, would do anything he asked. Yes, Vladimir had used compulsion on his followers, I was certain. A lot of Moroi had in those days, before it was banned, but they didn't use it on Moroi or dhampirs. They couldn't. Only Lissa could.

I shut the book and leaned back against my bed. Vladimir healed plants and animals. He could use compulsion on a massive scale. And by all accounts, using those sorts of powers had made him crazy and depressed.

Added into it all, making it that much weirder was that everyone kept describing his guardian as "shadow-kissed." That expression had bugged me ever since I first heard it. . . .

"You're *shadow-kissed*! You have to take care of her!"
Ms. Karp had shouted those words at me, her hands

clenching my shirt and jerking me toward her. It had happened on a night two years ago when I'd been inside the main part of the upper school to return a book. It was nearly past curfew, and the halls were empty. I'd heard a loud commotion, and then Ms. Karp had come tearing around the corner, looking frantic and wild-eyed.

She shoved me into a wall, still gripping me. "Do you understand?"

I knew enough self-defense that I could have probably pushed her away, but my shock kept me frozen. "No."

"They're coming for me. They'll come for her."

"Who?"

"Lissa. You have to protect her. The more she uses it, the worse it'll get. Stop her, Rose. Stop her before they notice, before they notice and take her away too. Get her out of here."

"I . . . what do you mean? Get her out of . . . you mean the Academy?"

"Yes! You have to leave. You're bound. It's up to you. Take her away from this place."

Her words were crazy. No one left the Academy. Yet as she held me there and stared into my eyes, I began to feel strange. A fuzzy feeling clouded my mind. What she said suddenly sounded very reasonable, like the most reasonable thing in the world. Yes. I needed to take Lissa away, take her—

Feet pounded in the hallway, and a group of guardians rounded the corner. I didn't recognize them; they weren't from the school. They pried her off of me, restraining her wild thrashing. Someone asked me if I was okay, but I could only keep staring at Ms. Karp.

"Don't let her use the power!" she screamed. "Save her. Save her from herself!"

The guardians had later explained to me that she wasn't well and had been taken to a place where she could recover. She would be safe and cared for, they assured me. She would recover.

Only she hadn't.

Back in the present, I stared at the books and tried to put it all together. Lissa. Ms. Karp. St. Vladimir.

What was I supposed to do?

Someone rapped at my door, and I jerked out of my memories. No one had visited me, not even staff, since my suspension. When I opened the door, I saw Mason in the hall.

"Twice in one day?" I asked. "And how'd you even get up here?"

He flashed his easy smile. "Someone put a lit match in one of the bathroom's garbage cans. Damn shame. The staff's kind of busy. Come on, I'm springing you."

I shook my head. Setting fires was apparently a new sign of affection. Christian had done it and now Mason. "Sorry, no saving me tonight. If I get caught—"

"Lissa's orders."

I shut up and let him smuggle me out of the building. He took me over to the Moroi dorm and miraculously got me in

and up to her room unseen. I wondered if there was a distract-
ing bathroom fire in this building too.

Inside her room, I found a party in full swing. Lissa, Camille,
Carly, Aaron, and a few other royals sat around laughing, listening to loud music, and passing around bottles of whiskey.
No Mia, no Jesse. Natalie, I noticed a few moments later, sat
apart from the group, clearly unsure how to act around all of
them. Her awkwardness was totally obvious.

Lissa stumbled to her feet, the fuzzy feelings in our bond
indicating she'd been drinking for a while. "Rose!" She turned
to Mason with a dazzling smile. "You delivered."

He swept her an over-the-top bow. "I'm at your command."

I hoped he'd done it for the thrill of it and not because of
any compulsion. Lissa slung an arm around my waist and
pulled me down with the others. "Join the festivities."

"What are we celebrating?"

"I don't know. Your escape tonight?"

A few of the others held up plastic cups, cheering and
toasting me. Xander Badica poured two more cups, handing them to Mason and me. I took mine with a smile, all the
while feeling uneasy about the night's turn of events. Not so
long ago, I would have welcomed a party like this and would
have downed my drink in thirty seconds. Too much bothered
me this time, though. Like the fact that the royals were treat-
ing Lissa like a goddess. Like how none of them seemed to
remember that I had been accused of being a blood whore.

Like how Lissa was completely unhappy despite her smiles and laughter.

"Where'd you get the whiskey?" I asked.

"Mr. Nagy," Aaron said. He sat very close to Lissa.

Everyone knew Mr. Nagy drank all the time after school and kept a stash on campus. He continually used new hiding places—and students continually found them.

Lissa leaned against Aaron's shoulder. "Aaron helped me break into his room and take them. He had them hidden in the bottom of the paint closet."

The others laughed, and Aaron gazed at her with complete and utter worship. Amusingly, I realized she hadn't had to use any compulsion on him. He was just that crazy for her. He always had been.

"Why aren't you drinking?" Mason asked me a little while later, speaking quietly into my ear.

I glanced down at my cup, half surprised to see it full. "I don't know. I guess I don't think guardians should drink around their charges."

"She's not your charge yet! You aren't on duty. You won't be for a long time. Since when did you get so responsible?"

I didn't really think I was all that responsible. But I *was* thinking about what Dimitri had said about balancing fun and obligation. It just seemed wrong to let myself go wild when Lissa was in such a vulnerable state lately. Wiggling out of my tight spot between her and Mason, I walked over and sat beside Natalie.

"Hey Nat, you're quiet tonight."

She held a cup as full as mine. "So are you."

I laughed softly. "I guess so."

She tilted her head, watching Mason and the royals like they were some sort of science experiment. They'd consumed a lot more whiskey since I'd arrived, and the silliness had shot up considerably. "Weird, huh? You used to be the center of attention. Now she is."

I blinked in surprise. I hadn't considered it like that. "I guess so."

"Hey, Rose," said Xander, nearly spilling his drink as he walked over to me. "What was it like?"

"What was what like?"

"Letting someone feed off you?"

The others fell quiet, a sort of anticipation settling over them.

"She didn't do that," said Lissa in a warning voice. "I told you."

"Yeah, yeah, I know nothing happened with Jesse and Ralf. But you guys did it, right? While you were gone?"

"Let it go," said Lissa. Compulsion worked best with direct eye contact, and his attention was focused on me, not her.

"I mean, it's cool and everything. You guys did what you had to do, right? It's not like you're a feeder. I just want to know what it was like. Danielle Szelsky let me bite her once. She said it didn't feel like anything."

There was a collective "ew" from among the girls. Sex and

blood with dhampirs was dirty; between Moroi, it was cannibalistic.

"You are such a liar," said Camille.

"No, I'm serious. It was just a small bite. She didn't get high like the feeders. Did *you*?" He put his free arm around my shoulder. "Did you like it?"

Lissa's face went still and pale. Alcohol muted the full force of her feelings, but I could read enough to know how she felt. Dark, scared thoughts trickled into me—underscored with anger. She usually had a good grip on her temper—unlike me—but I'd seen it flare up before. Once it had happened at a party very similar to this one, just a few weeks after Ms. Karp had been taken away.

Greg Dashkov—a distant cousin of Natalie's—had held the party in his room. His parents apparently knew someone who knew someone, because he had one of the biggest rooms in the dorm. He'd been friends with Lissa's brother before the accident and had been more than happy to take Andre's little sister into his social fold. Greg had also been happy to take me in, and the two of us had been all over each other that night. For a sophomore like me, being with a royal Moroi senior was a huge rush.

I drank a lot that night but still managed to keep an eye on Lissa. She always wore an edge of anxiety around this many people, but no one really noticed, because she could interact with them so well. My heavy buzz kept a lot of her feelings from me, but as long as she looked okay, I didn't worry.

Mid-kiss, Greg suddenly broke away and looked at something over my shoulder. We both sat in the same chair, with me on his lap, and I craned my neck to see. "What is it?"

He shook his head with a sort of amused exasperation. "Wade brought a feeder."

I followed his gaze to where Wade Voda stood with his arm around a frail girl about my age. She was human and pretty, with wavy blond hair and porcelain skin pale from so much blood loss. A few other guys had homed on her and stood with Wade, laughing and touching her face and hair.

"She's already fed too much today," I said, observing her coloring and complete look of confusion.

Greg slid his hand behind my neck and turned me back to him. "They won't hurt her."

We kissed a while longer and then I felt a tap on my shoulder. "Rose."

I looked up into Lissa's face. Her anxious expression startled me because I couldn't feel the emotions behind it. Too much beer for me. I climbed off of Greg's lap.

"Where are you going?" he asked.

"Be right back." I pulled Lissa aside, suddenly wishing I was sober. "What's wrong?"

"Them."

She nodded toward the guys with the feeder girl. She still had a group around her, and when she shifted to look at one of them, I saw small red wounds scattered on her neck. They were doing a sort of group feeding, taking turns biting her and making gross suggestions. High and oblivious, she let them.

"They can't do that," Lissa told me.

"She's a feeder. Nobody's going to stop them."

Lissa looked up at me with pleading eyes. Hurt, outrage, and anger filled them. "Will *you*?"

I'd always been the aggressive one, looking after her ever since we were little. Seeing her there now, so upset and looking at me to fix things, was more than I could stand. Giving her a shaky nod, I stumbled over to the group.

"You so desperate to get some that you've got to drug girls now, Wade?" I asked.

He glanced up from where he'd been running his lips over the human girl's neck. "Why? Are you done with Greg and looking for more?"

I put my hands on my hips and hoped I looked fierce. The truth was, I was actually starting to feel a little nauseous from all I'd drunk. "Aren't enough drugs in the world to get me near you," I told him. A few of his friends laughed. "But maybe you can go make out with that lamp over there. It seems to be out of it enough to make even you happy. You don't need *her* anymore." A few other people laughed.

"This isn't any of your business," he hissed. "She's just lunch." Referring to feeders as meals was about the only thing worse than calling dhampirs blood whores.

"This isn't a feeding room. Nobody wants to see this."

"Yeah," agreed a senior girl. "It's gross." A few of her friends agreed.

Wade glared at all of us, me the hardest. "Fine. None of you have to see it. Come on." He grabbed the feeder girl's arm and jerked her away. Clumsily, she stumbled along with him out of the room, making soft whimpering noises.

"Best I could do," I told Lissa.

She stared at me, shocked. "He's just going to take her to his room. He'll do even worse things to her."

"Liss, I don't like it either, but it's not like I can go chase him down or anything." I rubbed my forehead. "I could go punch him or something, but I feel like I'm going to throw up as it is."

Her face grew dark, and she bit her lip. "He can't do that."

"I'm sorry."

I returned to the chair with Greg, feeling a little bad about what had happened. I didn't want to see the feeder get taken advantage of anymore than Lissa did—it reminded me too much of what a lot of Moroi guys thought they cold do to dhampir girls. But I also couldn't win this battle, not tonight.

Greg had shifted me around to get a better angle on my neck when I noticed Lissa was gone a few minutes later. Practically falling, I clambered off his lap and looked around. "Where's Lissa?"

He reached for me. "Probably the bathroom."

I couldn't feel a thing through the bond. The alcohol had numbed it. Stepping out into the hallway, I breathed a sigh of relief at escaping the loud music and voices. It was quiet out here—except for a crashing sound a couple rooms down. The door was ajar, and I pushed my way inside.

The feeder girl cowered in a corner, terrified. Lissa stood with arms crossed, her face angry and terrible. She was staring at Wade intently, and he stared back, enchanted. He also held a baseball bat, and it looked like he'd used it already, because the room was trashed: bookshelves, the stereo, the mirror. . . .

"Break the window too," Lissa told him smoothly. "Come on. It doesn't matter."

Hypnotized, he walked over to the large, tinted window. I stared, my mouth nearly hitting the floor, as he pulled back and slammed the bat into the glass. It shattered, sending shards everywhere and letting in the early morning light it normally kept blocked out. He winced as it shone in his eyes, but he didn't move away.

"Lissa," I exclaimed. "Stop it. Make him stop."

"He should have stopped earlier."

I barely recognized the look on her face. I'd never seen her so upset, and I'd certainly never seen her do anything like this. I knew what it was, of course. I knew right away. Compulsion. For all I knew, she was seconds away from having him turn the bat on himself.

"Please, Lissa. Don't do it anymore. Please."

Through the fuzzy, alcoholic buzz, I felt a trickle of her emotions. They were strong enough to practically knock me over. Black. Angry. Merciless. Startling feelings to be coming from sweet and steady Lissa. I'd known her since kindergarten, but in that moment, I barely knew her.

And I was afraid.

"Please, Lissa," I repeated. "He's not worth it. Let him go."

She didn't look at me. Her stormy eyes were focused entirely on Wade. Slowly, carefully, he lifted up the bat, tilting it so that it lined up with his own skull.

"Liss," I begged. Oh God. I was going to have to tackle her or something to make her stop. "Don't do it."

"He should have stopped," Lissa said evenly. The bat quit moving. It was now at exactly the right distance to gain momentum and strike. "He shouldn't have done that to her. People can't treat other people like that—even feeders."

"But you're scaring her," I said softly. "Look at her."

Nothing happened at first, then Lissa let her gaze flick toward the feeder. The human girl still sat huddled in a corner, arms wrapped around herself protectively. Her blue eyes were enormous, and light reflected off her wet, tear-streaked face. She gave a choked, terrified sob.

Lissa's face stayed impassive. Inside her, I could feel the battle she was waging for control. Some part of her didn't want to hurt Wade, despite the blinding anger that otherwise filled her. Her face crumpled, and she squeezed her eyes shut. Her right hand reached out to her left wrist and clenched it, nails digging deep into the flesh. She flinched at the pain, but through the bond, I felt the shock of the pain distract her from Wade.

She let go of the compulsion, and he dropped the bat, suddenly looking confused. I let go of the breath I'd been holding. In the hallway, footsteps sounded. I'd left the door open, and the crash had attracted attention. A couple of dorm staff members burst into the room, freezing when they saw the destruction in front of them.

"What happened?"

The rest of us looked at each other. Wade looked completely lost. He stared at the room, at the bat, and then at Lissa and me. "I don't know. . . . I can't . . ." He turned his full attention to me and suddenly grew angry. "What the—it was you! You wouldn't let the feeder thing go."

The dorm workers looked at me questioningly, and in a few seconds, I made up my mind.

You have to protect her. The more she uses it, the worse it'll get. Stop her, Rose. Stop her before they notice, before they notice and take her away too. Get her out of here.

I could see Ms. Karp's face in my mind, pleading frantically. I gave Wade a haughty look, knowing full well no one would question a confession I made or even suspect Lissa.

"Yeah, well, if you'd let her go," I told him, "I wouldn't have had to do this."

Save her. Save her from herself.

After that night, I never drank again. I refused to let my guard down around Lissa. And two days later, while I was supposed to be suspended for "destruction of property," I took Lissa and broke out of the Academy.

Back in Lissa's room, with Xander's arm around me and her angry and upset eyes on us, I didn't know if she'd do anything drastic again. But the situation reminded me too much of that one from two years ago, and I knew I had to defuse it.

"Just a little blood," Xander was saying. "I won't take much. I just want to see what dhampir tastes like. Nobody here cares."

"Xander," growled Lissa, "leave her alone."

I slipped out from under his arm and smiled, looking for a funny retort rather than one that might start a fight. "Come on," I teased. "I had to hit the last guy who asked me that, and you're a hell of a lot prettier than Jesse. It'd be a waste."

"Pretty?" he asked. "I'm stunningly sexy but not *pretty*."

Carly laughed. "No, you're pretty. Todd told me you buy some kind of French hair gel."

Xander, distracted as so many drunk people easily are, turned around to defend his honor, forgetting me. The tension disappeared, and he took the teasing about his hair with a good attitude.

Across the room, Lissa met my eyes with relief. She smiled and gave me a small nod of thanks before she returned her attention to Aaron.

Sixteen

THE NEXT DAY, IT FULLY hit me how much things had changed since the Jesse-and-Ralf rumors first started. For some people, I remained a nonstop source of whispers and laughter. From Lissa's converts, I received friendliness and occasional defense. Overall, I realized, our classmates actually gave me very little of their attention anymore. This became especially true when something new distracted everyone.

Lissa and Aaron.

Apparently, Mia had found about the party and had blown up when she learned that Aaron had been there without her. She'd bitched at him and told him that if he wanted to be with her, he couldn't run around and hang out with Lissa. So Aaron had decided he didn't want to be with her. He'd broken up with her that morning . . . and moved on.

Now he and Lissa were all over each other. They stood around in the hall and at lunch, arms wrapped around one another, laughing and talking. Lissa's bond feelings showed only mild interest, despite her gazing at him as though he was the most fascinating thing on the planet. Most of this was for show, unbeknownst to him. He looked as though he could have built a shrine at her feet at any moment.

And me? I felt ill.

My feelings were nothing, however, compared to Mia's. At lunch, she sat on the far side of the room from us, eyes fixed pointedly ahead, ignoring the consolations of the friends near her. She had blotchy pink patches on her pale, round cheeks, and her eyes were red-rimmed. She said nothing mean when I walked past. No smug jokes. No mocking glares. Lissa had destroyed her, just as Mia had vowed to do us.

The only person more miserable than Mia was Christian. Unlike her, he had no qualms about studying the happy couple while wearing an open look of hatred on his face. As usual, no one except me even noticed.

After watching Lissa and Aaron make out for the tenth time, I left lunch early and went to see Ms. Carmack, the teacher who taught elemental basics. I'd been wanting to ask her something for a while.

"Rose, right?" She seemed surprised to see me but not angry or annoyed like half the other teachers did lately.

"Yeah. I have a question about, um, magic."

She raised an eyebrow. Novices didn't take magic classes. "Sure. What do you want to know?"

"I was listening to the priest talk about St. Vladimir the other day. . . . Do you know what element he specialized in? Vladimir, I mean. Not the priest."

She frowned. "Odd. As famous as he is around here, I'm surprised it never comes up. I'm no expert, but in all the stories I've heard, he never did anything that I'd say connects to any one of the elements. Either that or no one ever recorded it."

"What about his healings?" I pushed further. "Is there an element that lets you perform those?"

"No, not that I know of." Her lips quirked into a small smile. "People of faith would say he healed through the power of God, not any sort of elemental magic. After all, one thing the stories are certain about is that he was 'full of spirit.'"

"Is it possible he didn't specialize?"

Her smile faded. "Rose, is this really about St. Vladimir? Or is it about Lissa?"

"Not exactly . . ." I stammered.

"I know it's hard on her—especially in front of all her classmates—but she has to be patient," she explained gently. "It will happen. It always happens."

"But sometimes it doesn't."

"Rarely. But I don't think she'll be one of those. She's got a higher-than-average aptitude in all four, even if she hasn't hit specialized levels. One of them will shoot up any day now."

That gave me an idea. "Is it possible to specialize in more than one element?"

She laughed and shook her head. "No. Too much power. No one could handle all that magic, not without losing her mind."

Oh. Great.

"Okay. Thanks." I started to leave, then thought of something else. "Hey, do you remember Ms. Karp? What did she specialize in?"

Ms. Carmack got that uncomfortable look other teachers

did whenever anyone mentioned Ms. Karp. "Actually—"

"What?"

"I almost forgot. I think she really was one of the rare ones who never specialized. She just always kept a very low control over all four."

I spent the rest of my afternoon classes thinking about Ms. Carmack's words, trying to work them into my unified Lissa-Karp-Vladimir theory. I also watched Lissa. So many people wanted to talk to her now that she barely noticed my silence. Every so often, though, I'd see her glance at me and smile, a tired look in her eyes. Laughing and gossiping all day with people she only sort of liked was taking its toll on her.

"The mission's accomplished," I told her after school. "We can stop Project Brainwash."

We sat on benches in the courtyard, and she swung her legs back and forth. "What do you mean?"

"You've done it. You stopped people from making my life horrible. You destroyed Mia. You stole Aaron. Play with him for another couple weeks, then drop him and the other royals. You'll be happier."

"You don't think I'm happy now?"

"I know you aren't. Some of the parties are fun, but you hate pretending to be friends with people you don't like—and you don't like most of them. I know how much Xander pissed you off the other night."

"He's a jerk, but I can deal with that. If I stop hanging out with them, everything'll go back to the way it was. Mia will just start up again. This way, she can't bother us."

"It's not worth it if everything else is bothering you."

"Nothing's bothering me." She sounded a little defensive.

"Yeah?" I asked meanly. "Because you're so in love with Aaron? Because you can't wait to have sex with him again?"

She glared at me. "Have I mentioned you can be a huge bitch sometimes?"

I ignored that. "I'm just saying you've got enough shit to worry about without all this. You're burning yourself out with all the compulsion you're using."

"Rose!" She glanced anxiously around. "Be quiet!"

"But it's true. Using it all the time is going to screw with your head. For real."

"Don't you think you're getting carried away?"

"What about Ms. Karp?"

Lissa's expression went very still. "What about her?"

"You. You're just like her."

"No, I'm not!" Outrage flashed in those green eyes.

"She healed too."

Hearing me talk about this shocked her. This topic had weighed us down for so long, but we'd almost never spoken about it.

"That doesn't mean anything."

"You don't think it does? Do you know anyone else who can do that? Or can use compulsion on dhampirs *and* Moroi?"

"She never used compulsion like that," she argued.

"She did. She tried to use it on me the night she left. It started to work, but then they took her away before she finished." Or had they? After all, it was only a month later that Lissa and I had run away from the Academy. I'd always thought that was my own idea, but maybe Ms. Karp's suggestion had been the true force behind it.

Lissa crossed her arms. Her face looked defiant, but her emotions felt uneasy. "Fine. So what? So she's a freak like me. That doesn't mean anything. She went crazy because . . . well, that was just the way she was. That's got nothing to do with anything else."

"But it's not just her," I said slowly. "There's someone else like you guys, too. Someone I found." I hesitated. "You know St. Vladimir. . . ."

And that's when I finally let it all out. I told her everything. I told her about how she, Ms. Karp, and St. Vladimir could all heal and use super-compulsion. Although it made her squirm, I told her how they too grew easily upset and had tried to hurt themselves.

"He tried to kill himself," I said, not meeting her eyes. "And I used to notice marks on Ms. Karp's skin—like she'd claw at her own face. She tried to hide it with her hair, but I could see the old scratches and tell when she made new ones."

"It doesn't mean *anything*," insisted Lissa. "It—it's all a coincidence."

She sounded like she wanted to believe that, and inside,

some part of her really did. But there was another part of her, a desperate part of her that had wanted for so long to know that she wasn't a freak, that she wasn't alone. Even if the news was bad, at least now she knew there were others like her.

"Is it a coincidence that neither of them seems to have specialized?"

I recounted my conversation with Ms. Carmack and explained my theory about specializing in all four elements. I also repeated Ms. Carmack's comment about how that would burn someone out.

Lissa rubbed her eyes when I finished, smudging a little of her makeup. She gave me a weak smile. "I don't know what's crazier: what you're actually telling me or the fact that you actually *read* something to find all this out."

I grinned, relieved that she'd actually mustered a joke. "Hey, I know how to read too."

"I know you do. I also know it took you a year to read *The Da Vinci Code*." She laughed.

"That wasn't my fault! And don't try to change the subject."

"I'm not." She smiled, then sighed. "I just don't know what to think about all this."

"There's nothing to think about. Just don't do stuff that'll upset you. Remember coasting through the middle? Go back to that. It's a lot easier on you."

She shook her head. "I can't do that. Not yet."

"Why not? I already told you—" I stopped, wondering

why I hadn't caught on before. "It's not just Mia. You're doing all this because you feel like you're *supposed* to. You're still trying to be Andre."

"My parents would have wanted me to—"

"Your parents would have wanted you to be happy."

"It's not that easy, Rose. I can't ignore these people forever. I'm royal too."

"Most of them suck."

"And a lot of them are going to help rule the Moroi. Andre knew that. He wasn't like the others, but he did what he had to do because he knew how important they were."

I leaned back against the bench. "Well, maybe that's the problem. We're deciding who's 'important' based on family alone, so we end up with these screwed-up people making decisions. That's why Moroi numbers are dropping and bitches like Tatiana are queen. Maybe there needs to be a new royal system."

"Come on, Rose. This is the way it is; that's the way it's been for centuries. We have to live with that." I glared. "Okay, how about this?" she continued. "You're worried about me becoming like *them*—like Ms. Karp and St. Vladimir—right? Well, she said I shouldn't use the powers, that it would make things get worse if I did. What if I just stop? Compulsion, healing, everything."

I narrowed my eyes. "You could do that?" The convenient compulsion aside, that was what I'd wanted her to do the whole time. Her depression had started at the same time the powers emerged, just after the accident. I had to believe they were connected, particularly in light of the evidence and Ms. Karp's warnings.

"Yes."

Her face was perfectly composed, her expression serious and steady. With her pale hair woven into a neat French braid and a suede blazer over her dress, she looked like she could have taken her family's place on the council right now.

"You'd have to give up everything," I warned. "No healing, no matter how cute and cuddly the animal. And no more compulsion to dazzle the royals."

She nodded seriously. "I can do it. Will that make you feel better?"

"Yeah, but I'd feel even better if you stopped magic *and* went back to hanging out with Natalie."

"I know, I know. But I can't stop, not now at least."

I couldn't get her to budge on that—*yet*—but knowing that she would avoid using her powers relieved me.

"All right," I said, picking up my backpack. I was late for practice. Again. "You can keep playing with the brat pack, so long as you keep the 'other stuff' in check." I hesitated. "And you know, you really have made your point with Aaron and Mia. You don't have to keep him around to keep hanging out with the royals."

"Why do I keep getting the feeling you don't like him anymore?"

"I like him okay—which is about as much as you like him.

And I don't think you should get hot and sweaty with people you only like 'okay.'"

Lissa widened her eyes in pretend astonishment. "Is this Rose Hathaway talking? Have you reformed? Or do *you* have someone you like 'more than okay'?"

"Hey," I said uncomfortably, "I'm just looking out for you. That, and I never noticed how boring Aaron is before."

She scoffed. "You think everyone's boring."

"Christian isn't."

It slipped out before I could stop it. She quit smiling. "He's a *jerk*. He just stopped talking to me for no reason one day." She crossed her arms. "And don't you hate him anyway?"

"I can still hate him and think he's interesting."

But I was also starting to think that I might have made a big mistake about Christian. He was creepy and dark and liked to set people on fire, true. On the other hand, he was smart and funny—in a twisted way—and somehow had a calming effect on Lissa.

But I'd messed it all up. I'd let my anger and jealousy get the best of me and ended up separating them. If I'd let him go to her in the garden that night, maybe she wouldn't have gotten upset and cut herself. Maybe they'd be together now, away from all the school politics.

Fate must have been thinking the same thing, because five minutes after I left Lissa, I passed Christian walking across the quad. Our eyes locked for a moment before we passed each other. I nearly kept walking. Nearly. Taking a deep breath, I came to a stop.

"Wait . . . Christian." I called out to him. Damn, I was so late for training. Dimitri was going to kill me.

Christian spun around to face me, hands stuffed in the pockets of his long black coat, his posture slumped and uncaring.

"Yeah?"

"Thanks for the books." He didn't say anything. "The ones you gave to Mason."

"Oh, I thought you meant the other books."

Smartass. "Aren't you going to ask what they were for?"

"Your business. Just figured you were bored being suspended."

"I'd have to be pretty bored for that."

He didn't laugh at my joke. "What do you want, Rose? I've got places to be."

I knew he was lying, but my sarcasm no longer seemed as funny as usual. "I want you to, uh, hang out with Lissa again."

"Are you *serious*?" He studied me closely, suspicion all over him. "After what you said to me?"

"Yeah, well . . . Didn't Mason tell you? . . ."

Christian's lips turned up into a sneer. "He told me something."

"And?"

"And I don't want to hear it from Mason." His sneer

cranked up when I glared. "You sent him to apologize for you. Step up and do it yourself."

"You're a jerk," I informed him.

"Yeah. And you're a liar. I want to see you eat your pride."

"I've been eating my pride for two weeks," I growled.

Shrugging, he turned around and started to walk away.

"Wait!" I called, putting my hand on his shoulder. He stopped and looked back at me. "All right, all right. I lied about how she felt. She never said any of that stuff about you, okay? She *likes* you. I made it up because *I* don't like you."

"And yet you want me to talk to her."

When the next words left my lips, I could barely believe it. "I think . . . you might be . . . good for her."

We stared at each other for several heavy moments. His smirk dried up a little. Not much surprised him. This did.

"I'm sorry. I didn't hear you. Can you repeat that?" he finally asked.

I almost punched him in the face. "Will you stop it already? I want you to hang out with her again."

"No."

"Look, I told you, I lied—"

"It's not that. It's *her*. You think I can talk to her now? She's Princess Lissa again." Venom dripped off his words. "I can't go near her, not when she's surrounded by all those royals."

"You're royal too," I said, more to myself than him. I kept forgetting the Ozeras were one of the twelve families.

"Doesn't mean much in a family full of Strigoi, huh?"

"But *you're* not—wait. That's why she connects to you," I realized with a start.

"Because I'm going to become a Strigoi?" he asked snidely.

"No . . . because you lost your parents too. Both of you saw them die."

"She saw hers die. I saw mine murdered."

I flinched. "I know. I'm sorry. it must have been . . . well, I don't have any idea what it was like."

Those crystal-blue eyes went unfocused. "It was like seeing an army of Death invade my house."

"You mean . . . your parents?"

He shook his head. "The guardians who came to kill them. I mean, my parents were scary, yeah, but they still looked like my parents—a little paler, I guess. Some red in their eyes. But they walked and talked the same way. I didn't know anything was wrong with them, but my aunt did. She was watching me when they came for me."

"Were they going to convert you?" I'd forgotten my original mission here, too caught up in the story. "You were really little."

"I think they were going to keep me until I was older, then turn me. Aunt Tasha wouldn't let them take me. They tried to reason with her, convert her too, but when she wouldn't listen, they tried to take her by force. She fought them—got really messed up—and then the guardians showed up." His eyes drifted back to me. He smiled, but there was no happiness in it. "Like I said, an army of Death. I think you're crazy,

Rose, but if you turn out like the rest of them, you're going to be able to do some serious damage one day. Even I won't mess with you."

I felt horrible. He'd had a miserable life, and I'd taken away one of the few good things in it. "Christian, I'm sorry for screwing things up between you and Lissa. It was stupid. She wanted to be with you. I think she still does now. If you could just—"

"I told you, I can't."

"I'm worried about her. She's into all this royal stuff because she thinks it's going to get back at Mia—she's doing it for me."

"And you aren't grateful?" The sarcasm returned.

"I'm worried. She can't handle playing all these catty political games. It isn't good for her, but she won't listen to me. I could . . . I could use help."

"*She* could use help. Hey, don't look so surprised—I know there's something funny going on with her. And I'm not even talking about the wrist thing."

I jumped. "Did she tell you? . . ." Why not? She'd told him everything else.

"She didn't need to," he said. "I've got eyes." I must have looked pathetic, because he sighed and ran a hand through his hair. "Look, if I catch Lissa alone . . . I'll try to talk to her. But honestly . . . if you really want to help her . . . well, I know I'm supposed to be all anti-establishment, but you might get the best help talking to somebody else. Kirova. Your guardian guy. I don't know. Someone who knows something. Someone you trust."

"Lissa wouldn't like that." I considered. "Neither would I."

"Yeah, well, we all have to do things we don't like. That's life."

My snarky switch flipped on. "What are you, an after-school special?"

A ghostly smile flickered across his face. "If you weren't so psychotic, you'd be fun to hang around."

"Funny, I feel that way about you too."

He didn't say anything else, but the smile grew, and he walked away.

SEVENTEEN

A FEW DAYS LATER, LISSA found me outside the commons and delivered the most astonishing news.

"Uncle Victor's getting Natalie off campus this weekend to go shopping in Missoula. For the dance. They said I could come along."

I didn't say anything. She looked surprised at my silence.

"Isn't that cool?"

"For *you*, I guess. No malls or dances in my future."

She smiled excitedly. "He told Natalie she could bring two other people besides me. I convinced her to bring you and Camille."

I threw up my hands. "Well, thanks, but I'm not even supposed to go to the library after school. No one's going to let me go to Missoula."

"Uncle Victor thinks he can get Headmistress Kirova to let you go. Dimitri's trying too."

"Dimitri?"

"Yeah. He has to go with me if I leave campus." She grinned, taking my interest in Dimitri as interest in the mall. "They figured out my account finally—I got my allowance back. So we can buy other stuff along with dresses. And you know if they let you go to the mall, they'll have to let you go to the dance."

"Do we go to dances now?" I said. We never had before. School-sponsored social events? No way.

"Of course not. But you know there'll be all kinds of secret parties. We'll start at the dance and sneak off." She sighed happily. "Mia's so jealous she can barely stand it."

She went on about all the stores we'd go to, all the things we'd buy. I admit, I was kind of excited at the thought of getting some new clothes, but I doubted I'd actually get this mythical release.

"Oh hey," she said excitedly. "You should see these shoes Camille let me borrow. I never knew we wore the same size. Hang on." She opened her backpack and began rifling through it.

Suddenly, she screamed and threw it down. Books and shoes spilled out. So did a dead dove.

It was one of the pale brown mourning doves that sat on wires along the freeway and under trees on campus. It had so much blood on it that I couldn't figure out where the wound was. Who knew something so small even had that much blood? Regardless, the bird was definitely dead.

Covering her mouth, Lissa stared wordlessly, eyes wide.

"Son of a bitch," I swore. Without hesitating, I grabbed a stick and pushed the little feathered body aside. When it was out of the way, I started shoving her stuff back into the backpack, trying not to think about dead-bird germs. "Why the hell does this keep—Liss!"

I leapt over and grabbed her, pulling her away. She had

been kneeling on the ground, with her hand outstretched to the dove. I don't think she'd even realized what she was about to do. The instinct in her was so strong, it acted on its own.

"Lissa," I said, tightening my hand around hers. She was still leaning toward the bird. "Don't. Don't do it."

"I can save it."

"No, you can't. You promised, remember? Some things have to stay dead. Let this one go." Still feeling her tension, I pleaded. "Please, Liss. You promised. No more healings. You said you wouldn't. You promised me."

After a few more moments, I felt her hand relax and her body slump against mine. "I hate this, Rose. I hate all of this."

Natalie walked outside then, oblivious to the gruesome sight awaiting her.

"Hey, do you guys—oh my God!" she squealed, seeing the dove. "What is that?"

I helped Lissa as we rose to our feet. "Another, um, prank."

"Is it . . . dead?" She scrunched up her face in disgust.

"Yes," I said firmly.

Natalie, picking up on our tension, looked between the two of us. "What else is wrong?"

"Nothing." I handed Lissa her backpack. "This is just someone's stupid, sick joke, and I'm going to tell Kirova so they can clean this up."

Natalie turned away, looking a little green. "Why do people keep doing this to you? It's horrible."

Lissa and I exchanged looks.

"I have no idea," I said. Yet as I walked to Kirova's office, I started to wonder.

When we'd found the fox, Lissa had hinted that someone must know about the raven. I hadn't believed that. We'd been alone in the woods that night, and Ms. Karp wouldn't have told anyone. But what if someone actually had seen? What if someone kept doing this not to scare her, but to see if she'd heal again? What had the rabbit note said? *I know what you are.*

I didn't mention any of this to Lissa; I figured there were only so many of my conspiracy theories she could handle. Besides, when I saw her the next day, she'd practically forgotten the dove in light of other news: Kirova had given me permission to go on the trip that weekend. The prospect of shopping can brighten a lot of dark situations—even animal murder—and I put my own worries on hold.

Only, when the time came, I discovered my release came with strings attached.

"Headmistress Kirova thinks you've done well since coming back," Dimitri told me.

"Aside from starting a fight in Mr. Nagy's class?"

"She doesn't blame you for that. Not entirely. I convinced her you needed a break . . . and that you could use this as a training exercise."

"Training exercise?"

He gave me a brief explanation as we walked out to meet the others going with us. Victor Dashkov, as sickly as ever, was there with his guardians, and Natalie practically barreled into him. He smiled and gave her a careful hug, one that ended when a coughing fit took over. Natalie's eyes went wide with concern as she waited for it to pass.

He claimed he was fine to accompany us, and while I admired his resolve, I thought he'd be putting himself through a lot just to shop with a bunch of teenage girls.

We rode out the two-hour trip to Missoula in a large school van, leaving just after sunrise. Many Moroi lived separately from humans, but many also lived among them, and when shopping at their malls, you had to go during their hours. The back windows of the van had tinted glass to filter the light and keep the worst of it away from the vampires.

We had nine people in our group: Lissa, Victor, Natalie, Camille, Dimitri, me, and three other guardians. Two of the guardians, Ben and Spiridon, always traveled with Victor. The third was one of the school's guardians: Stan, the jerk who'd humiliated me on my first day back.

"Camille and Natalie don't have personal guardians yet," Dimitri explained to me. "They're both under the protection of their families' guardians. Since they are Academy students leaving campus, a school guardian accompanies them—Stan. I go because I'm Lissa's assigned guardian. Most girls her age wouldn't have a personal guardian yet, but circumstances make her unusual."

I sat in the back of the van with him and Spiridon, so they could dispense guardian wisdom to me as part of the "training exercise." Ben and Stan sat up front, while the others sat in the middle. Lissa and Victor talked to each other a lot, catching up on news. Camille, raised to be polite among older royals, smiled and nodded along. Natalie, on the other hand, looked left out and kept trying to shift her father's attention from Lissa. It didn't work. He'd apparently learned to tune out her chatter.

I turned back to Dimitri. "She's supposed to have two guardians. Princes and princesses always do."

Spiridon was Dimitri's age, with spiky blond hair and a more casual attitude. Despite his Greek name, he had a Southern drawl. "Don't worry, she'll have plenty when the time comes. Dimitri's already one of them. Odds are you'll be one too. And that's why you're here today."

"The training part," I guessed.

"Yup. You're going to be Dimitri's partner."

A moment of funny silence fell, probably not noticeable to anyone except Dimitri and me. Our eyes met.

"Guarding partner," Dimitri clarified unnecessarily, like maybe he too had been thinking of other kinds of partners.

"Yup," agreed Spiridon.

Oblivious to the tension around him, he went on to explain how guardian pairs worked. It was standard stuff, straight from my textbooks, but it meant more now that I'd be doing it in the real world. Guardians were assigned to Moroi based on importance. Two was a common grouping, one I'd probably work in a lot with Lissa. One guardian stayed close to the target; the other stood back and kept an eye on the surroundings.

Boringly, those holding these positions were called near and far guards.

"You'll probably always be near guard," Dimitri told me. "You're female and the same age as the princess. You can stay close to her without attracting any attention."

"And I can't ever take my eyes off her," I noted. "Or you."

Spiridon laughed again and elbowed Dimitri. "You've got a star student there. Did you give her a stake?"

"No. She's not ready."

"I would be if *someone* would show me how to use one," I argued. I knew every guardian in the van had a stake and a gun concealed on him.

"More to it than just using the stake," said Dimitri in his old-and-wise way. "You've still got to subdue them. And you've got to bring yourself to kill them."

"Why wouldn't I kill them?"

"Most Strigoi used to be Moroi who purposely turned. Sometimes they're Moroi or dhampirs turned by force. It doesn't matter. There's a strong chance you might know one of them. Could you kill someone you used to know?"

This trip was getting less fun by the minute.

"I guess so. I'd have to, right? If it's them or Lissa . . . "

"You might still hesitate," said Dimitri. "And that hesitation could kill you. And her."

"Then how do you make sure you don't hesitate?"

"You have to keep telling yourself that they *aren't* the same people you knew. They've become something dark and twisted. Something unnatural. You have to let go of attachments and do what's right. If they have any grain of their former selves left, they'll probably be grateful."

"Grateful for me killing them?"

"If someone turned you into a Strigoi, what would you want?" he asked.

I didn't know how to answer that, so I said nothing. Never taking his eyes off me, he kept pushing.

"What would you want if you knew you were going to be converted into a Strigoi against your will? If you knew you would lose all sense of your old morals and understanding of what's right and wrong? If you knew you'd live the rest of your life—your immortal life—killing innocent people? What would you want?"

The van had grown uncomfortably silent. Staring at Dimitri, burdened by all those questions, I suddenly understood why he and I had this weird attraction, good looks aside.

I'd never met anyone else who took being a guardian so seriously, who understand all the life-and-death consequences. Certainly no one my age did yet; Mason hadn't been able to understand why I couldn't relax and drink at the party. Dimitri had said I grasped my duty better than many older guardians, and I didn't get why—especially when they would have seen so much more death and danger. But I knew in that moment that he was right, that I had some weird sense of how life and death and good and evil worked with each other.

So did he. We might get lonely sometimes. We might have

to put our "fun" on hold. We might not be able to live the lives we wanted for ourselves. But that was the way it had to be. We understood each other, understood that we had others to protect. Our lives would never be easy.

And making decisions like this one was part of that.

"If I became Strigoi . . . I'd want someone to kill me."

"So would I," he said quietly. I could tell that he'd had the same flash of realization I'd just had, that same sense of connection between us.

"It reminds me of Mikhail hunting Sonya," murmured Victor thoughtfully.

"Who are Mikhail and Sonya?" asked Lissa.

Victor looked surprised. "Why, I thought you knew. Sonya Karp."

"Sonya Kar . . . you mean, Ms. Karp? What about her?" She looked back and forth between me and her uncle.

"She . . . became Strigoi," I said, not meeting Lissa's eyes. "By choice."

I'd known Lissa would find out some day. It was the final piece of Ms. Karp's saga, a secret I'd kept to myself. A secret that worried me constantly. Lissa's face and bond registered complete and utter shock, growing in intensity when she realized I'd known and never told.

"But I don't know who Mikhail is," I added.

"Mikhail Tanner," said Spiridon.

"Oh. Guardian Tanner. He was here before we left." I frowned. "Why is he chasing Ms. Karp?"

"To kill her," said Dimitri flatly. "They were lovers."

The entire Strigoi thing shifted into new focus for me. Running into a Strigoi I knew during the heat of battle was one thing. Purposely hunting down someone . . . someone I'd loved. Well, I didn't know if I could do that, even if it was technically the right thing.

"Perhaps it is time to talk about something else," said Victor gently. "Today isn't a day to dwell on depressing topics."

I think all of us felt relieved to get to the mall. Shifting into my bodyguard role, I stuck by Lissa's side as we wandered from store to store, looking at all the new styles that were out there. It was nice to be in public again and do to something with her that was just *fun* and didn't involve any of the dark, twisted politics of the Academy. It was almost like old times. I'd missed just hanging out. I'd missed my best friend.

Although it was only just past mid-November, the mall already had glittering holiday decorations up. I decided I had the best job ever. Admittedly, I did feel a little put out when I realized the older guardians got to stay in contact through cool little communication devices. When I protested my lack of one, Dimitri told me I'd learn better without one. If I could handle protecting Lissa the old-fashioned way, I could handle anything.

Victor and Spiridon stayed with us while Dimitri and Ben fanned out, somehow managing not to look like creepy stalker guys watching teenage girls.

"This is so you," said Lissa in Macy's, handing me a low-cut tank top embellished with lace. "I'll buy it for you."

I regarded it longingly, already picturing myself in it. Then, making my regular eye contact with Dimitri, I shook my head and handed it back. "Winter's coming. I'd get cold."

"Never stopped you before."

Shrugging, she hung it back up. She and Camille tried on a nonstop string of clothes, their massive allowances ensuring that price posed no problem. Lissa offered to buy me anything I wanted. We'd been generous with each other our whole lives, and I didn't hesitate to take her up on it. My choices surprised her.

"You've got three thermal shirts and a hoodie," she informed me, flipping through a stack of BCBG jeans. "You've gone all boring on me."

"Hey, I don't see you buying slutty tops."

"I'm not the one who wears them."

"Thanks a lot."

"You know what I mean. You're even wearing your hair up."

It was true. I'd taken Dimitri's advice and wrapped my hair up in a high bun, earning a smile when he'd seen me. If I'd had *molnija* marks, they would have shown.

Glancing around, she made sure none of the others could hear us. The feelings in the bond shifted to something more troubled.

"You knew about Ms. Karp."

"Yeah. I heard about it a month or so after she left."

Lissa tossed a pair of embroidered jeans over her arm, not looking at me. "Why didn't you tell me?"

"You didn't need to know."

"You didn't think I could handle it?"

I kept my face perfectly blank. As I stared at her, my mind was back in time, back to two years ago. I'd been on day two of my suspension for allegedly destroying Wade's room when a royal party visited the school. I'd been allowed to attend that reception too but had been under heavy guard to make sure I didn't "try anything."

Two guardians escorted me to the commons and talked quietly with each other along the way.

"She killed the doctor attending her and nearly took out half the patients and nurses on her way out."

"Do they have any idea where she went?"

"No, they're tracking her . . . but, well, you know how it is."

"I never expected her to do this. She never seemed like the type."

"Yeah, well, Sonya was crazy. Did you see how violent she was getting near the end? She was capable of anything."

I'd been trudging along miserably and jerked my head up.

"Sonya? You mean Ms. Karp?" I asked. "She killed somebody?"

The two guardians exchanged looks. Finally, one said gravely, "She became a Strigoi, Rose."

I stopped walking and stared. "Ms. Karp? No . . . she wouldn't have. . . ."

"I'm afraid so," the other one replied. "But . . . you should keep that to yourself. It's a tragedy. Don't make it school gossip."

I went through the rest of the night in a daze. Ms. Karp. Crazy Karp. She'd killed someone to become Strigoi. I couldn't believe it.

When the reception ended, I'd managed to sneak off from my guardians and steal a few precious moments with Lissa. The bond had grown strong by now, and I hadn't needed to see her face to know how miserable she was.

"What's wrong?" I asked her. We were in a corner of the hallway, just outside the commons.

Her eyes were blank. I could feel how she had a headache; its pain transferred to me. "I . . . I don't know. I just feel weird. I feel like I'm being followed, like I have to be careful, you know?"

I didn't know what to say. I didn't think she was being followed, but Ms. Karp used to say the same thing. Always paranoid. "It's probably nothing," I said lightly.

"Probably," she agreed. Her eyes suddenly narrowed. "But Wade isn't. He won't shut up about what happened. You can't believe the things he's saying about you."

I could, actually, but I didn't care. "Forget about him. He's nothing."

"I hate him," she said. Her voice was uncharacteristically sharp. "I'm on the committee with him for that fund-raiser, and I *hate* hearing him run his fat mouth every day and seeing him flirt with anything female that walks by. You shouldn't be punished for what he did. He needs to pay."

My mouth went dry. "It's okay . . . I don't care. Calm down, Liss."

"*I* care," she snapped, turning her anger on me. "I wish there was a way I could get back at him. Some way to hurt him like he hurt you." She put her hands behind her back and paced back and forth furiously, her steps hard and purposeful.

The hatred and anger boiled within her. I could feel it in the bond. It felt like a storm, and it scared the hell out of me. Wrapped around it all was an uncertainty, an instability that said Lissa didn't know what to do but that she wanted desperately to do something. Anything. My mind flashed to the night with the baseball bat. And then I thought about Ms. Karp. *She became a Strigoi, Rose.*

It was the scariest moment of my life. Scarier than seeing her in Wade's room. Scarier than seeing her heal that raven. Scarier than my capture by the guardians would be. Because just then, I didn't know my best friend. I didn't know what she was capable of. A year earlier, I would have laughed at anyone who said she'd want to go Strigoi. But a year earlier, I also would have laughed at anyone who said she'd want to cut her wrists or make someone "pay."

In that moment, I suddenly believed she might do the impossible. And I had to make sure she didn't. *Save her. Save her from herself.*

"We're leaving," I said, taking her arm and steering her down the hall. "Right now."

Confusion momentarily replaced her anger. "What do you mean? You want to go to the woods or something?"

I didn't answer. Something in my attitude or words must

have startled her, because she didn't question me as I led us out of the commons, cutting across campus toward the parking lot where visitors came. It was filled with cars belonging to tonight's guests. One of them was a large Lincoln Town Car, and I watched as its chauffeur started it up.

"Someone's leaving early," I said, peering at him from around a cluster of bushes. I glanced behind us and saw nothing. "They'll probably be here any minute."

Lissa caught on. "When you said, 'We're leaving,' you meant . . . no. Rose, we can't leave the Academy. We'd never get through the wards and checkpoints."

"We don't have to," I said firmly. "He does."

"But how does that help us?"

I took a deep breath, regretting what I had to say but seeing it as the lesser of evils. "You know how you made Wade do those things?"

She flinched but nodded.

"I need you to do the same thing. Go up to that guy and tell him to hide us in his trunk."

Shock and fear poured out of her. She didn't understand, and she was scared. Extremely scared. She'd been scared for weeks now, ever since the healing and the moods and Wade. She was fragile and on the edge of something neither of us understood. But through all of that, she trusted me. She believed I would keep her safe.

"Okay," she said. She took a few steps toward him, then looked back at me. "Why? Why are we doing this?"

I thought about Lissa's anger, her desire to do *anything* to get back at Wade. And I thought about Ms. Karp—pretty, unstable Ms. Karp—going Strigoi. "I'm taking care of you," I said. "You don't need to know anything else."

At the mall in Missoula, standing between racks of designer clothes, Lissa asked again, "Why didn't you tell me?"

"You didn't need to know," I repeated.

She headed toward the dressing room, still whispering with me. "You're worried I'm going to lose it. Are you worried I'll go Strigoi too?"

"No. No way. That was all her. You'd never do that."

"Even if I was crazy?"

"No," I said, trying to make a joke. "You'd just shave your head and live with thirty cats."

Lissa's feelings grew darker, but she didn't say anything else. Stopping just outside the dressing room, she pulled a black dress off the rack. She brightened a little.

"This is the dress you were born for. I don't care how practical you are now."

Made of silky black material, the dress was strapless and sleek, falling about to the knees. Although it had a slight flair at the hemline, the rest looked like it would definitely manage some serious clinging action. Super sexy. Maybe even challenge-the-school-dress-code sexy.

"That is my dress," I admitted. I kept staring at it, wanting it so badly that it ached in my chest. This was the kind of dress that changed the world. The kind of dress that started religions.

Lissa pulled out my size. "Try it on."

I shook my head and started to put it back. "I can't. It would compromise you. One dress isn't worth your grisly death."

"Then we'll just get it without you trying it on." She bought the dress.

The afternoon continued, and I found myself growing tired. Always watching and being on guard suddenly became a lot less fun. When we hit our last stop, a jewelry store, I felt kind of glad.

"Here you go," said Lissa, pointing at one of the cases. "The necklace made to go with your dress."

I looked. A thin gold chain with a gold-and-diamond rose pendant. Emphasis on the diamond part.

"I hate rose stuff."

Lissa had always loved getting me rose things—just to see my reaction, I think. When she saw the necklace's price, her smile fell away.

"Oh, look at that. Even you have limits," I teased. "Your crazy spending is stopped at last."

We waited for Victor and Natalie to finish up. He was apparently buying her something, and she looked like she might grow wings and fly away with happiness. I was glad. She'd been dying for his attention. Hopefully he was buying her something extra-expensive to make up for it.

We rode home in tired silence, our sleep schedules all messed up by the daylight trip. Sitting next to Dimitri, I leaned back against the seat and yawned, very aware that our arms were touching. That feeling of closeness and connection burned between us.

"So, I can't ever try on clothes again?" I asked quietly, not wanting to wake up the others. Victor and the guardians were awake, but the girls had fallen asleep.

"When you aren't on duty, you can. You can do it during your time off."

"I don't ever want time off. I want to always take care of Lissa." I yawned again. "Did you see that dress?"

"I saw the dress."

"Did you like it?"

He didn't answer. I took that as a yes.

"Am I going to endanger my reputation if I wear it to the dance?"

When he spoke, I could barely hear him. "You'll endanger the school."

I smiled and fell asleep.

When I woke up, my head rested against his shoulder. That long coat of his—the duster—covered me like a blanket. The van had stopped; we were back at school. I pulled the duster off and climbed out after him, suddenly feeling wide awake and happy. Too bad my freedom was about to end.

"Back to prison," I sighed, walking beside Lissa toward the commons. "Maybe if you fake a heart attack, I can make a break for it."

"Without your clothes?" She handed me a bag, and I

swung it around happily. "I can't wait to see the dress."

"Me either. If they let me go. Kirova's still deciding if I've been good enough."

"Show her those boring shirts you bought. She'll go into a coma. I'm about ready to."

I laughed and hopped up onto one of the wooden benches, pacing her as I walked along it. I jumped back down when I reached the end. "They aren't *that* boring."

"I don't know what to think of this new, responsible Rose."

I hopped up onto another bench. "I'm not that responsible."

"Hey," called Spiridon. He and the rest of the group trailed behind us. "You're still on duty. No fun allowed up there."

"No fun here," I called back, hearing the laughter in his voice. "I swear—shit."

I was up on a third bench, near the end of it. My muscles tensed, ready to jump back down. Only when I tried to, my foot didn't go with me. The wood, at one moment seemingly hard and solid, gave way beneath me, almost as though made of paper. It disintegrated. My foot went through, my ankle getting caught in the hole while the rest of my body tried to go in another direction. The bench held me, swinging my body to the ground while still seizing my foot. My ankle bent in an unnatural direction. I crashed down. I heard a cracking sound that wasn't the wood. The worst pain of my life shot through my body.

And then I blacked out.

EIGHTEEN

I WOKE UP STARING AT the boring white ceiling of the clinic. A filtered light—soothing to Moroi patients—shone down on me. I felt strange, kind of disoriented, but I didn't hurt.

"Rose."

The voice was like silk on my skin. Gentle. Rich. Turning my head, I met Dimitri's dark eyes. He sat in a chair beside the bed I lay on, his shoulder-length brown hair hanging forward and framing his face.

"Hey," I said, my voice coming out as a croak.

"How do you feel?"

"Weird. Kind of groggy."

"Dr. Olendzki gave you something for the pain—you seemed pretty bad when we brought you in."

"I don't remember that. . . . How long have I been out?"

"A few hours."

"Must have been strong. Must still be strong." Some of the details came back. The bench. My ankle getting caught. I couldn't remember much after that. Feeling hot and cold and then hot again. Tentatively, I tried moving the toes on my healthy foot. "I don't hurt at all."

He shook his head. "No. Because you weren't seriously injured."

The sound of my ankle cracking came back to me. "Are you sure? I remember . . . the way it bent. No. Something must be broken." I manage to sit up, so I could look at my ankle. "Or at least sprained."

He moved forward to stop me. "Be careful. Your ankle might be fine, but you're probably still a little out of it."

I carefully shifted to the edge of the bed and looked down. My jeans were rolled up. The ankle looked a little red, but I had no bruises or serious marks.

"God, I got lucky. If I'd hurt it, it would have put me out of practice for a while."

Smiling, he returned to his chair. "I know. You kept telling me that while I was carrying you. You were very upset."

"You . . . you carried me here?"

"After we broke the bench apart and freed your foot."

Man. I'd missed out on a lot. The only thing better than imagining Dimitri carrying me in his arms was imagining him shirtless while carrying me in his arms.

Then the reality of the situation hit me.

"I was taken down by a bench," I groaned.

"What?"

"I survived the whole day guarding Lissa, and you guys said I did a good job. Then, I get back here and meet my downfall in the form of a bench." Ugh. "Do you know how embarrassing it is? And all those guys saw, too."

"It wasn't your fault," he said. "No one knew the bench was rotted. It looked fine."

"Still. I should have just stuck to the sidewalk like a normal person. The other novices are going to give me shit when I get back."

His lips held back a smile. "Maybe presents will cheer you up."

I sat up straighter. "Presents?"

The smile escaped, and he handed me a small box with a piece of paper.

"This is from Prince Victor."

Surprised that Victor would have given me anything, I read the note. It was just a few lines, hastily scrawled in pen.

> *Rose—*
>
> *I'm very happy to see you didn't suffer any serious injuries from your fall. Truly, it is a miracle. You lead a charmed life, and Vasilisa is lucky to have you.*

"That's nice of him," I said, opening the box. Then I saw what was inside. "Whoa. Very nice."

It was the rose necklace, the one Lissa had wanted to get me but couldn't afford. I held it up, looping its chain over my hand so the glittering, diamond-covered rose hung free.

"This is pretty extreme for a get-well present," I noted, recalling the price.

"He actually bought it in honor of you doing so well on your first day as an official guardian. He saw you and Lissa looking at it."

"Wow." It was all I could say. "I don't think I did *that* good of a job."

"I do."

Grinning, I placed the necklace back in the box and set it on a nearby table. "You did say 'presents,' right? Like more than one?"

He laughed outright, and the sound wrapped around me like a caress. God, I loved the sound of his laugh. "This is from me."

He handed me a small, plain bag. Puzzled and excited, I opened it up. Lip gloss, the kind I liked. I'd complained to him a number of times how I was running out, but I'd never thought he was paying attention.

"How'd you manage to buy this? I saw you the whole time at the mall."

"Guardian secrets."

"What's this for? For my first day?"

"No," he said simply. "Because I thought it would make you happy."

Without even thinking about it, I leaned forward and hugged him. "Thank you."

Judging from his stiff posture, I'd clearly caught him by surprise. And yeah . . . I'd actually caught myself by surprise, too. But he relaxed a few moments later, and when he reached around and rested his hands on my lower back, I thought I was going to die.

"I'm glad you're better," he said. His mouth sounded like it was almost in my hair, just above my ear. "When I saw you fall . . ."

"You thought, 'Wow, she's a loser.'"

"That's not what I thought."

He pulled back slightly, so he could see me better, but we didn't say anything. His eyes were so dark and deep that I wanted to dive right in. Staring at them made me feel warm all over, like they had flames inside. Slowly, carefully, those long fingers of his reached out and traced the edge of my cheekbone, moving up the side of my face. At the first touch of his skin on mine, I shivered. He wound a lock of my hair around one finger, just like he had in the gym.

Swallowing, I dragged my eyes up from his lips. I'd been contemplating what it'd be like to kiss him. The thought both excited and scared me, which was stupid. I'd kissed a lot of guys and never thought much about it. No reason another one—even an older one—should be that big of a deal. Yet the thought of him closing the distance and bringing his lips to mine made the world start spinning.

A soft knock sounded at the door, and I hastily leaned back. Dr. Olendzki stuck her head in. "I thought I heard you talking. How do you feel?"

She walked over and made me lie back down. Touching and bending my ankle, she assessed it for damage and finally shook her head when finished.

"You're lucky. With all the noise you made coming in here, I thought your foot had been amputated. Must have just been shock." She stepped back. "I'd feel better if you sat out from your normal trainings tomorrow, but otherwise, you're good to go."

I breathed a sigh of relief. I didn't remember my hysteria—and was actually kind of embarrassed that I'd thrown such a fit—but I had been right about the problems this would have caused me if I'd broken or sprained it. I couldn't afford to lose any time here; I needed to take my trials and graduate in the spring.

Dr. Olendzki gave me the okay to go and then left the room. Dimitri walked over to another chair and brought me my shoes and coat. Looking at him, I felt a warm flush sweep me as I recalled what had happened before the doctor had entered.

He watched as I slipped one of the shoes on. "You have a guardian angel."

"I don't believe in angels," I told him. "I believe in what I can do for myself."

"Well then, you have an amazing body." I glanced up at him with a questioning look. "For healing, I mean. I heard about the accident. . . ."

He didn't specify which accident it was, but it could be only one. Talking about it normally bothered me, but with him, I felt I could say anything.

"Everyone said I shouldn't have survived," I explained. "Because of where I sat and the way the car hit the tree. Lissa was really the only one in a secure spot. She and I walked away with only a few scratches."

"And you don't believe in angels or miracles."

"Nope. I—"

Truly, it is a miracle. You lead a charmed life. . . .

And just like that, a million thoughts came slamming into my head. Maybe . . . maybe I had a guardian angel after all. . . .

Dimitri immediately noticed the shift in my feelings. "What's wrong?"

Reaching out with my mind, I tried to expand the bond and shake off the lingering effects of the pain medication. Some more of Lissa's feelings came through to me. Anxious. Upset.

"Where's Lissa? Was she here?"

"I don't know where she is. She wouldn't leave your side while I brought you in. She stayed right next the bed, right up until the doctor came in. You calmed down when she sat next to you."

I closed my eyes and felt like I might faint. I had calmed down when Lissa sat next to me because she'd taken the pain away. She'd healed me. . . .

Just as she had the night of the accident.

It all made sense now. I shouldn't have survived. Everyone had said so. Who knew what kind of injuries I'd actually suffered? Internal bleeding. Broken bones. It didn't matter because Lissa had fixed it, just like she'd fixed everything else. That was why she'd been leaning over me when I woke up.

It was also probably why she'd passed out when they took her to the hospital. She'd been exhausted for days afterward. And that was when her depression had begun. It had seemed like a normal reaction after losing her family, but now I wondered if there was more to it, if healing me had played a role.

Opening my mind again, I reached out to her, needing to find her. If she'd healed me, there was no telling what shape she could be in now. Her moods and magic were linked, and this had been a pretty intense show of magic.

The drug was almost gone from my system, and like that, I snapped into her. It was almost easy now. A tidal wave of emotions hit me, worse than when her nightmares engulfed me. I'd never felt such intensity from her before.

She sat in the chapel's attic, crying. She didn't entirely know why she was crying either. She felt happy and relieved that I'd been unharmed, that she'd been able to heal me. At the same time, she felt weak in both body and mind. She burned inside, like she'd lost part of herself. She worried I'd be mad because she'd used her powers. She dreaded going through another school day tomorrow, pretending she liked being with a crowd who had no other interests aside from spending their families' money and making fun of those less beautiful and less popular. She didn't want to go to the dance with Aaron and see him watch her so adoringly—and feel him touching her—when she felt only friendship for him.

Most of these were all normal concerns, but they hit her hard, harder than they would an ordinary person, I thought. She couldn't sort through them or figure out how to fix them.

"You okay?"

She looked up and brushed the hair away from where it stuck to her wet cheeks. Christian stood in the entrance to the attic. She hadn't even heard him come up the stairs. She'd been too lost in her own grief. A flicker of both longing and anger sparked within her.

"I'm fine," she snapped. Sniffling, she tried to stop her tears, not wanting him to see her weak.

Leaning against the wall, he crossed his arms and wore an unreadable expression. "Do . . . do you want to talk?"

"Oh . . ." She laughed harshly. "You want to talk now? After I tried so many times—"

"I didn't want that! That was Rose—"

He cut himself off and I flinched. I was totally busted.

Lissa stood up and strode toward him. "What about Rose?"

"Nothing." His mask of indifference slipped back into place. "Forget it."

"*What about Rose?*" She stepped closer. Even through her anger, she still felt that inexplicable attraction to him. And then she understood. "She *made* you, didn't she? She told you to stop talking to me?"

He stared stonily ahead. "It was probably for the best. I would have just messed things up for you. You wouldn't be where you are now."

"What's that supposed to mean?"

"What do you think it means? God. People live or die at your command now, Your Highness."

"You're being kind of melodramatic."

"Am I? All day, I hear people talking about what you're doing and what you're thinking and what you're wearing.

Whether you'll approve. Who you like. Who you hate. They're your puppets."

"It's not like that. Besides, I had to do it. To get back at Mia . . ."

Rolling his eyes, he looked away from her. "You don't even know what you're getting back at her for."

Lissa's anger flared. "She set up Jesse and Ralf to say those things about Rose! I couldn't let her get away with that."

"Rose is tough. She would have gotten over it."

"You didn't see her," she replied obstinately. "She was crying."

"So? People cry. *You're* crying."

"Not Rose."

He turned back to her, a dark smile curling his lips. "I've never seen anything like you two. Always so worried about each other. I get her thing—some kind of weird guardian hang-up—but you're just the same."

"She's my friend."

"I guess it's that simple. I wouldn't know." He sighed, momentarily thoughtful, then snapped back to sarcastic mode. "Anyway. Mia. So you got back at her over what she did to Rose. But you're missing the point. *Why* did she do it?"

Lissa frowned. "Because she was jealous about me and Aaron—"

"More to it than that, Princess. What did she have to be jealous about? She already had him. She didn't need to attack you to drive that home. She could have just made a big show of being all over him. Sort of like you are now," he added wryly.

"Okay. What else is there, then? Why did she want to ruin my life? I never did anything to her—before all this, I mean."

He leaned forward, crystal-blue eyes boring into hers.

"You're right. You didn't—but your brother did."

Lissa pulled away from him. "You don't know anything about my brother."

"I know he screwed Mia over. Literally."

"Stop it, stop lying."

"I'm not. Swear to God or whoever else you want to believe in. I used to talk to Mia now and then, back when she was a freshman. She wasn't very popular, but she was smart. Still is. She used to work on a lot of committees with royals—dances and stuff. I don't know all of it. But she got to know your brother on one of those, and they sort of got together."

"They did not. I would have known. Andre would have told me."

"Nope. He didn't tell anyone. He told her not to either. He convinced her it should be some kind of romantic secret when really, he just didn't want any of his friends to find out he was getting naked with a non-royal freshman."

"If Mia told you that, she was making it up," exclaimed Lissa.

"Yeah, well, I don't think she was making it up when I saw her crying. He got tired of her after a few weeks and dumped her. Told her she was too young and that he couldn't really get serious with someone who wasn't from a good family. From what I understand, he wasn't even nice about it either—didn't even bother with the 'let's be friends' stuff."

Lissa pushed herself into Christian's face. "You didn't even *know* Andre! He would never have done that."

"*You* didn't know him. I'm sure he was nice to his baby sister; I'm sure he loved you. But in school, with his friends, he was just as much of a jerk as the rest of the royals. I saw him because I see everything. Easy when no one notices you."

She held back a sob, unsure whether to believe him or not. "So *this* is why Mia hates me?"

"Yup. She hates you because of him. That, and because you're royal and she's insecure around all royals, which is why she worked so hard to claw up the ranks and be their friend. I think it's a coincidence that she ended up with your ex-boyfriend, but now that you're back, that probably made it worse. Between stealing him and spreading those stories about her parents, you guys really picked the best ways to make her suffer. Nice work."

The smallest pang of guilt lurched inside of her. "I still think you're lying."

"I'm a lot of things, but I'm not a liar. That's your department. And Rose's."

"We don't—"

"Exaggerate stories about people's families? Say that you hate me? Pretend to be friends with people you think are stupid? Date a guy you don't like?"

"I like him."

"Like or *like*?"

"Oh, there's a difference?"

"Yes. *Like* is when you date a big, blond moron and laugh at his stupid jokes."

Then, out of nowhere, he leaned forward and kissed her. It was hot and fast and furious, an outpouring of the rage and passion and longing that Christian always kept locked inside of him. Lissa had never been kissed like that, and I felt her respond to it, respond to *him*—how he made her feel so much more alive than Aaron or anyone else could.

Christian pulled back from the kiss but still kept his face next to hers.

"That's what you do with someone you *like*."

Lissa's heart pounded with both anger and desire. "Well, I don't like or *like* you. And I think you and Mia are both lying about Andre. *Aaron* would never make up anything like that."

"That's because Aaron doesn't say anything that requires words of more than one syllable."

She pulled away. "Get out. Get away from me."

He looked around comically. "You can't throw me out. We both signed the lease."

"Get. Out!" she yelled. "I hate you!"

He bowed. "Anything you want, Your Highness." With a final dark look, he left the attic.

Lissa sank to her knees, letting out the tears she'd held

back from him. I could barely make sense out of all the things hurting her. God only knew things upset me—like the Jesse incident—but they didn't attack me in the same way. They swirled within her, beating at her brain. The stories about Andre. Mia's hate. Christian's kiss. Healing me. This, I realized, was what real depression felt like. What madness felt like.

Overcome, drowning in her own pain, Lissa made the only decision she could. The only thing she could do to channel all of these emotions. She opened up her purse and found the tiny razor blade she always carried. . . .

Sickened, yet unable to break away, I felt as she cut her left arm, making perfectly even marks, watching as the blood flowed across her white skin. As always, she avoided veins, but her cuts were deeper this time. The cutting stung horribly, yet in doing it, she was able to focus on the physical pain, distract herself from the mental anguish so that she could feel like she was in control.

Drops of blood splattered onto the dusty floor, and her world began spinning. Seeing her own blood intrigued her. She had taken blood from others her entire life. Me. The feeders. Now, here it was, leaking out. With a nervous giggle, she decided it was funny. Maybe by letting it out, she was giving it back to those she'd stolen it from. Or maybe she was wasting it, wasting the sacred Dragomir blood that everyone obsessed over.

I'd forced my way into her head, and now I couldn't get

out. Her emotions had ensnared me now—they were too strong and too powerful. But I had to escape—I knew it with every ounce of my being. I had to stop her. She was too weak from the healing to lose this much blood. It was time to tell someone.

Breaking out at last, I found myself back in the clinic. Dimitri's hands were on me, gently shaking me as he said my name over and over in an effort to get my attention. Dr. Olendzki stood beside him, face dark and concerned.

I stared at Dimitri, truly seeing how much he worried and cared about me. Christian had told me to get help, to go to someone I trusted about Lissa. I'd ignored the advice because I didn't trust anyone except her. But looking at Dimitri now, feeling that sense of understanding we shared, I knew that I did trust someone else.

I felt my voice crack as I spoke. "I know where she is. Lissa. We have to help her."

NINETEEN

IT'S HARD TO SAY WHAT finally made me do it. I'd held on to so many secrets for so long, doing what I believed best protected Lissa. But hiding her cutting did nothing to protect her. I hadn't been able to make her stop—and really, I now wondered if it was my fault she'd ever started. None of this had happened until she healed me in the accident. What if she'd left me injured? Maybe I would have recovered. Maybe she would be all right today.

I stayed in the clinic while Dimitri went to get Alberta. He hadn't hesitated for a second when I told him where she was. I'd said she was in danger, and he'd left immediately.

Everything after that moved like some sort of slow-motion nightmare. The minutes dragged on while I waited. When he finally returned with an unconscious Lissa, a flurry arose at the clinic, one everyone wanted me kept out of. She had lost a lot of blood, and while they had a feeder on hand right away, rousing her to enough consciousness to drink proved difficult. It wasn't until the middle of the Academy's night that someone decided she was stable enough for me to visit.

"Is it true?" she asked when I walked into the room. She lay on the bed, wrists heavily bandaged. I knew they'd put a lot of blood back into her, but she still looked pale to me. "They said it was you. You told them."

"I had to," I said, afraid to get too close. "Liss . . . you cut yourself worse than you ever have. And after healing me . . . and then everything with Christian . . . you couldn't handle it. You needed help."

She closed her eyes. "Christian. You know about that. Of course you do. You know about everything."

"I'm sorry. I just wanted to help."

"What happened to what Ms. Karp said? About keeping it all secret?"

"She was talking about the other stuff. I don't think she'd want you to keep cutting yourself."

"Did you tell them about the 'other stuff'?"

I shook my head. "Not yet."

She turned toward me, eyes cold. "'Yet.' But you're going to."

"I have to. You can heal other people . . . but it's killing you."

"I healed *you.*"

"I would have been okay eventually. The ankle would have healed. It's not worth what it does to you. And I think I know how it started . . . when you first healed me. . . ."

I explained my revelation about the accident and how all of her powers and depression had started after that. I also pointed out how our bond had formed after the accident too, though I didn't fully understand why yet.

"I don't know what's going on, but this is beyond us. We need someone's help."

"They'll take me away," she said flatly. "Like Ms. Karp."

"I think they'll try to help you. They were all really worried. Liss, I'm doing this for you. I just want you to be okay."

She turned away from me. "Get out, Rose."

I did.

They released her the next morning on the condition that she'd have to come back for daily visits to the counselor. Dimitri told me they also planned on putting her on some sort of medication to help with the depression. I wasn't a big fan of pills, but I'd cheer on anything that would help her.

Unfortunately, some sophomore had been in the clinic for an asthma attack. He'd seen her come in with Dimitri and Alberta. He didn't know why she'd been admitted, but that hadn't stopped him from telling people in his hall what he'd seen. They then told others at breakfast. By lunch, all the upperclassmen knew about the late-night clinic visit.

And more importantly, everyone knew she wasn't speaking to me.

Just like that, whatever social headway I'd made plummeted. She didn't outright condemn me, but her silence spoke legions, and people behaved accordingly.

The whole day, I walked around the Academy like a ghost. People watched and occasionally spoke to me, but few made much more effort than that. They followed Lissa's lead, imitating her silence. No one was openly mean to me—they probably didn't want to risk it in case she and I patched things up. Still, I heard "blood whore" whispered here and there when someone thought I wasn't listening.

Mason would have welcomed me to his lunch table, but some of his friends might not have been so nice. I didn't want to be the cause of any fights between him and them. So I chose Natalie instead.

"I heard Lissa tried to run away again, and you stopped her," Natalie said. No one had a clue why she'd been in the clinic yet. I hoped it stayed that way.

Running away? Where in the world had that come from? "Why would she do that?"

"I don't know." She lowered her voice. "Why'd she leave before? It's just what I heard."

That story raged on as the day passed, as did all sorts of rumors about why Lissa might have gone to the med clinic. Pregnancy and abortion theories were eternally popular. Some whispered she might have gotten Victor's disease. No one even came close to guessing the truth.

Leaving our last class as quickly as possible, I was astonished when Mia started walking toward me.

"What do you want?" I demanded. "I can't come out and play today, little girl."

"You sure have an attitude for someone who doesn't exist right now."

"As opposed to you?" I asked. Remembering what Christian had said, I did feel a little sorry for her. That guilt disappeared after I took one look at her face. She might have been a victim, but now she was a monster. There was a cold, cunning look about her, very different from the desperate and depressed one from the other day. She hadn't stayed beaten after what Andre had done to her—if that was even true, and I believed it was—and I doubted she would with Lissa either. Mia was a survivor.

"She got rid of you, and you're too high and mighty to admit it." Her blue eyes practically bugged out. "Don't you want to get back at her?"

"Are you more psycho than usual? She's my best friend. And why are you still following me?"

Mia *tsk*ed. "She doesn't act like it. Come on, tell me what happened at the clinic. It's something big, isn't it? She really is pregnant, right? Tell me what it is."

"Go away."

"If you tell me, I'll get Jesse and Ralf to say they made all that stuff up."

I stopped walking and spun around to face her. Scared, she took a few steps backward. She must have recalled some of my past threats of physical violence.

"I already know they made it all up, because I didn't *do* any of it. And if you try to turn me against Lissa one more time, the stories are going to be about *you* bleeding, because I'll have ripped your throat out!"

My voice grew louder with each word until I practically shouted. Mia stepped back further, clearly terrified.

"You really are crazy. No wonder she dropped you." She shrugged. "Whatever. I'll find out what's going on without you."

When the dance came that weekend, I decided I really didn't want to go. It had sounded stupid to begin with, and I'd only been interested in going to the after-parties anyway. But without Lissa, I wasn't likely to gain admission to those. Instead, I holed up in my room, trying—and failing—to do some homework. Through the bond, I felt all sorts of mixed emotions from her, particularly anxiety and excitement. It had to be hard hanging out all night with a guy you didn't really like.

About ten minutes after the dance's start time, I decided to clean up and take a shower. When I came back down the hall from the bathroom, a towel wrapped around my head, I saw Mason standing outside my door. He wasn't exactly dressed up, but he also wasn't wearing jeans. It was a start.

"There you are, party girl. I was about ready to give up."

"Did you start another fire? No guys allowed in this hall."

"Whatever. Like that makes a difference." True. The school might be able to keep Strigoi out, but they did a horrible job at keeping the rest of us away from each other. "Let me in. You've got to get ready."

It took me a minute to realize what he meant. "No. I'm not going."

"Come on," he prodded, following me inside. "'Cause you

had a fight with Lissa? You guys are going to make up soon. No reason for you to stay here all night. If you don't want to be around her, Eddie's getting a group together over in his room later."

My old, fun-loving spirit perked its head up just a bit. No Lissa. Probably no royals. "Yeah?"

Seeing that he was starting to get me, Mason grinned. Looking at his eyes, I realized again how much he liked me. And again I wondered, Why couldn't I just have a normal boyfriend? Why did I want my hot, older mentor—the mentor I'd probably end up getting fired?

"It'll just be novices," Mason continued, oblivious to my thoughts. "And I have a surprise for you when we get there."

"Is it in a bottle?" If Lissa wanted to ignore me, I had no reason to keep myself sober.

"No, that's at Eddie's. Hurry up and get dressed. I know you aren't wearing that."

I looked down at my ripped jeans and University of Oregon T-shirt. Yeah. Definitely not wearing this.

Fifteen minutes later, we cut across the quad back over to the commons, laughing as we recounted how a particularly clumsy classmate of ours had given himself a black eye in practice this week. Moving quickly over the frozen ground wasn't easy in heels, and he kept grabbing my arm to keep me from falling over, half-dragging me along. It made us laugh that much more. A happy feeling started to well up in me—I wasn't entirely rid of the ache for Lissa, but this was a start.

Maybe I didn't have her and her friends, but I had my own friends. It was also very likely that I was going to get head-over-heels drunk tonight, which, while not a great way to solve my problems, would at least be really fun. Yeah. My life could be worse.

Then we ran into Dimitri and Alberta.

They were on their way somewhere else, talking guardian business. Alberta smiled when she saw us, giving us the kind of indulgent look older people always give to younger people who appear to be having fun and acting silly. Like she thought we were cute. The nerve. We stumbled to a halt, and Mason put a hand on my arm to steady me.

"Mr. Ashford, Miss Hathaway. I'm surprised you aren't already in the commons."

Mason gave her an angelic, teacher's-pet smile. "Got delayed, Guardian Petrov. You know how it is with girls. Always got to look perfect. You especially must know all about that."

Normally I would have elbowed him for saying something so stupid, but I was staring at Dimitri and incapable of speech. Perhaps more importantly, he was staring at me too.

I had on the black dress, and it was everything I'd hoped it could be. In fact, it was a wonder Alberta didn't call me on the dress code right there and then. The fabric clung everywhere, and no Moroi girl's chest could have held this dress up. Victor's rose hung around my neck, and I'd done a hasty blow-dry of my hair, leaving it down the way I knew

Dimitri liked it. I hadn't worn tights because no one wore tights with dresses like this anymore, so my feet were freezing in the heels. All for the sake of looking good.

And I was pretty sure I looked damn good, but Dimitri's face wasn't giving anything away. He just looked at me—and looked and looked. Maybe that said something about my appearance in and of itself. Remembering how Mason sort of held my hand, I pulled away from him. He and Alberta finished up their joking remarks, and we all went our separate ways.

Music blasted inside the commons when we arrived, white Christmas lights and—ugh—a disco ball casting the only light in the otherwise darkened room. Gyrating bodies, mostly underclassmen, packed the dance floor. Those who were our age stood in too-cool clusters along the edges of the room, waiting for an opportune time to sneak off. An assortment of chaperones, guardians and Moroi teachers alike, patrolled around, breaking up those dancers who did a little too much gyrating.

When I saw Kirova in a sleeveless plaid dress, I turned to Mason and said, "Are you sure we can't hit the hard liquor yet?"

He snickered and took my hand again. "Come on, time for your surprise."

Letting him lead me, I walked across the room, cutting through a cluster of freshmen who looked way too young to be doing the kind of pelvic thrusts they were attempting.

Where were the chaperones when you needed them? Then I saw where he was leading me and came to a screeching halt.

"No," I said, not budging when he tugged my hand.

"Come on, it's going to be great."

"You're taking me to Jesse and Ralf. The only way I can *ever* be seen with them is if I've got a blunt object, and I'm aiming between their legs."

He pulled me again. "Not anymore. Come on."

Reluctant, I finally started moving: my worst fears were realized when a few pairs eyes turned our way. Great. Everything was starting all over again. Jesse and Ralf didn't notice us at first, but when they did, an amusing array of expressions played over their faces. First they saw my body and the dress. Testosterone took over as pure male lust shone out of their faces. Then they seemed to realize it was me and promptly turned terrified. Cool.

Mason gave Jesse a sharp poke in the chest with the end of his finger. "All right, Zeklos. Tell her."

Jesse didn't say anything, and Mason repeated the gesture, only harder.

"Tell her."

Not meeting my eyes, Jesse mumbled, "Rose, we know none of that stuff happened."

I almost choked on my own laughter. "*Do* you? Wow. I'm really glad to hear that. Because you see, until you said that, I'd been thinking it *had* happened. Thank God you guys are here to set me straight and tell me what the hell I have or haven't done!"

They flinched, and Mason's light expression darkened to something harder.

"She knows that," he growled. "Tell her the rest."

Jesse sighed. "We did it because Mia told us to."

"And?" prompted Mason.

"And we're sorry."

Mason turned to Ralf. "I want to hear it from you, big boy."

Ralf wouldn't meet my eyes either, but he mumbled something that sounded vaguely like an apology.

Seeing them defeated, Mason turned chipper. "You haven't heard the best part yet."

I cut him a sidelong look. "Yeah? Like the part where we rewind time and none of this ever happened?"

"Next best thing." He tapped Jesse again. "Tell her. Tell her *why* you did it."

Jesse looked up and exchanged uneasy looks with Ralf.

"Boys," warned Mason, clearly delighted about something, "you're making Hathaway and me very angry. Tell her why you did it."

Wearing the look of one who realized things couldn't get any worse, Jesse finally met my eyes. "We did it because she slept with us. Both of us."

TWENTY

My MOUTH DROPPED OPEN. "Uh . . . wait . . . you mean *sex*?"

My astonishment prevented me from thinking of a better response. Mason thought it was hysterical. Jesse looked like he wanted to die.

"Of course I mean sex. She said she'd do it if we said that we'd . . . you know. . . ."

I made a face. "You guys didn't both, uh, do it at the same time, did you?"

"No," said Jesse in disgust. Ralf kind of looked like he wouldn't have minded.

"God," I muttered, pushing hair out of my face. "I can't believe she hates us that much."

"Hey," exclaimed Jesse, reading into my insinuation. "What's that supposed to mean? We're not that bad. And you and me—we were pretty close to—"

"No. We weren't *even* close to that." Mason laughed again, and something struck me. "If this . . . if this happened back then, though . . . she must have still been dating Aaron."

All three guys nodded.

"Oh. Whoa."

Mia *really* hated us. She'd just moved beyond poor-girl-wronged-by-girl's-brother and well into sociopath territory. She'd slept with these two and cheated on a boyfriend whom she seemed to adore.

Jesse and Ralf looked incredibly relieved when we walked away. Mason slung a lazy arm around my shoulders. "Well? What do you think? I rule, right? You can tell me. I won't mind."

I laughed. "How'd you finally find that out?"

"I called in a lot of favors. Used some threats. The fact that Mia can't retaliate helped too."

I recalled Mia accosting me the other day. I didn't think she was entirely helpless yet but didn't say so.

"They'll start telling people on Monday," he continued. "They promised. Everyone'll know by lunch."

"Why not now?" I asked sulkily. "They slept with a girl. Hurts her more than them."

"Yeah. True. They didn't want to deal with it tonight. You could start telling people if you wanted to. We could make a banner."

With as many times as Mia had called me a slut and a whore? Not a bad idea. "You got any markers and paper? . . ."

My words trailed off as I stared across the gym to where Lissa stood surrounded by admirers, Aaron's arm around her waist. She wore a sleek pink cotton sheath in a shade I never could have pulled off. Her blond hair had been pulled up in a bun that she'd used little crystal hairpins on. It almost looked like she wore a crown. Princess Vasilisa.

The same feelings as earlier hummed through to me, anxiety and excitement. She just couldn't quite enjoy herself tonight.

Watching her from the other side of the room, lurking in the darkness, was Christian. He practically blended into the shadows.

"Stop it," Mason chided me, seeing my stare. "Don't worry about her tonight."

"Hard not to."

"It makes you look all depressed. And you're too hot in that dress to look depressed. Come on, there's Eddie."

He dragged me away, but not before I cast one last glance at Lissa over my shoulder. Our eyes met briefly. Regret flashed through the bond.

But I pushed her out of my head—figuratively speaking—and managed to put on a good face when we joined a group of other novices. We earned a lot of mileage by telling them about the Mia scandal and, petty or not, seeing my name cleared and getting revenge on her felt amazingly good. And as those in our group wandered off and mingled with others, I could see the news spreading and spreading. So much for waiting until Monday.

Whatever. I didn't care. I was actually having a good time. I fell into my old role, happy to see I hadn't grown too dusty in making funny and flirty remarks. Yet, as time passed and Eddie's party grew closer, I started to feel Lissa's anxiety pick up in intensity. Frowning, I stopped talking and turned around, scanning the room for her.

There. She was still with a group of people, still the sun in her little solar system. But Aaron was leaning very close to her, saying something in her ear. A smile I recognized as fake was plastered across her face, and the annoyance and anxiety from her increased further.

Then it spiked. Mia had walked up to them.

Whatever she'd come to say, she didn't waste any time in saying it. With the eyes of Lissa's admirers on her, little Mia in her red dress gestured wildly, mouth working animatedly. I couldn't hear the words from across the room, but the feelings grew darker and darker through the bond.

"I've got to go," I told Mason.

I half walked, half ran over to Lissa's side, catching only the tail end of Mia's tirade. She was yelling at Lissa full force now and leaning into her face. From what I could tell, word must have reached her about Jesse and Ralf selling her out.

"—you and your slutty friend! I'm going to tell everyone what a psycho you are and how they had to lock you in the clinic because you're so crazy. They're putting you on medication. That's why you and Rose left before anyone else could find out you cut—"

Whoa, not good. Just like at our first meeting in the cafeteria, I grabbed her and jerked her away.

"Hey," I said. "Slutty friend here. Remember what I said about standing too close to her?"

Mia snarled, baring her fangs. As I'd noted before, I couldn't feel too sorry for her anymore. She was dangerous.

She had stooped low to get back at me. Now, somehow, she knew about Lissa and the cutting. *Really* knew, too; she wasn't just guessing. The information she had now sounded both like what the guardians on the scene had reported, as well as what I'd told them about Lissa's history. Maybe some confidential doctor's stuff too. Mia'd snagged the records somehow.

Lissa realized it too, and the look on her face—scared and fragile, no more princess—made my decision for me. It didn't matter that Kirova had spoken the other day about giving me my freedom, that I'd been having a good time, and that I could have let my worries go and partied tonight. I was going to ruin everything, right here and right now.

I'm really not good with impulse control.

I punched Mia as hard as I could—harder, I think, than I'd even hit Jesse. I heard a crunch as my fist impacted her nose, and blood spurted out. Someone screamed. Mia shrieked and flew backwards into some squealing girls who didn't want to get blood on their dresses. I swooped in after her, getting in one more good punch before somebody peeled me off her.

I didn't fight restraint as I had when they'd taken me from Mr. Nagy's classroom. I'd expected this as soon as I'd swung at her. Stopping all signs of resistance, I let two guardians lead me out of the dance while Ms. Kirova tried to bring some semblance of order. I didn't care what they did to me. Not anymore. Punish or expel. Whatever. I could handle—

Ahead of us, through the ebbing and flowing waves of students passing through the double doors, I saw a figure in pink dart out. Lissa. My own out-of-control emotions had overridden hers, but there they were, flooding back into me. Devastation. Despair. Everyone knew her secret now. She'd face more than just idle speculation. Pieces would fall together. She couldn't handle that.

Knowing I wasn't going anywhere, I frantically searched for some way to help her. A dark figure caught my eye. "Christian!" I yelled. He'd been staring at Lissa's retreating figure but glanced up at the sound of his name.

One of my escorts shushed me and took my arm. "Be quiet."

I ignored her. "Go after her," I called to Christian. "Hurry."

He just sat there, and I suppressed a groan.

"Go, you idiot!"

My guardians snapped at me to be quiet again, but something inside of Christian woke up. Springing up from his lounging position, he tore off in the direction Lissa had traveled.

No one wanted to deal with me that night. There'd be hell to pay tomorrow—I heard talk of suspension or possibly even expulsion—but Kirova had her hands full with a bleeding Mia and a hysterical student body. The guardians escorted me to my room under the watchful eye of the dorm matron who informed me she'd check on me every hour to make sure I stayed in my room. A couple guardians would also hang out around the dorm's entrances. Apparently I was now a high-security risk. I'd probably just ruined Eddie's party; he'd never sneak a group up to his room now.

Heedless of my dress, I flounced onto the floor of my room, crossing my legs underneath me. I reached out to Lissa. She was calmer now. The events from the dance still hurt her terribly, but Christian was soothing her somehow, although whether it was through simple words or physical mojo, I couldn't say. I didn't care. So long as she felt better and wouldn't do anything stupid. I returned to myself.

Yes, things were going to get messy now. Mia and Jesse's respective accusations were going to set the school on fire. I probably would get thrown out and have to go live with a bunch of skanky dhampir women. At least Lissa might realize Aaron was boring and that she wanted to be with Christian. But even if that was the right thing, it still meant—

Christian. Christian.

Christian was hurt.

I snapped back into Lissa's body, suddenly sucked in by the terror pounding through her. She was surrounded, surrounded by men and women who had come out of nowhere, bursting up into the attic of the chapel where she and Christian had gone to talk. Christian leapt up, fire flaring from his fingers. One of the invaders hit him on the head with something hard, making his body slump to the ground.

I desperately hoped he was okay, but I couldn't waste any more energy worrying about him. All my fear was for Lissa now. I couldn't let the same thing happen to her. I couldn't let them hurt her. I needed to save her, to get her out of there. But I didn't know how. She was too far away, and I couldn't even escape her head at the moment, let alone run over there or get help.

The attackers approached her, calling her Princess and telling her not to worry, and that they were guardians. And they *did* seem like guardians. Definitely dhampirs. Moving in precise, efficient ways. But I didn't recognize them as any of the guardians from school. Neither did Lissa. Guardians wouldn't have attacked Christian. And guardians certainly wouldn't be binding and gagging her—

Something forced me out of her head, and I frowned, staring around my room. I needed to go back to her and find out what had happened. Usually the connection just faded or I closed it off, but this—this was like something had actually removed me and pulled me. Pulled me back here.

But that made no sense. What could pull me back from . . . wait.

My mind blanked.

I couldn't remember what I'd just been thinking about. It was gone. Like static in my brain. Where had I been? With Lissa? What about Lissa?

Standing up, I wrapped my arms around myself, confused, trying to figure out what was going on. Lissa. Something with Lissa.

Dimitri, a voice inside my head suddenly said. *Go to Dimitri.*

Yes. Dimitri. My body and spirit burned for him all of a sudden, and I wanted to be with him more than I ever had before. I couldn't stay away from him. He'd know what to do.

And he'd told me before I should come to him if something was wrong with Lissa. Too bad I couldn't remember what that was. Still. I knew he'd take care of everything.

Getting up to the staff wing of the dorm wasn't hard, since they wanted to keep me inside tonight. I didn't know where his room was, but it didn't matter. *Something* was pulling me to him, urging me closer. An instinct pushed me toward one of the doors, and I beat the living daylights out of it.

After a few moments, he opened it, brown eyes widening when he saw me.

"Rose?"

"Let me in. It's Lissa."

He immediately stepped aside for me. I'd apparently caught him in bed, because the covers were peeled back on one side and only a small tableside lamp shone in the darkness. Plus, he wore only cotton pajama bottoms; his chest—which I'd never seen before, and wow, did it look great—was bare. The ends of his dark hair curled near his chin and appeared damp, like he'd taken a shower not so long ago.

"What's wrong?"

The sound of his voice thrilled me, and I couldn't answer. I couldn't stop staring at him. The force that had pulled me up here pulled me to him. I wanted him to touch me so badly, so badly I could barely stand it. He was so amazing. So unbelievably gorgeous. I knew somewhere something was wrong, but it didn't seem important. Not when I was with him.

With almost a foot separating us, there was no way I could

easily kiss his lips without his help. So instead, I aimed for his chest, wanting to taste that warm, smooth skin.

"Rose!" he exclaimed, stepping back. "What are you doing?"

"What do you think?"

I moved toward him again, needing to touch him and kiss him and do so many other things.

"Are you drunk?" he asked, holding his hand out in a warding gesture.

"Don't I wish." I tried to dodge around him, then paused, momentarily uncertain. "I thought you wanted to—don't you think I'm pretty?" In all the time we'd known each other, in all the time this attraction had built, he'd never told me I was pretty. He'd hinted at it, but that wasn't the same. And despite all the assurances I had from other guys that I was hotness incarnate, I needed to hear it from the one guy I actually wanted.

"Rose, I don't know what's going on, but you need to go back to your room."

When I moved toward him again, he reached out and gripped my wrists. With that touch, an electric current shot through both of us, and I saw him forget whatever he'd just been worrying about. Something seized him too, something that made him suddenly want me as much I wanted him.

Releasing my wrists, he moved his hands up my arms, sliding slowly along my skin. Holding me in his dark, hungry gaze, he pulled me to him, pressing me right up to his body.

One of his hands moved up the back of my neck, twining his fingers in my hair and tipping my face up to his. He brought his lips down, barely brushing them against mine.

Swallowing, I asked again, "Do you think I'm pretty?"

He regarded me with utter seriousness, like he always did. "I think you're beautiful."

"Beautiful?"

"You are so beautiful, it hurts me sometimes."

His lips moved to mine, gentle at first, and then hard and hungry. His kiss consumed me. His hands on my arms slid down, down my hips, down to the edge of my dress. He gathered up the fabric in his hands and began pushing it up my legs. I melted into that touch, into his kiss and the way it burned against my mouth. His hands kept sliding up and up, until he'd pulled the dress over my head and tossed it on the floor.

"You . . . you got rid of that dress fast," I pointed out between heavy breaths. "I thought you liked it."

"I do like it," he said. His breathing was as heavy as mine. "I love it."

And then he took me to the bed.

TWENTY-ONE

I'D NEVER BEEN COMPLETELY NAKED around a guy before. It scared the hell out of me—even though it excited me, too. Lying on the covers, we clung to each other and kept kissing—and kissing and kissing and kissing. His hands and lips took possession of my body, and every touch was like fire on my skin.

After yearning for him for so long, I could barely believe this was happening. And while the physical stuff felt great, I also just liked being close to him. I liked the way he looked at me, like I was the sexiest, most wonderful thing in the world. I liked the way he would say my name in Russian, murmured like a prayer: *Roza, Roza . . .*

And somewhere, somewhere in all of this, was that same urging voice that had driven me up to his room, a voice that didn't sound like my own but that I was powerless to ignore. *Stay with him, stay with him. Don't think about anything else except him. Keep touching him. Forget about everything else.*

I listened—not that I really needed any extra convincing.

The burning in his eyes told me he wanted to do a lot more than we were, but he took things slow, maybe because he knew I was nervous. His pajama pants stayed on. At one point, I shifted so that I hovered over him, my hair hanging around him. He tilted his head slightly, and I just barely caught sight of the back of his neck. I brushed my fingertips over the six tiny marks tattooed there.

"Did you really kill six Strigoi?" He nodded. "Wow."

He brought my own neck down to his mouth and kissed me. His teeth gently grazed my skin, different from a vampire but every bit as thrilling. "Don't worry. You'll have a lot more than me someday."

"Do you feel guilty about it?"

"Hmm?"

"Killing them. You said in the van that it was the right thing to do, but it still bothers you. It's why you go to church, isn't it? I see you there, but you aren't really into the services."

He smiled, surprised and amused I'd guessed another secret about him. "How do you know these things? I'm not guilty exactly . . . just sad sometimes. All of them used to be human or dhampir or Moroi. It's a waste, that's all, but as I said before, it's something I have to do. Something we all have to do. Sometimes it bothers me, and the chapel is a good place to think about those kinds of things. Sometimes I find peace there, but not often. I find more peace with you."

He rolled me off of him and moved on top of me again. The kissing picked up once more, harder this time. More urgent. *Oh God*, I thought. *I'm finally going to do it. This is it. I can feel it.*

He must have seen the decision in my eyes. Smiling, he slid his hands behind my neck and unfastened Victor's necklace.

He set it on the bedside table. As soon as the chain left his fingers, I felt like I'd been slapped in the face. I blinked in surprise.

Dimitri must have felt the same way. "What happened?" he asked.

"I—I don't know." I felt like I was trying to wake up, like I'd been asleep for two days. I needed to remember something.

Lissa. Something with Lissa.

My head felt funny. Not pain or dizziness, but . . . the voice, I realized. The voice urging me toward Dimitri was gone. That wasn't to say I didn't want him anymore because hey, seeing him there in those sexy pajama bottoms, with that brown hair spilling over the side of face was pretty fine. But I no longer had that outside influence pushing me to him. Weird.

He frowned, no longer turned on. After several moments of thought, he reached over and picked up the necklace. The instant his fingers touched it, I saw desire sweep over him again. He slid his other hand onto my hip, and suddenly, that burning lust slammed back into me. My stomach went queasy while my skin started to prickle and grow warm again. My breathing became heavy. His lips moved toward mine again.

Some inner part of me fought through.

"Lissa," I whispered, squeezing my eyes shut. "I have to tell you something about Lissa. But I can't . . . remember . . . I feel so strange. . . ."

"I know." Still holding onto me, he rested his cheek against my forehead. "There's something . . . something here. . . ." He pulled his face away, and I opened my eyes. "This necklace. That's the one Prince Victor gave you?"

I nodded and could see the sluggish thought process trying to wake up behind his eyes. Taking a deep breath, he removed his hand from my hip and pushed himself away.

"What are you doing?" I exclaimed. "Come back. . . ."

He looked like he wanted to—very badly—but instead he climbed out of the bed. He and the necklace moved away from me. I felt like he'd ripped part of me away, but at the same time, I had that startling sensation of waking up, like I could think clearly once more without my body making all the decisions.

On the other hand, Dimitri still wore a look of animal passion on him, and it seemed to take a great deal of effort for him to walk across the room. He reached the window and managed to open it one-handed. Cold air blasted in, and I rubbed my hands over my arms for warmth.

"What are you going to—?" The answer hit me, and I sprang out of bed, just as the necklace flew out the window. "No! Do you know how much that must have—?"

The necklace disappeared, and I no longer felt like I was *waking* up. I *was* awake. Painfully, startlingly so.

I took in my surroundings. Dimitri's room. Me naked. The rumpled bed.

But all that was nothing compared to what hit me next.

"Lissa!" I gasped out. It all came back, the memories and

the emotions. And, in fact, her held-back emotions suddenly poured into me—at staggering levels. More terror. Intense terror. Those feelings wanted to suck me back into her body, but I couldn't let them. Not quite yet. I fought against her, needing to stay here. With the words coming out in a rush, I told Dimitri everything that had happened.

He was in motion before I finished, putting on clothes and looking every bit like a badass god. Ordering me to get dressed, he tossed me a sweatshirt with Cyrillic writing on it to wear over the skimpy dress.

I had a hard time following him downstairs; he made no effort to slow for me this time. Calls were made when we got there. Orders shouted. Before long, I ended up in the guardians' main office with him. Kirova and other teachers were there. Most of the campus's guardians. Everyone seemed to speak at once. All the while, I felt Lissa's fear, felt her moving farther and farther away.

I yelled at them to hurry up and do something, but no one except Dimitri would believe my story about her abduction until someone retrieved Christian from the chapel and then verified Lissa really wasn't on campus.

Christian staggered in, supported by two guardians. Dr. Olendzki appeared shortly thereafter, checking him out and wiping blood away from the back of his head.

Finally, I thought, something would happen.

"How many Strigoi were there?" one of the guardians asked me.

"How in the world did they get in?" muttered someone else.

I stared. "Wh—? There weren't any Strigoi."

Several sets of eyes stared at me. "Who else would have taken her?" asked Ms. Kirova primly. "You must have seen it wrong through the . . . vision."

"No. I'm positive. It was . . . they were . . . guardians."

"She's right," mumbled Christian, still under the doctor's ministrations. He winced as she did something to the back of his head. "Guardians."

"That's impossible," someone said.

"They weren't school guardians." I rubbed my forehead, fighting hard to keep from leaving the conversation and going back to Lissa. My irritation grew. "Will you guys get moving? She's getting farther away!"

"You're saying a group of privately retained guardians came in and kidnapped her?" The tone in Kirova's voice implied I was playing some kind of joke.

"Yes," I replied through gritted teeth. "They . . ."

Slowly, carefully, I slipped my mental restraint and flew into Lissa's body. I sat in a car, an expensive car with tinted windows to keep out most of the light. It might be "night" here, but it was full day for the rest of the world. One of the guardians from the chapel drove; another sat beside him in the front—one I recognized. Spiridon. In the back, Lissa sat with tied hands, another guardian beside her, and on the other side—

"They work for Victor Dashkov," I gasped out, focusing back on Kirova and the others. "They're his."

"Prince Victor Dashkov?" asked one of the guardians with a snort. Like there was any other freaking Victor Dashkov.

"Please," I moaned, hands clutching my head. "Do something. They're getting so far away. They're on . . ." A brief image, seen outside the car window, flared in my vision. "Eighty-three. Headed south."

"Eighty-three already? How long ago did they leave? Why didn't you come sooner?"

My eyes turned anxiously to Dimitri.

"A compulsion spell," he said slowly. "A compulsion spell put into a necklace he gave her. It made her attack me."

"No one can use that kind of compulsion," exclaimed Kirova. "No one's done that in ages."

"Well, someone did. By the time I'd restrained her and taken the necklace, a lot of time had passed," Dimitri continued, face perfectly controlled. No one questioned the story.

Finally, finally, the group moved into action. No one wanted to bring me, but Dimitri insisted when he realized I could lead them to her. Three details of guardians set out in sinister black SUVs. I rode in the first one, sitting in the passenger seat while Dimitri drove. Minutes passed. The only times we spoke was when I gave a report.

"They're still on Eighty-three . . . but their turn is coming. They aren't speeding. They don't want to get pulled over."

He nodded, not looking at me. He most definitely *was* speeding.

Giving him a sidelong glance, I replayed tonight's earlier events. In my mind's eye, I could see it all again, the way he'd looked at me and kissed me.

But what had it been? An illusion? A trick? On the way to the car, he'd told me there really had been a compulsion spell in the necklace, a lust one. I had never heard of such a thing, but when I'd asked for more information, he just said it was a type of magic earth users once practiced but never did anymore.

"They're turning," I said suddenly. "I can't see the road name, but I'll know when we're close."

Dimitri grunted in acknowledgment, and I sank further into my seat.

What had it all meant? Had it meant anything to him? It had definitely meant a lot to me.

"There," I said about twenty minutes later, indicating the rough road Victor's car had turned off on. It was unpaved gravel, and the SUV gave us an edge over his luxury car.

We drove on in silence, the only sound coming from the crunching of the gravel under the tires. Dust kicked up outside the windows, swirling around us.

"They're turning again."

Farther and farther off the main routes they went, and we followed the whole time, led by my instructions. Finally, I felt Victor's car come to a stop.

"They're outside a small cabin," I said. "They're taking her—"

"Why are you doing this? What's going on?"

Lissa. Cringing and scared. Her feelings had pulled me into her.

"Come, child," said Victor, moving into the cabin, unsteady on his cane. One of his guardians held the door open. Another pushed Lissa along and settled her into a chair near a small table inside. It was cold in here, especially in the pink dress. Victor sat across from her. When she started to get up, a guardian gave her a warning look. "Do you think I'd seriously hurt you?"

"What did you do to Christian?" she cried, ignoring the question. "Is he dead?

"The Ozera boy? I didn't mean for that to happen. We didn't expect him to be there. We'd hoped to catch you alone, to convince others you'd run away again. We'd made sure rumors already circulated about that."

We? I recalled how the stories had resurfaced this week . . . from Natalie.

"Now?" He sighed, spreading his hands wide in a help-less gesture. "I don't know. I doubt anyone will connect it to us, even if they don't believe you ran away. Rose is the biggest liability. We'd intended to . . . dispatch her, letting others think she'd run away as well. The spectacle she created at your dance made that impossible, but I had another plan in place to make sure she stays occupied for some time . . . probably until tomorrow. We will have to contend with her later."

He hadn't counted on Dimitri figuring out the spell. He'd figured we'd be too busy getting it on all night.

"Why?" asked Lissa. "Why are you doing all this?"

His green eyes widened, reminding her of her father's. They might be distant relatives, but that jade-green color ran in both the Dragomirs and the Dashkovs. "I'm surprised you even have to ask, my dear. I need you. I need you to heal me."

TWENTY-TWO

"*H*EAL YOU?"

Heal him? My thoughts echoed hers.

"You're the only way," he said patiently. "The only way to cure this disease. I've been watching you for years, waiting until I was certain."

Lissa shook her head. "I can't . . . no. I can't do anything like that."

"Your healing powers are incredible. No one has any idea just how powerful."

"I don't know what you're talking about."

"Come now, Vasilisa. I know about the raven—Natalie saw you do it. She'd been following you. And I know how you healed Rose."

She realized the pointlessness of denying it. "That . . . was different. Rose wasn't that hurt. But you . . . I can't do anything about Sandovsky's Syndrome."

"Not *that* hurt?" he laughed. "I'm not talking about her ankle—which was still impressive. I'm talking about the car accident. Because you're right, you know. Rose didn't get 'that hurt.' She *died*."

He let the words sink in.

"That's . . . no. She lived," Lissa finally managed.

"No. Well, yes, she did. But I read all the reports. There was *no way* she should have survived—especially with so many injuries. You healed her. You brought her back." He sighed, half wistful and half weary. "I'd suspected you could do this for so long, and I tried so hard to repeat it . . . to see how much you could control. . . ."

Lissa caught on and gasped. "The *animals*. It was you."

"With Natalie's help."

"Why would you do that? How could you?"

"Because I had to know. I have only a few more weeks to live, Vasilisa. If you can truly bring back the dead, then you can cure Sandovsky's. I had to know before I took you away that you could heal at will and not just in moments of panic."

"Why take me at all?" A spark of anger flared up in her. "You're my near-uncle. If you wanted me to do this—if you really think I can . . . " Her voice and feelings showed me she didn't really entirely believe she could heal him. "Then why kidnap me? Why didn't you just ask?"

"Because it's not a onetime affair. It took a long time to figure out what you are, but I managed to acquire some of the old histories . . . scrolls kept out of Moroi museums. When I read about how wielding spirit works—"

"Wielding what?"

"Spirit. It's what you've specialized in."

"I haven't specialized in anything! You're crazy."

"Where else do you think these powers of yours have

come from? Spirit is another element, one few people have any more."

Lissa's mind was still reeling from the kidnapping and the possible truth that she'd brought me back from the dead. "That doesn't make any sense. Even if it wasn't common, I still would have heard of another element! Or of someone having it."

"No one knows about spirit anymore. It's been forgotten. When people do specialize in it, nobody realizes it. They think the person simply hasn't specialized at all."

"Look, if you're just trying to make me feel—" She abruptly cut herself off. She was angry and afraid, but behind those emotions, her higher reasoning had been processing what he'd said about spirit users and specializing. It now caught up with her. "Oh my God. Vladimir and Ms. Karp."

He gave her a knowing look. "You've known about this all along."

"No! I swear. It's just something Rose was looking into. . . . She said they were like me. . . ." Lissa was starting to change from a little scared to all scared. The news was too shocking.

"They *are* like you. The books even say Vladimir was 'full of spirit.'" Victor seemed to find that funny. Seeing that smile made me want to slap him.

"I thought . . ." Lissa still wanted him to be wrong. The idea of not specializing was safer than specializing in some freakish element. "I thought that meant, like, the Holy Spirit."

"So does everyone else, but no. It's something else entirely. An element that's within all of us. A master element that can give you indirect control over the others." Apparently my theory about her specializing in all the elements wasn't so far off.

She worked hard to get a grip on this news and her own self-control. "That doesn't answer my question. It doesn't matter if I have this spirit thing or whatever. You didn't have to kidnap me."

"Spirit, as you've seen, can heal physical injuries. Unfortunately, it's only good on acute injuries. Onetime things. Rose's ankle. The accident wounds. For something chronic— say, a genetic disease like Sandovsky's—continual healings are required. Otherwise it will keep coming back. That's what would happen to me. I need you, Vasilisa. I need you to help me fight this and keep it away. So I can live."

"That still doesn't explain why you took me," she argued. "I would have helped you if you'd asked."

"They never would have let you do it. The school. The council. Once they got over the shock of finding a spirit user, they'd get hung up on ethics. After all, how does one choose who gets to be healed? They'd say it wasn't fair. That it was like playing God. Or else they'd worry about the toll it'd take on you."

She flinched, knowing exactly what toll he referred to.

Seeing her expression, he nodded. "Yes. I won't lie to you. It will be hard. It will exhaust you—mentally and physically.

But I must do it. I *am* sorry. You'll be provided with feeders and other entertainments for your services."

She leapt from the chair. Ben immediately stepped forward and pushed her back into it. "And then what? Are you going to just make me a prisoner here? Your own private nurse?"

He made that annoying open-palmed gesture again. "I'm sorry. I have no choice."

White-hot anger blasted away the fear inside of her. She spoke in a low voice. "Yes. *You* don't have the choice, because this is *me* we're talking about."

"It's better for you this way. You know how the others turned out. How Vladimir spent the last of his days stark, raving mad. How Sonya Karp had to be taken away. The trauma you've experienced since the accident comes from more than just your family's loss. It's from using spirit. The accident woke the spirit in you; your fear over seeing Rose dead made it burst out, allowing you to heal her. It forged your bond. And once it's out, you can't put it back. It's a powerful element—but it's also dangerous. Earth users get their power from the earth, air users from the air. But spirit? Where do you think that comes from?"

She glared.

"It comes from you, from your own essence. To heal another, you must give part of yourself. The more you do that, the more it will destroy you over time. You must be noticing that already. I've seen how much certain things upset you, how fragile you are."

"I'm not fragile," snapped Lissa. "And I'm not going to go

crazy. I'm going to stop using spirit before things get worse."

He smiled. "Stop using it? You might as well stop breathing. Spirit has its own agenda. . . . You'll always have the urge to help and heal. It's part of you. You resisted the animals, but you didn't think twice about helping Rose. You can't even help compulsion—which spirit also gives you special strength in. And that's how it will always be. You can't avoid spirit. Better to stay here, in isolation, away from further sources of stress. You'd either have become increasingly unstable at the Academy, or they would have put you on some pill that would have made you feel better but stunted your power."

A calm core of confidence settled inside her, one very different from what I'd observed over the last couple of years. "I love you, Uncle Victor, but *I'm* the one who has to deal with that and decide what to do. Not you. You're making me give up my life for yours. That's not fair."

"It's a matter of which life means more. I love you too. Very much. But the Moroi are falling apart. Our numbers are dropping as we let the Strigoi prey upon us. We used to actively seek them out. Now Tatiana and the other leaders hide away. They keep you and your peers isolated. In the old days, you were trained to fight alongside your guardians! You were taught to use magic as a weapon. Not any longer. We wait. We are *victims*." As he stared off, both Lissa and I could see how caught up in his passion he was. "I would have changed that if I were king. I would have brought about a revolution the likes of which neither Moroi nor Strigoi have ever seen. *I* should have been Tatiana's heir. She was ready to name me before they dis-covered the disease, and then she would not. If I were cured . . . if I were cured, I could take my rightful place. . . ."

His words triggered something inside of Lissa, a sudden consideration for the state of the Moroi. She'd never con-templated what he'd said, about how different it might be if Moroi and their guardians fought side by side to rid the world of the Strigoi and their evil. It reminded her of Christian and what he'd said about using magic as a weapon too. But even if she did appreciate Victor's convictions, neither of us thought it was worth what he wanted her to do.

"I'm sorry," she whispered. "I'm sorry for you. But please don't make me do this."

"I have to."

She looked him straight in the eye. "I won't do it."

He inclined his head, and someone stepped forward from the corner. Another Moroi. No one I knew. Walking around behind Lissa, he untied her hands.

"This is Kenneth." Victor held his hands out toward her free ones. "Please, Vasilisa. Take my hands. Send the magic through me just as you did with Rose."

She shook her head. "No."

His voice was less kindly when he spoke again. "Please. One way or another, you will heal me. I'd rather it be on your terms, not ours."

She shook her head again. He made a slight gesture toward Kenneth.

And that's when the pain started.

Lissa screamed. I screamed.

In the SUV, Dimitri's grip on the wheel jerked in surprise, making us veer. Casting me an alarmed look, he started to pull over.

"No, no! Keep going!" I pressed my palms to my temples. "We have to get there!"

From behind my seat, Alberta reached forward and rested a hand on my shoulder. "Rose, what's happening?"

I blinked back tears. "They're torturing her . . . with air. This guy . . . Kenneth . . . he's making it press against her . . . into her head. The pressure's insane. It feels like my—her—skull's gonna explode." I started sobbing.

Dimitri looked at me out of the corner of his eye and pressed the gas pedal down harder.

Kenneth didn't stop with just the physical force of air. He also used it to affect her breathing. Sometimes he'd smother her with it; other times he'd take it all away and leave her gasping. After enduring all that firsthand—and it was bad enough secondhand—I felt pretty confident I would have done anything they wanted.

And finally, she did.

Hurting and bleary-eyed, Lissa took Victor's hands. I'd never been in her head when she worked magic and didn't know what to expect. At first, I felt nothing. Just a sense of concentration. Then . . . it was like . . . I don't even know how to describe it. Color and light and music and life and joy and love . . . so many wonderful things, all the lovely things that make up the world and make it worth living in.

Lissa summoned up all of those things, as many as she could, and sent them into Victor. The magic flowed through both of us, brilliant and sweet. It was alive. It was her life. And as wonderful as it all felt, she was growing weaker and weaker. But as all of those elements—bound by the mysterious spirit element—flowed into Victor, he grew stronger and stronger.

The change was startling. His skin smoothed, no longer wrinkled and pocked. The gray, thinning hair filled out, turning dark and lustrous once more. The green eyes—still jade-like—sparkled again, turning alert and lively.

He'd become the Victor she remembered from her childhood.

Exhausted, Lissa passed out.

In the SUV, I tried to relate what was happening. Dimitri's face grew darker and darker, and he spat out a string of Russian swear words he *still* hadn't taught me the meanings of.

When we were a quarter mile from the cabin, Alberta made a call on her cell phone, and our whole convoy pulled over. All of the guardians—more than a dozen—got out and stood huddled, planning strategy. Someone went ahead to scout and returned with a report on the number of people inside and outside of the cabin. When the group seemed ready to disperse, I started to get out of the car. Dimitri stopped me.

"No, Roza. You stay here."

"The hell with that. I have to go help her."

He cupped my chin with his hands, fixing me with his eyes. "You have helped her. Your job is done. You did it well. But this isn't any place for you. She and I both need you to stay safe."

Only the realization that arguing would delay the rescue kept me quiet. Swallowing back any protests, I nodded. He nodded back and joined the others. All of them slipped off into the woods, blending with the trees.

Sighing, I kicked the passenger seat back and lay down. I was so tired. Even though the sun poured through the windshield, it was night for me. I'd been up for most of it, and a lot had happened in that time. Between the adrenaline of my own role and sharing Lissa's pain, I could have passed out just like she had.

Except that she was awake now.

Slowly, her perceptions dominated mine once more. She lay on a couch in the cabin. One of Victor's henchmen must have carried her there after she'd fainted. Victor himself—alive and well now, thanks to his abuse of her—stood in the kitchen with the others as they all spoke in low voices about their plans. Only one stood near Lissa, keeping watch. He'd be easy to take down when Dimitri and the Badass Team burst inside.

Lissa studied the lone guardian and then glanced at a window beside the couch. Still dizzy from the healing, she managed to sit up. The guardian turned around, watching her warily. She met his eyes and smiled.

"You're going to stay quiet no matter what I do," she told him. "You aren't going to call for help or tell anyone when I leave. Okay?"

The thrall of compulsion slid over him. He nodded in agreement.

Moving toward the window, she unlocked it and slid the glass up. As she did, a tumble of considerations played through her mind. She was weak. She didn't know how far from the Academy—from anything, really—she was. She had no clue how far she could get before someone noticed.

But she also knew she might not get another chance at escape. She had no intention of spending the rest of her life in this cabin in the woods.

At any other time, I would have cheered on her boldness, but not this time. Not when all those guardians were about to save her. She needed to stay put. Unfortunately, she couldn't hear my advice.

Lissa climbed out the window, and I swore out loud.

"What? What'd you see?" asked a voice behind me.

I jerked up from my reclining position in the car, banging my head on the ceiling. Glancing behind me, I found Christian peering up from the cargo space behind the farthest back-seats.

"What are you doing here?" I asked.

"What's it look like? I'm a stowaway."

"Don't you have a concussion or something?"

He shrugged like it didn't matter. What a great pair he

and Lissa were. Neither afraid to take on crazy feats while seriously injured. Still, if Kirova had made me stay behind, I would have been right beside him in the back.

"What's happening?" he asked. "Did you see something new?

Hastily, I told him. I also got out of the car as I spoke. He followed.

"She doesn't know our guys are already coming for her. I'm going to go get her before she kills herself with exhaustion."

"What about the guardians? The school's, I mean. Are you going to tell them she's gone?"

I shook my head. "They're probably already busting down the cabin's door. I'm going after her." She was somewhere off to the right side of the cabin. I could head in that direction but wouldn't be able to get very precise until I was much closer to her. Still, it didn't matter. I had to find her. Seeing Christian's face, I couldn't resist giving him a dry smile. "And yeah, I know. You're going with me."

TWENTY-THREE

I'D NEVER HAD SO MUCH trouble staying out of Lissa's head before, but then, we'd never been through anything like this together either. The strength of her thoughts and feelings kept trying to pull me in as I hurried through the forest.

Running through the brush and woods, Christian and I moved farther and farther from the cabin. Man, how I wished Lissa had stayed back there. I would have loved to see the raid through her eyes. But that was behind us now, and as I ran, Dimitri's push on laps and stamina paid off. She wasn't moving very quickly, and I could feel the distance closing between us, giving me a more precise idea of her location. Likewise, Christian couldn't keep up with me. I started to slow for him but soon realized the foolishness of that.

So did he. "Go," he gasped out, waving me on.

When I reached a point close enough to her that I thought she could hear me, I called out her name, hoping to get her to turn around. Instead, what answered me was a set of howls—a soft canine baying.

Psi-hounds. Of course. Victor had said he hunted with them; he could control those beasts. I suddenly understood why no one at school recalled sending psi-hounds after Lissa and me in Chicago. The Academy hadn't arranged that; Victor had.

A minute later, I reached a clearing where Lissa cringed, back against a tree. From her looks and bond feelings, she should have fainted long ago. Only the barest scraps of will-power kept her hanging on. Wide-eyed and pale, she stared in horror at the four psi-hounds cornering her. Noticing the full sunlight, it occurred to me that she and Christian had another obstacle to contend with out here.

"Hey," I yelled at the hounds, trying to draw them toward me. Victor must have sent them to trap her, but I hoped they'd sense and respond to another threat—especially a dhampir. Psi-hounds didn't like us any better than other animals did.

Sure enough, they turned on me, teeth bared and drool coming out of their mouths. They resembled wolves, only with brown fur and eyes that glowed like orange fire. He'd probably ordered them not to harm her, but they had no such instructions regarding me.

Wolves. Just like in science class. What had Ms. Meissner said? A lot of confrontations were all about willpower? Bearing this mind, I tried to project an alpha attitude, but I don't think they fell for it. Any one of them outweighed me. Oh yeah—they also outnumbered me. No, they didn't have any-thing to be scared of.

Trying to pretend this was just a free-for-all match with Dimitri, I picked up a branch from the ground that had about the same heft and weight as a baseball bat. I'd just positioned it in my hands when two of the hounds jumped me. Claws and teeth bit into me, but I held my own surprisingly well as I tried to remember everything I'd learned in the last two months about fighting bigger and stronger opponents.

I didn't like hurting them. They reminded me too much of dogs. But it was me or them, and survival instincts won out. One of them I managed to beat to the ground, dead or unconscious I didn't know. The other was still on me, still coming on fast and furious. His companions looked ready to join him, but then a new competitor burst on the scene—sort of. Christian.

"Get out of here," I yelled at him, shaking off my hound as its claws ripped into the bare skin of my leg, nearly toppling me over. I was still wearing the dress, though I'd shed the heels a while ago.

But Christian, like any lovesick guy, didn't listen. He picked up a branch as well and swung it at one of the hounds. Flames burst from the wood. The hound backed up, still compelled to follow Victor's orders, though also clearly afraid of the fire.

Its companion, the fourth hound, circled away from the torch and came up behind Christian. Smart little bastard. It sprang at Christian, hitting him back first. The branch flew from his hands, the fire immediately going out. Both hounds then leapt onto his fallen form. I finished my hound—again feeling sick over what I had to do to subdue it—and moved toward the other two, wondering if I had the strength to take on these last ones.

But I didn't have to. Rescue appeared in the form of Alberta, emerging through some trees.

With a gun in hand, she shot the hounds without hesitation. Boring as hell perhaps—and completely useless against Strigoi—but against other things? Guns were tried and true. The hounds stopped moving and slumped next to Christian's body.

And Christian's body . . .

All three of us made our way over to it—Lissa and I practically crawling. When I saw it, I had to look away. My stomach lurched, and it took a lot of effort not to throw up. He wasn't dead yet, but I didn't think he had much longer.

Lissa's eyes, wide and distraught, drank him in. Tentatively, she reached out toward him and then dropped her hand.

"I can't," she managed in a small voice. "I don't have the strength left."

Alberta, leathery face both hard and compassionate, gently tugged her arm. "Come on, Princess. We need to get out of here. We'll send help."

Turning back to Christian, I forced myself to look at him and let myself feel how much Lissa cared about him.

"Liss," I said hesitantly. She looked over at me, like she'd forgotten I was even there. Wordlessly, I brushed my hair away from my neck and tilted it toward her.

She stared for a moment, blank-faced; then understanding shone in her eyes.

Those fangs that lurked behind her pretty smile bit into my neck, and a small moan escaped my lips. I hadn't realized how much I'd missed it, that sweet, wonderful pain followed by glorious wonder. Bliss settled over me. Dizzying. Joyful. Like being in a dream.

I don't entirely remember how long Lissa drank from me. Probably not that long. She would never even consider drinking the quantities that would kill a person and make her a Strigoi. She finished, and Alberta caught me as I started to sway.

Dizzily, I watched as Lissa leaned over Christian and rested her hands on him. In the distance, I heard the other guardians crashing through the forest.

No glowing or fireworks surrounded the healing. It all took place invisibly, occurring between Lissa and Christian. Even though the bite's endorphins had numbed my connection to her, I remembered Victor's healing and the wonderful colors and music she must be bringing forth.

A miracle unfolded before my eyes, and Alberta gasped. Christian's wounds closed. The blood dried up. Color—as much as a Moroi ever had, at least—returned to his cheeks. His eyelids fluttered, and his eyes regained their life again. Focusing on Lissa, he smiled. It was like watching a Disney movie.

I must have keeled over after that, because I don't remember anything else.

Eventually, I woke up in the Academy's clinic, where they forced fluids and sugar into me for two days. Lissa stayed by my side almost the entire time, and slowly, the events of the kidnapping unfolded.

We had to tell Kirova and a few choice others about Lissa's powers, how she'd healed Victor and Christian and, well, me. The news was shocking, but the administrators agreed to keep it secret from the rest of the school. No one even considered taking Lissa away like they had Ms. Karp.

Mostly all the other students knew was that Victor Dashkov had kidnapped Lissa Dragomir. They didn't know why. Some of his guardians had died when Dimitri's band attacked—a damned shame, when guardian numbers were so low already. Victor was now being held under 24/7 guard at the school, waiting for a royal regiment of guardians to carry him away. The Moroi rulers might be a mostly symbolic government within another country's larger government, but they had systems of justice, and I'd heard about Moroi prisons. Not any place I'd want to be.

As for Natalie . . . that was trickier. She was still a minor, but she'd conspired with her father. She'd brought in the dead animals and kept an eye on Lissa's behavior—even before we left. Being an earth user like Victor, she'd also been the one to rot the bench that broke my ankle. After she'd seen me hold Lissa back from the dove, she and Victor realized that they needed to injure *me* to get to her—it was their only chance to get her to heal again. Natalie had simply waited for a good opportunity. She wasn't locked up or anything yet, and the Academy didn't know what to do with her until a royal command came.

I couldn't help but feel sorry for her. She was so awkward

and self-conscious. Anyone could have manipulated her, let alone her father, whom she loved and from whom she so desperately wanted attention. She would have done anything. Rumor said she'd stood screaming outside the detention center, begging them to let her see him. They'd refused and hauled her away.

Meanwhile, Lissa and I slipped back into our friendship like nothing had happened. In the rest of her world, a lot had happened. After all that excitement and drama, she seemed to gain a new sense of what mattered to her. She broke up with Aaron. I'm sure she did it very nicely, but it still had to be hard on him. She'd dropped him twice now. The fact that his last girlfriend had cheated on him probably wasn't helping his confidence any.

And without any more hesitation, Lissa started dating Christian, not caring about the consequences to her reputation. Seeing them out in public, holding hands, made me do a double take. He didn't seem able to believe it himself. The rest of our classmates were almost too stunned to even comprehend it yet. They could barely process acknowledging his existence, let alone him being with someone like her.

My own romantic state was less rosy than hers—if you could even *call* it a romantic state. Dimitri hadn't visited me during my recovery, and our practices were indefinitely suspended. It wasn't until the fourth day after Lissa's kidnapping that I ran into him in the gym. We were alone.

I had come back for my gym bag and froze when I saw him, unable to speak. He started to walk past and then stopped.

"Rose . . ." he began after several uncomfortable moments. "You need to report what happened. With us."

I'd been waiting a long time to talk to him, but this wasn't the conversation I'd imagined.

"I can't do that. They'll fire you. Or worse."

"They should fire me. What I did was wrong."

"You couldn't help it. It was the spell. . . ."

"It doesn't matter. It was wrong. And stupid."

Wrong? Stupid? I bit my lip, and tears threatened to fill my eyes. I quickly tried to regain my composure. "Look, it's not a big deal."

"It *is* a big deal! I took advantage of you."

"No," I said evenly. "You didn't."

There must have been something telling in my voice because he met my eyes with a deep and serious intensity.

"Rose, I'm seven years older than you. In ten years, that won't mean so much, but for now, it's huge. I'm an adult. You're a child."

Ouch. I flinched. Easier if he'd just punched me.

"You didn't seem to think I was a child when you were all over me."

Now he flinched. "Just because your body . . . well, that doesn't make you an adult. We're in two very different places. I've been out in the world. I've been on my own. I've killed, Rose—*people*, not animals. And you . . . you're just starting out. Your life is about homework and clothes and dances."

"That's all you think I care about?"

"No, of course not. Not entirely. But it's all part of your world. You're still growing up and figuring out who you are and what's important. You need to keep doing that. You need to be with boys your own age."

I didn't want boys my own age. But I didn't say that. I didn't say anything.

"Even if you choose not to tell, you need to understand that *it was a mistake*. And it isn't ever going to happen again," he added.

"Because you're too old for me? Because it isn't responsible?"

His face was perfectly blank. "No. Because I'm just not interested in you in that way."

I stared. The message—the rejection—came through loud and clear. Everything from that night, everything I'd believed so beautiful and full of meaning, turned to dust before my eyes.

"It only happened because of the spell. Do you understand?"

Humiliated and angry, I refused to make a fool of myself by arguing or begging. I just shrugged. "Yeah. Understood."

I spent the rest of the day sulking, ignoring both Lissa and Mason's attempts to draw me out of my room. It was ironic that I should want to stay inside. Kirova had been impressed enough by my performance with the rescue to end my house arrest.

Before school the next day, I made my way to where Victor

was being held. The Academy had honest-to-goodness cells, complete with bars, and two guardians stood watch in the hallway nearby. It took a little bit of finagling on my part to get them to let me inside to talk to him. Even Natalie wasn't allowed in. But one of the guardians had ridden with me in the SUV and watched me undergo Lissa's torture. I told him I needed to ask Victor about what he'd done to Lissa. It was a lie, but the guardians bought it and felt sorry for me. They allowed me five minutes to speak, backing up a discrete distance down the hall where they could see but not hear.

Standing outside Victor's cell, I couldn't believe I'd once felt sorry for him. Seeing his new and healthy body enraged me. He sat cross-legged on a narrow bed, reading. When he heard me approach, he looked up.

"Why Rose, what a nice surprise. Your ingenuity never fails to impress me. I didn't think they'd allow me any visitors."

I crossed my arms, trying to put on a look of total guardian fierceness. "I want you to break the spell. Finish it off."

"What do you mean?"

"The spell you did on me and Dimitri."

"That spell is done. It burned itself out."

I shook my head. "No. I keep thinking about him. I keep wanting to . . ."

He smiled knowingly when I didn't finish. "My dear, that was already there, long before I set that up."

"It wasn't like this. Not this bad."

"Maybe not consciously. But everything else . . . the attraction—physical and mental—was already in you. And in him. It wouldn't have worked otherwise. The spell didn't really add anything new—it just removed inhibitions and strengthened the feelings you already had for each other."

"You're lying. He said he didn't feel that way about me."

"*He's* lying. I tell you, the spell wouldn't have worked otherwise, and honestly, he should have known better. He had no right to let himself feel that way. You can be forgiven for a schoolgirl's crush. But him? He should have demonstrated more control in hiding his feelings. Natalie saw it and told me. After just a few observations of my own, it was obvious to me too. It gave me the perfect chance to distract you both. I keyed the necklace's charm for each of you, and you two did the rest."

"You're a sick bastard, doing that to me and him. And to Lissa."

"I have no regrets about what I did with her," he declared, leaning against the wall. "I'd do it again if I could. Believe what you want, I love my people. What I wanted to do was in their best interest. Now? Hard to say. They have no leader, no *real* leader. There's no one worthy, really." He cocked his head toward me, considering. "Vasilisa actually might have been such a one—if she could ever have found it within herself to believe in something and overcome the influence of spirit. It's ironic, really. Spirit can shape someone into a leader and also crush her ability to remain one. The fear, depression, and uncertainty take over, and keep her true strength buried deep within her. Still, she has the blood of the Dragomirs, which is no small thing. And of course, she has you, her shadow-kissed guardian. Who knows? She may surprise us yet."

"'Shadow-kissed'?" There it was again, the same thing Ms. Karp had called me.

"You've been kissed by shadows. You've crossed into Death, into the other side, and returned. Do you think something like that doesn't leave a mark on the soul? You have a greater sense of life and the world—far greater than even I have—even if you don't realize it. You should have stayed dead. Vasilisa brushed Death to bring you back and bound you to her forever. You were actually in its embrace, and some part of you will always remember that, always fight to cling to life and experience all it has. That's why you're so reckless in the things you do. You don't hold back your feelings, your passion, your anger. It makes you remarkable. It makes you dangerous."

I didn't know what to say to that. I was speechless, which he seemed to like.

"It's what created your bond, too. Her feelings always press out of her, onto others. Most people can't pick up on them unless she's actually directing her thoughts toward them with compulsion. You, however, have a mind sensitive to extrasensory forces—hers in particular." He sighed, almost happily, and I remembered reading that Vladimir had saved Anna from death. That must have made *their* bond, too. "Yes, this ridiculous Academy has no idea what they have in either you or her. If not for the fact that I needed to kill you, I would have made you part of my royal guard when you were older."

"You never would've had a royal guard. Don't you think people would have been weirded out by you suddenly recovering like that? Even if no one found out about Lissa, Tatiana never would have made you king."

"You may be right, but it doesn't matter. There are other ways of taking power. Sometimes it's necessary to go outside the established channels. Do you think Kenneth is the only Moroi who follows me? The greatest and most powerful revolutions often start very quietly, hidden in the shadows." He eyed me. "Remember that."

Odd sounds came from the detention center's entrance, and I glanced toward where I'd come in. The guardians who had let me in were gone. From around the corner, I heard a few grunts and thumps. I frowned and craned my head to get a better look.

Victor stood up. "Finally."

Fear spiked down my spine—at least until I saw Natalie round the corner.

Mixed sympathy and anger flitted through me, but I forced a kind smile. She probably wouldn't see her father again once they took him. Villain or no, they should be allowed to say goodbye.

"Hey," I said, watching her stride toward me. There was an unusual purpose in her movements that some part of me whispered wasn't right. "I didn't think they'd let you in." Of course, they weren't supposed to have let me in either.

She walked right up to me and—no exaggeration—*launched* me against the far wall. My body hit it hard, and black starbursts danced across my vision.

"What? . . ." I put a hand to my forehead and tried to get up.

Unconcerned about me now, Natalie unlocked Victor's cell with a set of keys I'd seen on one of the guardian's belts. Staggering to my feet, I approached her.

"What are you doing?"

She glanced up at me, and that's when I saw it. The faint ring of red around her pupils. Skin too pale, even for a Moroi. Blood smudged around her mouth. And most telling of all, the look in her eyes. A look so cold and so evil, my heart nearly came to a standstill. It was a look that said she no longer walked among the living—a look that said she was now one of the Strigoi.

TWENTY-FOUR

IN SPITE OF ALL THE training I'd received, all the lessons on Strigoi habits and how to defend against them, I'd never ever actually seen one. It was scarier than I'd expected.

This time, when she swung at me again, I was ready. Sort of. I dodged back, slipping out of reach, wondering what chance I had. I remembered Dimitri's joke about the mall. No silver stake. Nothing to cut her head off with. No way to set her on fire. Running seemed like the best option after all, but she was blocking my way.

Feeling useless, I simply backed down the hall as she advanced on me, her movements far more graceful than they'd ever been in life.

Then, also faster than she'd ever moved in life, she leapt out, grabbed me, and slammed my head against the wall. Pain exploded in my skull, and I felt pretty sure that was blood I tasted in the back of my mouth. Frantically, I fought against her, trying to mount some kind of defense, but it was like fighting Dimitri on crack.

"My dear," murmured Victor, "try not to kill her if you don't have to. We might be able to use her later."

Natalie paused in her attack, giving me a moment to back up, but she never took her cold eyes off me. "I'll *try* not to."

There was a skeptical tone in her voice. "Get out of here now. I'll meet you there when I'm done."

"I can't believe you!" I yelled after him. "You got your own daughter to turn Strigoi?"

"A last resort. A necessary sacrifice made for the greater good. Natalie understands." He left.

"Do you?" I hoped I could stall her with talking, just like in the movies. I also hoped my questions would hide how utterly and completely terrified I was. "Do you understand? God, Natalie. You . . . you turned. Just because he told you to?"

"My father's a great man," she replied. "He's going to save the Moroi from the Strigoi."

"Are you insane?" I cried. I was backing up again and suddenly hit the wall. My nails dug into it, as though I could dig my way through. "You *are* a Strigoi."

She shrugged, almost seeming like the old Natalie. "I had to do it to get him out of here before the others came. One Strigoi to save all of the Moroi. It's worth it, worth giving up the sun and the magic."

"But you'll want to kill Moroi! You won't be able to help it."

"He'll help me stay in control. If not, then they'll have to kill me." She reached out and grabbed my shoulders, and I shuddered at how casually she talked about her own death. It was almost as casual as the way she was no doubt contemplating *my* death.

"You *are* insane. You can't love him that much. You can't really—"

She threw me into a wall again, and as my body collapsed in a heap on the floor, I had a feeling I wouldn't be getting up this time. Victor had told her not to kill me . . . but there was a look in her eyes, a look that said she wanted to. She wanted to feed off me; the hunger was there. It was the Strigoi way. I shouldn't have talked to her, I realized. I'd hesitated, just as Dimitri had warned.

And then, suddenly, he was there, charging down the hallway like Death in a cowboy duster.

Natalie spun around. She was fast, so fast. But Dimitri was fast too and avoided her attack, a look of pure power and strength on his face. With an eerie fascination, I watched them move, circling each other like partners in a deadly dance. She was stronger than him, clearly, but she was also a fresh Strigoi. Gaining superpowers doesn't mean you know how to use them.

Dimitri, however, knew how to use the ones he had. After both giving and receiving some vicious hits, he made his move. The silver stake flashed in his hand like a streak of lightning, then it snaked forward—into her heart. He yanked it out and stepped back, his face impassive as she screamed and fell to the floor. After a few horrible moments, she stopped moving.

Just as quickly, he was leaning over me, slipping his arms under my body. He stood up, carrying me like he had when I hurt my ankle.

"Hey, Comrade," I murmured, my own voice sounding

sleepy. "You were right about Strigoi." The world started to darken, and my eyelids drooped.

"Rose. Roza. Open your eyes." I'd never heard his voice so strained, so frantic. "Don't go to sleep on me. Not yet."

I squinted up at him as he carried me out of the building, practically running toward the clinic. "Was he right?"

"Who?"

"Victor . . . he said it couldn't have worked. The necklace."

I started to drift off, lost in the blackness of my mind, but Dimitri prompted me back to consciousness.

"What do you mean?"

"The spell. Victor said you had to want me . . . to care about me . . . for it to work." When he didn't say anything, I tried to grip his shirt, but my fingers were too weak. "Did you? Did you want me?"

His words came out thickly. "Yes, Roza. I did want you. I still do. I wish . . . we could be together."

"Then why did you lie to me?"

We reached the clinic, and he managed to open the door while still holding me. As soon as he stepped inside, he began yelling for help.

"Why did you lie?" I murmured again.

Still holding me in his arms, he looked down at me. I could hear voices and footsteps getting closer.

"Because we can't be together."

"Because of the age thing, right?" I asked. "Because you're my mentor?"

His fingertip gently wiped away a tear that had escaped down my cheek. "That's part of it," he said. "But also . . . well, you and I will both be Lissa's guardians someday. I need to protect her at all costs. If a pack of Strigoi come, I need to throw my body between them and her."

"I know that. Of course that's what you have to do." The black sparkles were dancing in front of my eyes again. I was fading out.

"No. If I let myself love you, I won't throw myself in front of her. I'll throw myself in front of you."

The medical team arrived and took me out of his arms.

And that was how, two days after being discharged, I ended up back in the clinic. My third time in the two months we'd been back at the Academy. It had to be some kind of record. I definitely had a concussion and probably internal bleeding, but we never really found out. When your best friend is a kick-ass healer, you sort of don't have to worry about those things.

I still had to stay there for a couple of days, but Lissa—and Christian, her new sidekick—almost never left my side when they weren't in class. Through them, I learned bits and pieces about the outside world. Dimitri had realized there was a Strigoi on campus when they'd found Natalie's victim dead and drained of blood: Mr. Nagy of all people. A surprising choice, but since he was older, he'd been able to put up less of a fight. No more Slavic art for us. The guardians in the detention center had been injured but not killed. She'd simply slammed them around as she had me.

Victor had been found and recaptured while trying to escape campus. I was glad, even though it meant Natalie's sacrifice had been for nothing. Rumors said that Victor hadn't seemed afraid at all when the royal guards came and carried him away. He'd simply smiled the whole time, like he had some secret they didn't know about.

Inasmuch as it could, life returned to normal after that. Lissa did no more cutting. The doctor prescribed her something—an anti-depressant or anti-anxiety drug, I couldn't remember which—that made her feel better. I'd never really known anything about those kinds of pills. I thought they made people silly and happy. But it was a pill like any other, meant to fix something, and mostly it just kept her normal and feeling stable.

Which was a good thing—because she had some other issues to deal with. Like Andre. She'd finally believed Christian's story, and allowed herself to acknowledge that Andre might not have been the hero she'd always believed him to be. It was hard on her, but she finally reached a peaceful decision, accepting that he could have had both good and bad sides, like we all do. What he'd done to Mia saddened her, but it didn't change the fact that he'd been a good brother who loved her. Most importantly, it finally freed her from feeling like she needed to be *him* to make her family proud. She could be herself—which she proved daily in her relationship with Christian.

The school still couldn't get over that. She didn't care. She laughed it off, ignoring the shocked looks and disdain from the royals who couldn't believe she'd date someone from a humiliated family. Not all of them felt that way, though. Some who had gotten to know her during her brief social whirlwind actually liked her for *her*, no compulsion necessary. They liked her honesty and openness, preferring it to the games most royals played.

A lot of royals ignored her, of course, and talked viciously about her behind her back. Most surprising of all, Mia—despite being utterly humiliated—managed to wiggle back into the good graces of a couple of these royals. It proved my point. She wouldn't stay down for long. And, in fact, I saw the first signs of her revenge lurking again when I walked past her one day on the way to class. She stood with a few other people and spoke loudly, clearly wanting me to hear.

"—perfect match. Both of them are from *completely* disgraced and rejected families."

I clenched my teeth and kept walking, following her gaze to where Lissa and Christian stood. They were lost in their own world and formed a gorgeous picture, she blond and fair and he blue-eyed and black-haired. I couldn't help but stare too. Mia was right. Both of their families were disgraced. Tatiana had publicly denounced Lissa, and while no one "blamed" the Ozeras for what had happened to Christian's parents, the rest of the royal Moroi families continued to keep their distance.

But Mia had been right about the other part too. In some

ways, Lissa and Christian were perfect for each other. Maybe they were outcasts, but the Dragomirs and Ozeras had once been among the most powerful Moroi leaders. And in only a very short time, Lissa and Christian had started shaping one another in ways that could put them right up there with their ancestors. He was picking up some of her polish and social poise; she was learning to stand up for her passions. The more I watched them, the more I could see an energy and confidence radiating around them.

They weren't going to stay down either.

And I think that, along with Lissa's kindness, may have been what attracted people to her. Our social circle began to steadily grow. Mason joined, of course, and made no secret of his interest in me. Lissa teased me a lot about that, and I didn't yet know what to do about him. Part of me thought maybe it was time to give him a shot as a serious boyfriend, even though the rest of me yearned for Dimitri.

For the most part, Dimitri treated me just like anyone would expect of a mentor. He was efficient. Fond. Strict. Understanding. There was nothing out of the ordinary, nothing that would make anyone suspect what had passed between us—save for an occasional meeting of our eyes. And once I overcame my initial emotional reaction, I knew he was—technically—right about us. Age was a problem, yes, particularly while I was still a student at the Academy. But the other thing he'd mentioned . . . it had never entered my mind. It should have. Two guardians in a relationship could distract each other from the Moroi they were supposed to protect. We couldn't allow that to happen, couldn't risk her life for our own wants. Otherwise, we'd be no better than the Badica guardian who'd run off. I'd told Dimitri once that my own feelings didn't matter. She came first.

I just hoped I could prove it.

"It's too bad about the healing," Lissa told me.

"Hmm?" We sat in her room, pretending to study, but my mind was off thinking about Dimitri. I'd lectured her about keeping secrets, but I hadn't told her about him or about how close I'd come to losing my virginity. For some reason, I couldn't bring myself to tell.

She dropped the history book she'd been holding. "That I had to give up the healing. And the compulsion." A frown crossed her face at that last part. The healing had been regarded as a wondrous gift in need of further study; the compulsion had met with serious reprimands from Kirova and Ms. Carmack. "I mean, I'm happy now. I should have gotten help a long time ago—you were right about that. I'm glad I'm on the medication. But Victor was right too. I can't use spirit anymore. I can still sense it, though. . . . I miss being able to touch it."

I didn't entirely know what to say. I liked her better like this. Losing that threat of madness had made her whole again, confident and outgoing, just like the Lissa I'd always known and loved. Seeing her now, it was easy to believe what Victor had said about her becoming a leader. She reminded me of her parents and of Andre—how they used to inspire devotion in those who knew them.

"And that's another thing," she continued. "He said I couldn't give it up. He was right. It hurts, not having the magic. I want it so badly sometimes."

"I know," I said. I could feel that ache within her. The pills had dulled her magic, but not our bond.

"And I keep thinking about all the things I could do, all the people I could help." She looked regretful.

"You have to help yourself first," I told her fiercely. "I don't want you getting hurt again. I won't let you."

"I know. Christian says the same thing." She got that dopey smile she always did when she thought about him. If I'd known what idiots being in love would make them, I might not have been so keen to get them back together. "And I guess you guys are right. Better to want the magic and be sane than to have it and be a lunatic. There's no middle ground."

"No," I agreed. "Not with this."

Then, out of nowhere, a thought smacked me in the head. There *was* a middle ground. Natalie's words reminded me of it. *It's worth it, worth giving up the sun and the magic.*

The magic.

Ms. Karp hadn't become Strigoi simply because she'd gone crazy. She'd become Strigoi to stay sane. Becoming Strigoi cut a person completely off from magic. In doing that, she couldn't use it. She couldn't feel it. She wouldn't want it anymore. Staring at Lissa, I felt a knot of worry coil within me.

What if she figured that out? Would she want to do it too? No, I quickly decided. Lissa would never do that. She was too strong a person, too moral. And so long as she stayed on the pills, her higher reasoning would keep her from doing something so drastic.

Still, the whole concept prodded me to find out one last thing. The following morning, I went to the chapel and waited in one of the pews until the priest showed up.

"Hello, Rosemarie," he said, clearly surprised. "Can I help you with something?"

I stood up. "I need to know more about St. Vladimir. I read that book you gave me and a couple others." Best not to tell him about stealing the ones in the attic. "But nobody told how he died. What happened? How did his life end? Was he, like, martyred?"

The priest's bushy eyebrows rose. "No. He died of old age. Peacefully."

"You're sure? He didn't become Strigoi or kill himself?"

"No, of course not. Why would you think that?"

"Well . . . he was holy and everything, but he was also kind of crazy, right? I read about it. I thought he might have, I don't know, given into that."

His face was serious. "It's true he fought demons—insanity—his whole life. It was a struggle, and he did want to die sometimes. But he overcame it. He didn't let it defeat him."

I stared in wonder. Vladimir wouldn't have had pills, and he'd clearly continued to use magic.

"How? How did he do that?"

"Willpower, I guess. Well . . ." He paused. "That and Anna."

"Shadow-kissed Anna," I murmured. "His guardian."

The priest nodded. "She stayed with him. When he grew weak, she was the one who held him up. She urged him to stay strong and to never give in to his madness."

I left the chapel in a daze. Anna had done it. Anna had let Vladimir walk that middle ground, helping him to work miracles in the world without meeting a horrible end. Ms. Karp hadn't been as lucky. She hadn't had a bound guardian. She hadn't had anyone to hold her up.

Lissa *did*.

Smiling, I cut across the quadrangle toward the commons. I felt better about life than I had in a very long time. We could do this, Lissa and me. We could do it together.

Just then, I saw a dark figure out of the corner of my eye. It swooped past me and landed on a nearby tree. I stopped walking. It was a raven, large and fierce-looking, with shining black feathers.

A moment later, I realized it wasn't just *a* raven; it was *the* raven. The one Lissa had healed. No other bird would land so close to a dhampir. And no other bird would be looking at me in such an intelligent, familiar way. I couldn't believe he was still around. A chill ran down my spine, and I started to back up. Then the truth hit me.

"You're bound to her too, aren't you?" I asked, fully aware

that anyone who saw me would think I was crazy. "She brought you back. You're shadow-kissed."

That was actually pretty cool. I held out my arm to it, half hoping it'd come land on me in some sort of dramatic, movie-worthy gesture. All it did was look at me like I was an idiot, spread its wings, and fly off.

I glared as it flew off into the twilight. Then I turned around and headed off to find Lissa. From far away, I heard the sound of cawing, almost like laughter.

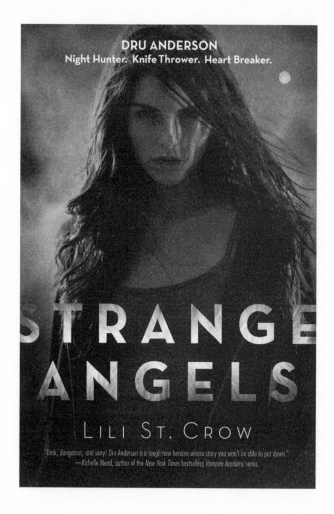

PROLOGUE

didn't tell Dad about Granmama's white owl. I know I should have.

There's that space between sleep and dreaming where things—not quite dreams, not fully fledged precognition, but weird little blends of both—sometimes get in. Your eyes open, slow and dreamy, when the sense of *someone looking* rises through the cotton-wool fog of being warm and tired.

That's when I saw it.

The owl ruffled itself up on my windowsill drenched in moonglow, each pale feather sharp and clear under icy light. I hadn't bothered to pull the cheap blinds down or hang up the curtains. Why bother, when we—Dad and me—only spend a few months in any town?

I blinked at the yellow-eyed bird. Instead of the comfort that means Gran is thinking about me—and don't ask how I know the dead think of the living; I've seen too much *not* to know—I felt a sharp annoyance, like a glass splinter under the surface of my brain.

The owl's beak was black, and its feathers had ghostly spots like cobwebs, shadows against snowy down. It stared into my sleepy eyes for what seemed like eternity, ruffling just a bit, puffing up the way Gran always used to when she thought anyone was messing with me.

Not again. Go away.

It usually only showed up when something interesting or really foul was about to happen. Dad had never seen it, or at least I didn't think so. But he could tell when I had, and it would make him reach for a weapon until I managed to open my mouth and say whether we were going to meet an old friend—or find ourselves in deep shit.

The night Gran died the owl had sat inside the window while she took her last few shallow, sipping breaths, but I don't think the nurses or the doctor saw it. They would have said something. By that point I knew enough to keep my mouth shut, at least. I just sat there and held Gran's hand until she drained away; then I sat in the hall while they did things to her empty body and wheeled it off. I curled up inside myself when the doctor or the social worker tried to talk to me, and just kept repeating that my dad would know, that he was on his way—even though I had no clue *where* he was, really. He'd been gone a good three months, off ridding the world of nasty things while I watched Gran slide downhill.

Of course, that morning Dad showed up, haggard and unshaven, his shoulder bandaged and his face bruised. He had all the ID, signed all the papers, and answered all the questions. Everything turned out okay, but sometimes I dream about that night, wondering if I'm going to get left behind again in some fluorescent-lit corridor smelling of Lysol and cold pain.

I don't like thinking about that. I settled further into the pillow, watching the owl's fluffing, each feather edged with cold moonlight.

My eyes drifted closed. Warm darkness swallowed me, and when the alarm clock went off it was morning, weak winter sunshine spilling through the window and making a square on the brown carpet. I'd thrashed out of the covers and was about to freeze my ass off. Dad hadn't turned the heater up.

It took a good twenty minutes in the shower before I felt anything *close* to awake. *Or* human. By the time I stamped down the stairs, I was already pissed off and getting worse. My favorite jeans weren't clean and I had a zit the size of Mount Pinatubo on my temple under a hank of dishwater brown hair. I opted for a gray T-shirt and a red hoodie, a pair of combat boots and no makeup.

Why bother, right? I wasn't going to be here long enough for anyone to care.

My bag smacked the floor. Last night's dishes still crouched in the sink. Dad was at the kitchen table, his shoulders hunched over the tray as he loaded clips, each bullet making a little clicking sound. "Hi, sweetheart."

I snorted, snagging the orange juice and opening the carton, taking a long cold draft. I wiped my mouth and belched musically.

"Ladylike." His bloodshot blue eyes didn't rise from the clip, and I knew what that meant.

"Going out tonight?" That's what I said. What I meant was, *without me?*

Click. Click. He set the full clip aside and started on the next. The bullets glinted, silver-coated. He must have been up all night with that, making them and loading them. "I won't be in for dinner. Order a pizza or something."

Which meant he was going somewhere more-dangerous, not just kinda-dangerous. And that he didn't need me to zero the target. So he must've gotten some kind of intel. He'd been gone every night this week, always reappearing in time for dinner smelling of cigarette smoke and danger. In other towns he'd mostly take me with him; people either didn't care about a teenage girl drinking a Coke in a bar, or we went places where Dad was reasonably sure he could stop any trouble with an ice-cold military stare or a drawled word.

But in this town he hadn't taken me anywhere. So if he'd gotten intel, it was on his own.

How? Probably the old-fashioned way. He likes that better, I guess. "I could come along."

"Dru." Just the one word, a warning in his tone. Mom's silver locket glittered at his throat, winking in the morning light.

"You might need me. I can carry the ammo." *And tell you when something invisible's in the corner, looking at you.* I heard the stubborn whine in my voice and belched again to cover it, a nice sonorous one that all but rattled the window looking out onto the scrubby backyard with its dilapidated swing set. There was a box of dishes sitting in front of the cabinets next to the stove; I suppressed the urge to kick at it. Mom's cookie jar—the one shaped like a fat grinning black-and-white cow—was next to the sink, the first thing unpacked in every new house. I always put it in the bathroom box with the toilet paper and shampoo; that's always the last in and first one out.

I've gotten kind of used to packing and unpacking, you could say. And trying to find toilet paper after a thirty-six-hour drive is no fun.

"Not this time, Dru." He looked up at me, though, the bristles of his cropped hair glittering blond under fluorescent light. "I'll be home late. Don't wait up."

I was about to protest, but his mouth had turned into a thin, hard line and the bottle sitting on the table warned me. Jim Beam. It had been almost full last night when I went to bed, and the dregs of amber liquid in it glowed warmer than his hair. Dad was pale blond, almost a towhead, even if his stubble was brown and gold.

I've got a washed-out version of Mom's curls and a better copy of Dad's blue eyes. The rest of me, I guess, is up for grabs. Except maybe Gran's nose, but she could have just been trying to make me feel better. I'm no prize. Most girls go through a gawky stage, but I'm beginning to think mine will be a lifelong thing.

It doesn't bother me too much. Better to be strong than pretty and useless. I'll take a plain girl with her head screwed on right over a cheerleader any day.

So I just leaned down and scooped up my messenger bag, the strap scraping against my fingerless wool gloves. They're scratchy but they're warm, and if you slip small stuff under the cuff, it's damn near invisible. "Okay."

"You should have some breakfast." *Click.* Another bullet slid into the clip. His eyes dropped back down to it, like it was the most important thing in the world.

Eat something? When he was about to go out and deal with bad news alone? Was he *kidding*?

My stomach turned over hard. "I'll miss the bus. Do you want some eggs?"

I don't know why I offered. He liked them sunny-side up, but neither Mom or me could ever get them done right. I've been breaking yolks all my life, even when he tried to teach me the right way to gently jiggle with a spatula to get them out of the pan. Mom would just laugh on Sunday mornings and tell him scrambled or over-hard was what he was going to get, and he'd come up behind her and put his arms around her waist and nuzzle her long, curling chestnut hair. I would always yell, *Ewwww! No kissing!*

And they would both laugh.

That was Before. A thousand years ago. When I was little.

Dad shook his head a little. "No thanks, kiddo. You have money?"

I spotted his billfold on the counter and scooped it up. "I'm taking twenty."

"Take another twenty, just in case." *Click. Click.* "How's school going?"

Just fine, Dad. Just freaking dandy. Two weeks in a new town is enough to make me all sorts of friends. "Okay."

I took two twenties out of his billfold, rubbing the plastic sleeve over Mom's picture with my thumb like I always did. There was a shiny space on the sleeve right over her wide, bright smile. Her chestnut hair was as wildly curly as mine, but pulled back into a loose ponytail, blonde-streaked ringlets falling into her heart-shaped face. She was beautiful. You could see why Dad fell for her in that picture. You could almost smell her perfume.

"Just okay?" *Click.*

"It's fine. It's stupid. Same old stuff." I toed the linoleum and set his billfold down. "I'm going."

Click. He didn't look up. "Okay. I love you." He was wearing his Marines sweatshirt and the pair of blue sweats he always worked out in, with the hole in the knee. I stared at the top of his head while he finished the clip, set it aside, and picked up a fresh one. I could almost feel the noise of each bullet being slid home in my own fingers.

My throat had turned to stone. "'Kay. Whatever. Bye." *Don't get killed.* I stamped out of the kitchen and down the hall, one of the stacked boxes barking me in the shin. I still hadn't unpacked the living room yet. Why bother? I'd just have to box it all up in another couple months.

I slammed the front door, too, and pulled my hood up, shoving my hair back. I hadn't bothered with much beyond dragging a comb through it. Mom's curls had been loose pretty ringlets, but mine were pure frizz. The Midwest podunk humidity made it worse; it was a wet blanket of cold that immediately turned my breath into a white cloud and nipped at my elbows and knees.

The rental was on a long, ruler-straight block of similar houses, all dozing under watery sunlight managing to fight its way through overcast. The air tasted like iron and I shivered. We'd been in Florida before this, always sticky, sweaty, sultry heat against the skin like oil. We'd cleared out four poltergeists in Pensacola and a haunting apparition of a woman even Dad could see in some dead-end town north of Miami, and there was a creepy woman with cottonmouths and copperheads in glass cages who sold Dad the silver he needed to take care of something else. I hadn't had to go to school there—we were so busy staying mobile, moving from one hotel to the next, so whatever Dad needed the silver for couldn't get a lock on us.

Now it was the Dakotas, and snow up to our knees. Great.

Our yard was the only one with weeds and tall grass. We had a picket fence, too, but the paint was flaking and peeling off and parts of it were missing, like a gap-toothed smile. Still, the porch was sturdy and the house was even sturdier. Dad didn't believe in renting crappy bungalows. He said it was a bad way to raise a kid.

I walked away with my head down and my hands stuffed in my pockets.

I never saw Dad alive again.

Will Dru discover just how special she really is?

Find out in BETRAYALS coming November 2009